THE
GIRL
WHO
FOUND
HER
NAME

A NOVEL

JS BELLATORRE

The Girl Who Found Her Name
Published by The All Roses Company
Los Angeles, California

ISBN: 978-1-7364932-0-5
FICTION / Literary

Cover and Interior design by Victoria Wolf,
wolfdesignandmarketing.com

the **ALL ROSES**
COMPANY

Includes explicit descriptions of sexual and violent situations.

CHAPTER ONE

Silky

THE SILVER PORSCHE pulled up to the curb and sat idling, like a sleeper caught between dreaming and waking.

The group of teens watched in silence. Dressed in jeans, T-shirts, and sneakers they looked like regular kids out past their bedtime. Their clothes were costumes devised by their leader to hide them in plain sight. His name was Skunk, and he had a strip of hair down his head from front to back dyed an unearthly yellow.

Silky watched as he drifted over to the car and knocked on the passenger-side window. It slid down, and Skunk talked to the driver. Silky looked away, hoping to make herself invisible. It was late and she didn't want to go out again.

Picking at the dead ends of her long, naturally blonde hair, she remembered how it had once been gloriously golden and thick. The dark purple polish on her nails had started to chip; she would have to steal another bottle from the drugstore at the corner of Sunset and El Centro. It was her favorite color and matched her lip-gloss perfectly. Silky wore makeup like a mask, with a heavy layer of foundation and eyes rimmed with black liner. Her customers didn't need to see the girl underneath.

Skunk rose from his crouching position beside the car, turned, and fixed her with his steely gaze.

Shit. I knew it. She took a drag off her cigarette.

The older boy approached. "Come on," he said. "You got a chance to do good."

Silky shouldered her fringed bag. It held her cosmetics, hairbrush, a dozen condoms, a pack of cigarettes, and, at the bottom, a knife kept razor-sharp. Dropping her smoke, she ground it into the pavement with the toe of her sneaker. There were pink stars in the sidewalk with the names of actors on them, stained with spit and gum. "David Niven" read the one below her foot. She had no idea who that was.

"Don't take less than a hundred," Skunk added.

A light changed and traffic started moving. Silky walked toward the curb, emerging from the shadows into the harsh glow of street lamps. Drawing close, she took a better look at the vehicle. Cars this nice never stopped for what she was about to do. The driver was rich, and might even be a producer or director. He could also be a cop. Better to stay on guard.

Silky dropped into the passenger seat. She hated small cars like this; they made it harder to get to the guy and the job took longer.

The driver put the Porsche in gear and pulled away.

"Turn left on Las Palmas," Silky instructed. "Go in the alley."

"No," he said. "Nothing like that."

"There's a motel on Sunset. You pay for the room."

"How old are you?" he asked.

"What the fuck does that matter?"

"I'm not taking you anywhere until I know."

"Eighteen," she lied.

"Okay." The driver paused, and then said: "I want you to come to my place."

"Fuck you," she snapped. "Pull over!" Silky pushed buttons on the door, found the lock, heard it snick open. Her other hand, deep in her bag, grasped the knife tightly.

"I need to talk to you," he said.

He needs to talk? He'd take her somewhere far off, with no way for her to get back. Maybe he had some buddies waiting and they'd all be on her at once.

"Pull over and let me out!"

The man held out a white envelope with bills inside. "I will give you that to come with me," he said. "Please."

The Porsche stopped at a red light. The man waited quietly, holding out the envelope.

He had offered her money, and that meant he wasn't a cop. Skunk had said that the police always waited for the girl to mention a price and what she would do for it. It was called solicitation, and they needed it for evidence in court.

Silky snatched the envelope from his hand. Inside were ten one-hundred-dollar bills, crisp and new. Returning with so much cash would send Skunk over the moon.

The door was unlocked. All she had to do was take the envelope and run. But a chance like this might never come again. Silky had been waiting for so long she had almost forgotten escape was possible. The man might be her way out. Going with him was a big risk, but she decided to take it.

"Don't try anything funny," she warned.

"I wouldn't dream of it." The light turned green and traffic inched forward.

Silky looked more closely at the driver. He was maybe thirty or thirty-five—not as old as some of the men who picked her up. His blonde hair was thinning on top, and he had a soft body that wasn't actually fat. In a white shirt and dress pants, he looked ready for a business meeting, not a night doing *this*.

"What's your name?" he asked.

"Silky," she offered. It was the name Skunk had given her.

The man, turning right and distracted by the traffic, asked "Susie?" Silky did not correct him. Let him think she'd said "Susie."

A minute later they entered the highway. The driver reached over to press a button on the dashboard, his hand shaking. It reminded Silky of something her father said long ago, about an opossum that had come into their yard: *He's more scared of you than you are of him.*

Rich sounds filled the car, music with clarity like she'd never heard. Yet it made no sense, all jumbled and no words.

"Miles Davis," the driver said. "I don't suppose you know him."

"Sounds fucking stupid."

The driver turned off the music. They rode in silence, hearing only the rumble of the tires on the highway.

Thirty minutes later they pulled on to a long, winding road that that took them to the Pacific Ocean. The man rolled down the windows, and the roar of the waves and smell of salt air poured in. She had not been to the beach for many years, and never in California, and could not see much now but the white line of breakers under the moonlight.

The man turned into a driveway, to a house hidden behind some trees. They entered the garage, parking beside an SUV. Getting out, he paused to press buttons on a security panel and then led her inside.

They entered a kitchen. Brass-bottomed pots hung from racks above the stove. Towels were draped in neat rows. The scent of food made Silky's stomach rumble. The only thing she'd eaten that day was a couple of Twinkies stolen from a convenience store.

"Smells nice in here," she said.

"Are you hungry?"

She put the ice back into her voice: "Just get on with it."

He took her into a huge living room. The ceiling was two stories high. A fireplace took up half of one wall. The rest of that wall was filled with books from top to bottom. The far end had a sweeping stairway up to a second story landing. The furniture was spotless white, the carpet thick as mountain snow.

Before she fell in with Skunk, Silky would read novels about the olden times, stories about princes and countesses, with servants and muscled horsemen. This house would have fit right in. She had once dreamed about living in a place like this.

Silky put the thought aside. The man surely had some perversion in mind. Why else would he have brought her to a place so far away from everything?

He stood waiting beside a wall made of glass. A blue light shone from a computer on a desk in front of it. Silky didn't know anyone back home who had their own computer. The school had them, and the doctor's office, but no one *she* knew. If the man had one, he was rich *and* important.

"So, okay," she said, fixing him with a cold gaze. "You wanna do it on the sofa?"

The man opened a sliding door in the glass wall. The scent of salt air swept into the room, the roar of the surf with it. Silky followed him out, onto a wooden deck with the beach beyond. Digging into her bag, she took out her last cigarette and lit it.

"The sea will tell you stories," the man said, looking into the darkness. "Tales of enchanted ships, and a sailor condemned to search for a woman who will love him without question, in spite of his calloused hands and briny heart."

This guy is too weird.

"This way," he said, and walked up a wooden stairway. Silky

followed. When they reached the upper deck, he slid open another glass door. "Please. No smoking inside."

Silky crushed her cigarette underfoot.

They entered a bedroom with white furniture, including a bed. There was a television, and paintings on the walls made of colors and shapes all jumbled and making no sense.

This is where he wants to fuck.

A guy this weird had to be kinky. He would chain her wrists to hidden bolts and submit her body to his whip. She'd done it before, long ago in Las Vegas when she could see no other way. It must be something like that. After all, he'd already given her a thousand dollars.

"Would you like to freshen up?" he asked.

Through an open door Silky saw a tiled bath with frosted glass and thick towels. It had been ages since she had taken a real shower. Her answer welled from her eyes like tears.

"Take as long as you like," he said. "I'll put out a robe."

Without another thought Silky dropped the bag from her shoulder. Taking the bottom of the T-shirt into her hands, she pulled it over her head. The man could now see her bare breasts and her flat stomach. It didn't matter. She had been naked for men a thousand times before.

He wasn't there. In the moment when her shirt covered her head the man had vanished. Silky had not been alone in a room for ages. The absolute silence of privacy surrounded her.

Leaving her clothes in a pile on the floor she entered the bathroom. A mirror covered the whole wall over the sink. A stranger looked back from it. Her once beautiful hair was now stringy and matted, her naturally large breasts smaller from the weight she had lost, her ribs visible beneath the skin. Thick makeup covered her face but the rest of her body was dotted with bruises, sores, and tiny red pimples.

There was a reason the man hadn't touched her. She looked like crap and stank like vomit from the streets.

Stepping into the shower, Silky turned on the silver faucets. The water shot out in a hot, firm stream. Lathering up, she watched the dirt run down her body into the drain. The filthy water flowed into the vast ocean, becoming nothing, one part in a million billion. She loaded her hair with shampoo, scrubbing until her scalp tingled, and then applied conditioner.

A wire basket held a razor and a can of Barbasol. Silky worked slowly and carefully, shaving her legs, her armpits, and the thick patch that had grown back in her crotch.

Stepping out, she found a blow-dryer and comb and began working through her knotted hair. The mirror showed another person. The girl who had run away from home at fourteen, with a boy she barely knew, was not there. The woman she had become, one of Skunk's kids working the streets, had vanished as well.

Eventually Silky shut off the blow-dryer. Her hair was fuller, although it still didn't shine like before. Her face had been scrubbed clean, making her look like some kind of farm girl. She had left her makeup on the other side of the bathroom door, where the man would be waiting. Now that she was clean, he would be ready.

He would force himself between her legs, and she would do as she had done a thousand times before: close her eyes and dream of the river, the long, slow St. Johns from her childhood, where she had spent lazy summer days in the shade of tall cypress draped with hanging moss—

Might as well get it over with.

Dropping the towel, she reached for the knob.

The man was not in the room. A thick white robe lay on the bed. Leaving her clothes on the floor, Silky slipped her arms into the robe's soft embrace. She needed her knife, didn't feel right without it, and dug it out of her bag. The robe's pocket was large enough to hold it. Curling her fingers around the handle, she was ready to meet him.

Music whirled around the room as she walked down the inside staircase. The man saw her, touched something on the wall, and the music softened.

"I warmed up some stew," he said. A bowl sat on the grand wooden table, and silverware on a napkin. There was also bread, butter in a small cup, and a glass of milk. The man brought out a copper-bottomed pot and spooned chunks of meat, potatoes, peas, and carrots into her bowl. She didn't like him standing there, and shot one of her "Don't fuck with me" looks at him. The man returned to the kitchen and began wiping down the spotless counter.

Hunger growled inside her like a trapped animal. The car, the house, the white-tiled shower, and the meal were part of a dream that had suddenly become real. Yet it wasn't real, because it wasn't *hers*. People didn't just give stuff like this away. Everyone wanted something in return, and they usually took it in the most awful ways.

Maybe the food was drugged. She would wake up tomorrow trapped in a whorehouse, forced to endure one stinking brute after another.

The powerful aroma broke through her resistance. Dropping into the chair, she scooped meat into her mouth. The heat seared her tongue. Grabbing the milk, she drank to ease the pain, and then swallowed huge mouthfuls stew, bread smeared with butter, barely stopping to breathe. She had not tasted anything so delicious in years.

Her head hummed and spun. The man looked at her from across the room.

The bastard had done it. He'd drugged her.

His voice sounded like it came down a long tunnel: "Go upstairs and get into bed."

Zombie-like she followed his command. He watched from below as she stepped carefully up, hand grasping the rail.

Alone in the bedroom, Silky pulled back the white cover and blanket. The knife in her pocket went under a pillow. Dropping the robe, she slipped between the sheets.

She expected to feel his clammy hands on her breasts, his hard cock forcing its way into her. But the man never entered the room. Silky dropped off, and slept more deeply than she had ever known.

CHAPTER TWO

Skunk

SKUNK WATCHED the club goers spill into the streets after last call. Bratwurst sizzled on the grill of a pushcart next to him. Across the street, the glaring lights of a pizza place announced that it was still open. The partiers stood on the sidewalk smoking and eating. Occasionally one would drift over and talk to him and, if it felt right, Skunk would slip him a small packet in exchange for twenty dollars.

Only one car stopped at the curb. Skunk ordered LightLight, a blonde girl with pale blue eyes, to go. She came back twenty minutes later and handed Skunk fifty dollars. He told his kids to call it a night. They went off to their hotel room, which Skunk rented by the week.

He waited until 3:00 am for Silky to return. The man in the Porsche had probably gotten a room, and Silky had stayed to enjoy a night sleeping alone. She would be back in the morning.

Rising, Skunk stretched out his wiry body and walked toward his apartment, passing the sleeping bodies of homeless people. For a Monday, it had been a good night.

CHAPTER THREE

Charlie

CHARLIE ROSE EARLY, AS ALWAYS. Most people needed a full eight hours, but for him six was usually enough. He always slept deeply, like a child.

When writing screenplays, he used his full name: Charles Anderson Warren. His friends (of which there were few these days) called him Charlie. He wondered, not for the first time, why he had brought the girl back to his home, his refuge, his Fortress of Solitude. A street whore like her would be racked with diseases, infected with fungus, riddled with lice. He would have to disinfect his entire house after he took her back to Hollywood.

And yet he knew her presence in his life was an absolute necessity.

Charlie had experienced what other people called "a mete-oric rise to success." The phrase made no sense to him. Meteors didn't rise; they fell, usually burning up in the process. Those that made it to earth slammed into the ground with devastating force. Destruction had indeed come upon him, not in the phys-ical sense, but creatively.

Two years prior, he had sold a screenplay. The movie became a box office smash. Charlie found himself thrust into a spot-light, and the glare burned his eyes. His agent insisted he attend parties and premieres to advance his career, which he did with the greatest unease. He simply wasn't comfortable unless alone with a book.

The studio had given him a huge advance for his next script, which he used as a down payment on a secluded residence in Malibu. Charlie furnished it quickly by ordering everything in white, and then locked himself away. Invitations went unan-swered until they stopped coming. When his agent phoned, Charlie's machine recorded the message, which he would return in the middle of the night. He spoke only to the deliveryman who brought groceries.

The deadline for the new screenplay was three months away. Charlie hadn't written a thing. Each morning he would sit at his computer and stare out at the ocean. From time to time he would rise and clean his already spotless house, hoping for inspiration. None came.

He had grown more anxious as the days passed. He couldn't read, couldn't sleep, couldn't *think*. One evening, around eleven o'clock, the telephone rang and he nearly jumped out of his skin. Picking up the receiver, a feminine voice asked a question in Spanish. It took him a moment to realize the woman had dialed the wrong number. He heard a soft *click* followed by a dial tone, and stood for some time listening to it.

How have I come to this?

He lived in an emptiness of his own making, his life a blank page. It had to be the source of his dilemma. Immersing himself in the noise and swirl and mess of the world was essential if he were to ever write again.

The silver Porsche 911 had been a gift from a studio executive, fully loaded with the latest technology including a mobile phone. Charlie had tried to return it, but his agent insisted that he keep it to maintain an edifice of success. He drove it now as a way of kicking himself out his comfortable nest.

Speeding along the Pacific Coast Highway, he switched on music and listened to the haunting notes of the brilliant trumpeter Miles Davis. Charlie drove until he reached Beverly Hills, filled with beautiful people dining in outdoor cafes. Instantly, he knew it would not do.

He then headed for Hollywood, not "Hollywood" of the movie business but the real Hollywood, with its eclectic mix of street life and strangers. Stopping at a red light he searched the faces for stimulation. Sounds came to him through the window: the banging boom box of sidewalk performers. When the light changed, he drove on.

Pulling up to a curb, Charlie considered going into a bar. He had not touched alcohol in years, and knew it would not solve his problem. He needed to do something radically different, something *electric*.

A sharp rap on the passenger side window startled him. A kid with a yellow stripe down his head stared back. Charlie pressed a button and the window slid down.

"What's up, man?" the kid said.

Who was this? What did he want?

"Come on," the punk urged. "The cops will see us."

Charlie noticed a small group of teenagers huddled in the shadows, dressed in T-shirts and sneakers. The kid was a pimp, the kids his merchandise. One was a woman, more than a child and yet not fully adult. He heard himself say: "I'd like to talk to that girl. The one in the blue shirt."

The pimp walked away. Charlie took an envelope of cash from the glove compartment that he kept there for emergencies. He never dreamed of using it for *this*, but knew it would entice the young woman into coming with him. A few moments later she was in his car.

Now, in the bright light of the next morning, Charlie wondered what the hell he had done. She was still asleep, upstairs in his bedroom. He had to get her out as soon as possible.

After climbing the stairway, Charlie carefully opened the door. The girl lay with her hair splayed across his pillow, her sleeping face the essence of innocence. Her appearance belied what Charlie knew: she was tough as leather and not to be trusted.

Her clothing sat in a pile on the floor like a vile dump on his white carpet. The girl's fringed bag lay heaped beside the clothes. Charlie had to do something. He couldn't just let the filthy things lie there.

He went into the bathroom where he kept a pair of thick rubber gloves. Putting them on, he first lifted the girl's bag and hung it on a chair. Concerned that it might contain drugs, he looked inside. It held only condoms, the envelope filled with money, a brush matted with old hair, and cosmetics. The mascara was smeared and there was a crust around the top of the foundation bottle.

Good lord, how could the girl put that contagion on her face?

He wrapped the makeup and the brush in a handkerchief, leaving the condoms and the envelope of money. Scooping up the clothes and her shoes from the floor, he took everything downstairs.

Charlie dumped the makeup into his trash compacter. The girl's clothes and sneakers went into the washer, which he set to the hottest water and poured in detergent. The brush went into a bucket to soak in bleach. His guest would be thankful.

His heart pounded, and his mind raced a thousand miles an hour. Going to the computer, he slid a floppy disk into the slot and, for the first time in nearly a year, began to type.

CHAPTER FOUR

Silky

SILKY DREAMED OF AIRPLANES buzzing overhead. Brightness forced its way through her eyelids. Waking, there was whiteness all around. The sound was the surf; the light was the morning sun. It felt wrong. This was not her world.

Where are my things?

Reaching under the pillow, she found her knife where she had left it. A clock on the nightstand read 10:04. Skunk would kill her! He would have expected her back within an hour. She'd just have to show him the thousand dollars and hope for the best.

The money!

She had left it in her bag, which wasn't where she dropped it. Her clothes were gone, too. The robe lay draped across the bed and she threw it on. Seething with anger, she strode toward the sliding glass doors, stopping at the sight of her bag hanging on a chair. It still held the envelope, with the money inside. Her condoms were there, but no makeup or hairbrush.

Stepping onto the deck, Silky squinted in the brilliance of the morning sun. People lay tanning, and in the distance some surfers waited for a wave. The sandy beach and soft roll of the ocean was so different from what she usually saw in the morning: dirty buildings, their black windows staring at her like blind eyes.

God, I need a smoke.

She descended the wooden stairs and went into living room. On the dining table, a white vase filled with yellow flowers.

"Good morning," the man said from somewhere behind her. Silky turned to see him sitting at his computer, smiling.

What the fuck?!

"Where are my clothes?" she demanded.

"Just put them in the dryer."

"My makeup, my shoes!" she said, her voice rising.

"The makeup looked contaminated. I threw it out."

"You had no right! That was my stuff! Mine! Fucking bastard! Son of a bitch!"

Silky felt the sting of tears in her eyes. A thousand guys had fucked her, but she had never felt so violated as when the man said he had thrown out her makeup. He had stripped her face away. She forced the tears back and glared at him in defiance.

"I-I-I'm sorry," he stammered. "I-I...only wanted to help."

"Give me my clothes. Drive me back to Hollywood."

"Uh-uh-okay," he said. "The, uh, the dryer will take twenty minutes. Let me, uh, fix you something to eat." He headed for the kitchen as if seeking its safety.

"I'm not going to let you dope me again, you sick freak."

"*Dope* you?"

"Drugs, shithead. You put something in the food."

"I-I-I would never—"

"Then why did I pass out?"

"You needed sleep." He poured coffee into a mug and held it out to her. The aroma stunned her nostrils. She wanted it desperately but glared at him with distrust.

He took a sip. "See? No drugs."

Silky accepted the coffee. Drinking it black, she stared at him over the rim of the mug. Last night he had been a mystery, and a potential danger. Today he seemed harmless.

"Are you queer?" she asked.

"No, I . . . I'm completely heterosexual."

"You never touched me."

"Do…do you want breakfast?"

Silky did want breakfast, and a smoke. Without waiting for an answer, he turned to the refrigerator and spooned fresh fruit into a white bowl.

The man had not hurt her. And, he had money.

"What's your name?" she asked, as the man placed the bowl on the table.

"Charlie. Uh-uh-it's Charlie."

She sat, and spooned chunks of sweet melon into her mouth.

Charlie watched, like he had never seen a girl eat before. Silky swallowed and said, "Are you going to fuck me or not?"

"I-I-I…" Silky waited until he found the words. "I should start breakfast," he finally answered, and went into the kitchen.

He cracked eggs into boiling water, and put round slices of bread in a toaster. When they popped up he put them on a plate, layered on ham and eggs and poured a smooth, yellow sauce over everything.

Charlie set the plate before her. She cut into the eggs and a golden yolk sprang out.

"I could use a drink," Silky said. "Like maybe some vodka."

"You aren't old enough," he replied.

"Stupid fuck," she said. "I had my first beer when I was fourteen."

"I -uh-uh, d-don't have any alcohol in the house," he said.

Charlie disappeared into the garage. She finished the breakfast, every tasty bite, and would have killed for a cigarette. It was pointless to ask. Charlie wouldn't have any. A guy like him would never let his lungs get dirty.

He returned with her clothes folded, holding her canvas sneakers with a handkerchief. Even her brush was clean, the matted hair removed from the bristles.

"Get dressed," he said. "I'll take you back now."

Silky went upstairs. Her clothes felt soft and warm. She put her hairbrush into her bag, and then looked around for anything worth taking. Opening drawers, she found a fancy pen, a watch, tie tacks, and cuff links. Silky shoved them all into her fringed bag.

Returning to the living room, Charlie waited with keys in his hand. Silky strode past him, through the kitchen and into the garage. They climbed into the Porsche and he started the engine.

"I want to buy you something," he said as they drove. "I would like you to have a souvenir of our evening."

Wasn't a thousand dollars enough? Hell, if he wants to buy me something, I'll let him. I can always sell it back on the street.

Charlie parked in front of a small store. It had the kind of clothes rich women wear to a beachside cafe. A silver bell over the door tinkled as they entered. The place was empty except for a saleslady. She gave Silky a snotty look and turned to Charlie.

"May I help you?" she asked, as if Silky wasn't there.

"She needs some nicer clothes," Charlie said. Then to Silky, "Choose something."

There was nothing in the place that Skunk would let her wear. Walking over to a rack, she selected a T-shirt with a colorful bird on the front. Looking at the price, she saw it cost fifty-nine dollars. That had to be a joke. It was a *shirt*, for God's sake. She gave blowjobs for less. Silky took it to the man.

"Let me see you in it," he said.

It hit her like a flash: The guy's kink was to watch her put on different clothes. She'd heard about guys who peeped in windows, or drilled holes to look at girls in the shower. Well, he'd paid plenty for the privilege.

Entering a dressing stall, Silky took off her blue T-shirt and put on the new one. She then came out to find Charlie waiting. His eyes sparkled when he saw her.

"Try on something else," he said. "Anything you want."

A memory stirred from long ago. She had once dreamed of walking on a red carpet like the movie stars she saw in magazines. Silky searched the racks, but there were no evening gowns. She found a summer dress that looked like something a Hollywood celebrity would wear, put it on in the changing room and paraded around for Charlie.

He handed her a Hawaiian shirt and white shorts, saying, "Try these." She took them and went into the stall.

Coming out, Silky found him holding tiny bikini on a hanger. Taking the bathing suit, she went back inside and changed.

"Nice," Charlie said, when she came out again. "Pick out a pair of sandals."

He obviously had a thing for feet, too. Silky chose a pair and slipped them on.

He had her try on two more outfits, both with a matching skirt and blouse.

Dressed in her own clothes again, Silky watched the saleslady ring up the order. Craving a smoke worse than ever, she decided to ask:

"I need cigarettes."

"You can't smoke in the car," Charlie said.

"Fuck you," she replied. "I dance around in those ridiculous clothes and you can't even buy me a goddamn pack of smokes?"

The saleslady glared. "What's the matter, bitch?" Silky said. "Charlie's buying me a bunch of shit here."

"S-S-S-S-Susie, please," Charlie stammered. "I'll g-g-g-get you a…p-p-pack when we leave."

Silky could feel the saleslady's eyes boring into the back of her head as they walked out of the store.

They drove in silence. Charlie pulled into the parking lot of a mini-mart. He handed her a twenty and she went inside. At the counter, an issue of *People* magazine with a picture of Cybill Shepherd on the cover caught her eye. The date said October 8, 1990.

October already? Shit, it would be getting cold again.

Silky set it on the counter and asked for a pack of Winstons. The clerk, an old guy with a huge belly, took them down from a rack above his head.

"You got ID?" the clerk asked.

"I didn't bring it."

"No ID, no cigarettes."

Silky snatched the pack from his hand. Leaving the twenty on the counter, she ran out of the store. Silky heard the fat clerk shout, "Hey! Hey!" but knew he would never catch her. She had been doing this sort of thing for a long time.

Silky got in the car and Charlie started the engine. The clerk came out of the store, but Charlie was looking over his shoulder to back up and didn't see him. Over the noise of the engine he could not hear the clerk shouting, "Get back here!"

Silky gave him the finger.

As they drove Charlie said, "I want you to spend another night with me."

She considered the offer. The idea of getting away from Skunk had never been far from her mind, and suddenly she had been offered the opportunity. But what would happen after? The man would drop her back on the street. No matter how much money she brought, Skunk would be mad as hell. And when he was mad, he hurt people.

"Nah. I got to get back."

"I'll give you another thousand dollars."

Jesus! Another thousand?

He didn't want to fuck her, just feed her and buy her clothes. There had to be some angle she hadn't figured out.

The dream of walking on a red carpet came to mind again. Staying would be a risk, but if she didn't take this chance there might never be another.

"You got it in cash?" she asked.

"I can get it."

Charlie stopped at a bank and went inside. Silky stayed in the car fidgeting nervously with the pages of her magazine. She kept thinking about what Skunk would do when she returned. Hopefully, two thousand dollars would be enough to keep him from going ballistic.

He returned and handed her another envelope with ten crisp one-hundred-dollar bills.

As they drove back the way they had come Silky said, "I don't get you."

"I don't understand myself," Charlie answered.

"You gonna fuck me this time?"

"I want something else."

"What?" she asked, putting the cold edge back into her voice.

Charlie pulled into the garage. He got out of the car and went inside without answering her question.

CHAPTER FIVE

Skunk

SKUNK AWOKE A LITTLE PAST NOON. He hit the streets, bought a muffin and coffee, and then set out to find what had happened to Silky.

Information could be had from his regular sources, like Shirley Goodness. Skunk found the black transvestite standing in her usual spot: Duncan Renaldo's star. Shirley once told Skunk that she couldn't bear to stand on Marilyn Monroe or Bette Davis. They lived during the Golden Age and had dignity. Duncan Renaldo was a B-list actor and didn't matter. In fact, Shirley thought that Renaldo *liked* it when she stood on him.

Skunk found her with another tranny named Mercy; they sometimes worked as a team. He slipped Shirley some money.

"Silky ain't been here," she responded. Skunk moved on, leaving Shirley Goodness and Mercy to their business.

Next, he talked to Lawshanda. She was the bouncer for Club Kaboom, which opened every morning at 6:00 a.m. With a body like a bull elephant, Skunk always kept on Lawshanda's good side.

"Ask China Girl," Lawshanda suggested. "In the Spotlight."

Skunk entered the windowless gloom of the Spotlight Club and searched for the skinny hooker called China Girl. She was actually Korean, but someone once called her "China girl" and the name stuck. She had been one of Skunk's kids until Lawshanda had taken her as her lover. Skunk dared not intimidate China Girl. She would complain to Lawshanda, and he needed the bouncer as a source of information.

Skunk found her watching *The People's Court* on a television over the bar.

"Hey, China," he said.

"I don't need your shit, Skunk," she said.

"Have you seen Silky?"

"Fuck no."

"You see her, tell Lawshanda."

"You gonna give me money?"

"No."

"Then fuck you, too."

China Girl slid off the barstool and walked over to the juke-box, making a big show of tuning her back on Skunk.

China Girl loved causing trouble. If China saw Silky, she

would tell everyone. One way or another, he'd find out what happened to the little blonde who brought in so much cash.

CHAPTER SIX

Silky

SILKY FOLLOWED CHARLIE into the house. He stood in the kitchen cutting the price tags from her new clothes. She waited for him to tell her what he wanted her to do.

"Go to the beach," he said. "I'll call you when lunch is ready."

"Jesus. Whatever." Silky gathered up the bathing suit and went upstairs to change. Maybe he would have liked watching her put it on, but he hadn't asked and she wasn't about to offer. When she came down he handed her a beach towel and a tube of sun block.

Silky spent the morning reading her magazine. Charlie watched through the glass wall, working on his computer. Apparently, all he wanted to do was look at her. Now that she understood his perversion she could dismiss it as harmless. She never dreamed two thousand dollars would be so easy to make.

He called her in for lunch, and had prepared crisp, green salad with grated cheese and slices of tangerine. Before they finished the doorbell rang, and Charlie rose to take a box of groceries from a deliveryman.

After they finished eating, Charlie showed her how to turn on the jets in the upstairs bathtub. The warm water and gentle bubbling made her drowsy. She took a nap, and then watched television for the first time in ages.

As darkness came she put on the new white shorts and T-shirt, and then went downstairs to find Charlie still on his computer.

He made dinner: chicken with mushroom sauce. Silky hated mushrooms and picked them out. The greasy little potatoes were delicious. She even liked the broccoli, which had spices on it.

Charlie also opened a bottle of wine. "I don't suppose it would hurt," he said. "In Europe, people your age have it the time." Silky noticed he drank only water.

"I would like to hear your story," he continued, as they ate. "Start at the beginning. Where were you born?"

Silky did not answer him right away. She did not want to revisit her past. He did not press her and they ate in silence. She finished the wine and poured herself more. After a delicious dessert of strawberries and vanilla ice cream they went onto the deck so she could smoke.

Silky took her glass with her and said, "Bring the bottle."

Charlie had paid her a lot of money, and she thought that she should try to give him what he wanted. Even the most innocent events would be hard to revisit. The wine would be necessary for her to keep going.

CHAPTER SEVEN

Jolene

SHE WAS RAISED AS "JOLENE." Her parents named her after a grandmother she never met. There were no brothers or sisters, and when Momma was angry she would tell Jolene that her being born had been "an accident."

They lived in a two-story, beaten-down house deep in the woods at the end of a long dirt road. Every now and then Daddy would try to fix it up, but the screens on the porch sagged, and the paint was old and faded.

Jolene knew little of the world beyond the forest around their house. Once a week Momma would take her into the tiny town of Enterprise to shop for groceries. She drove the rusty old pick-up truck, which was the family's only transportation, through narrow streets lined with moss-draped oaks. The Winn-Dixie store by the highway provided them with groceries, which Momma loaded into the truck bed for the ride home.

On Sundays, the family would go to church. Daddy, uncomfortable in a white shirt and tie, Momma in a faded blue dress, and Jolene would ride together in the front seat. She didn't like going because church was scary. The chapel was dark inside, with wooden pews that hurt to sit on. Only a dozen other people came regular, most of them old. The minister delivered sermons filled with hellfire and damnation, the congregation responding "Amen!" and "Hallelujah!" Momma would sing hymns with her eyes closed, and a look on her face like she was somewhere else. When the service was over, Jolene would play with two other girls whose parents also attended. The three boys who came didn't mix with them. She liked after-church, because was the only time that she saw other kids.

Jolene was punished for the slightest thing. Momma would make her kneel before a crucifix in her bedroom. The cross had a horribly tortured Jesus, his body covered in wounds, his hands contorted claws. Momma would force her to repeat "The Lord's Prayer" until she was satisfied the sin had been cleansed.

Sometimes Momma told Daddy to whip her with his belt. When he was done, Jolene would be sent to her own room. On those nights, she could hear her parents making strange noises through their closed door. There were no other families so far out in the woods and Jolene thought her life was the only way.

Daddy worked as a janitor at Enterprise Elementary. When

Jolene turned five and started kindergarten, she would ride to school with him. Momma made her wear drab-colored sack dresses that covered her entire body; anything else would be prideful, and pride was a deadly sin. The town was small, but the school had over a thousand students. Most were bussed in from Deltona, which people called a "bedroom community."

Jolene didn't get along with the kids from Deltona. They made fun of her clothes. Teachers would sometimes try to get her to play with the others, and she tried her best, but was always afraid of doing something wrong. It sometimes got so bad she would burst into tears.

Her body began to change the summer of her twelfth birthday. Her breasts became bigger, and hair grew in places where she never had it before. One morning she woke up and there was blood on the sheets. Momma said it was the curse, and that maybe it wouldn't happen a lot at first but by and by it would come every month. She gave Jolene a cotton pad to put in her underwear. Then, they knelt together and prayed to resist temptation. Momma did not explain what kind of temptation her daughter should be strong against.

Daddy began giving her a small allowance. On Saturdays, she would walk to a Handy-Mart store two miles away and buy movie-star magazines, hiding them under her mattress because she knew Momma would never approve. Jolene didn't know much about movies, because she had never been to see one. The magazines attracted her because they had pictures of the most beautiful people Jolene could imagine. They lived in a magical world, wearing colorful clothes, walking on red carpets, always smiling. Their lives were filled with light and joy.

In the fall of 1985 Jolene started attending middle school. Momma explained that she would have to ride a bus and gave her a class schedule that had come in the mail. On the first day, she rose early and walked to the end of the dirt road. When the bus arrived, she climbed the steps to find it almost full. No one wanted to make room for her. The other kids said, "It's taken" everywhere she tried to sit. The bus driver had to order someone to make a space.

The size of the school overwhelmed her. The other teens swarmed around greeting friends with happy voices. Clutching her notebook, Jolene went in to look for her classroom. The schedule said it was Cochran 208.

Taking a deep breath, she walked up to a group of girls her age. They were dressed in crisp, white blouses and plaid skirts, talking to each other like Jolene wasn't there. After the longest time one of the girls turned to her and said, "What?"

"Do you know where Cochran 208 is?" Jolene asked.

"Of course I do," the girl answered. She turned back to her friends saying, "So anyway, he kept calling me—"

"Could you tell me?" Jolene pressed.

"I don't socialize with trailer trash," the girl replied.

Jolene felt her face grow hot. She walked quickly away, the girls laughing behind her. A teacher saw her wandering and directed her to the room.

Jolene hated middle school. Exponents and fractions made

no sense to her. In English class, the teacher made each student read aloud from the book. She could hear the others snickering as she sorted out words in her thick Southern drawl. But at night, at home in her room, she would read the stories again and found them fascinating.

One day she wandered into the library, and came across a shelf of books with the pictures of beautiful women and muscular men on the covers. They looked like the people she saw in the magazines. The stories were set in faraway places where people lived in mansions and rode horses. There was always a beautiful young woman whose father was a "Baron" or a "Squire." There were bandits and swordfights and heroes who saved the day. The library became her refuge, where she went at lunch, and after classes until the bus came. Nobody bothered her there.

She could not completely avoid others. There was one girl in particular named Audrey who went out of her way to be cruel. She came up to Jolene mid-year and handed her a piece of paper. Then just as quickly she walked away.

The note read: "*You're ugly and weird. You should just kill yourself.*"

Tears welling in her eyes, Jolene tore the paper into pieces and threw it in the trash.

Another time she came across some boys hanging out at the end of a hall. They were laughing and shoving each other. One of them walked up, grabbed her breasts, and squeezed.

Jolene slapped him and cursed him. The noise attracted the attention of a teacher. The boys feigned innocence, saying that

Jolene had suddenly started acting crazy. The teacher sent her to the principal's office where she refused to answer any questions. Momma was called, and Daddy came to pick her up. She spent an hour in prayer as punishment.

Summer came rushing at her like a wild angel. She spent warm days alone in the forest, wandering among the fragrant pines. School had a summer reading program and she took books home, hiding them from Momma in her closet. Sneaking them out, she would walk to the St. John's River and read in the shade of fragrant cypress trees.

She turned thirteen that August, and her parents threw a little party with a homemade cake and presents. Jolene wished that her friends at church, Rebecca and Mary, could have been there but didn't want to say anything that might sound like a complaint.

Jolene felt better going back to school in the fall. She knew how to find her way around, and continued to hide out in the library. When it came time to get on the bus for home she would wait until all the other kids had left, and then go into the hall and out the back door. There was an alley between Cochran and another building, where she would linger until the last minute.

By keeping her eyes and ears open, Jolene picked up things that Momma would never teach her. Some of the other girls had also begun to change into women, and she would sneak looks at their bodies in gym class. Michelle Packard and Terry Sullivan had sprouted tiny breasts and wore bras, not the bland ones that her Momma bought for her but dainty, lacy things. Connie Townsend made a big show of shaving in the shower, smearing the cream down her legs and carefully drawing the razor along them.

Jolene had noticed that the ladies in her movie magazines, like Connie, didn't have hair on their legs or in their armpits. She made up her mind to try it herself. One Saturday she walked to the Handy-Mart, as she often did. This time, instead of buying a magazine and a cold drink, Jolene got a can of shaving cream and a bag of plastic razors. Sneaking them into the house, she waited until Momma was busy and locked herself in the bathroom. In the yellow light, Jolene stood in the claw-foot bathtub and did as she had seen Connie do, smiling with satisfaction that she had done something to make herself into a glamorous lady.

At dinner, she listened to her Daddy as he complained (as usual) about the "niggers" and "beaners" who were ruining the country. Momma never said much, unless Daddy took the Lord's name in vain. Jolene sat feeling the fabric of her dress against her newly shaved skin, delighted with herself because she had done something forbidden right under Momma's nose.

When summer came Jolene spent it as she had before, reading her books and dreaming of beautiful movie stars. On her fourteenth birthday, Momma and Daddy gave her a backpack for her schoolbooks. They celebrated with another homemade cake around the kitchen table, again just the three of them. Rebecca and Mary weren't coming to church so much anymore. They were both older, and Jolene rarely saw them at school.

On a hot night, Jolene could not sleep. Getting up around midnight, she went to the kitchen and poured a glass of milk. As she drank it, Daddy pulled into the yard in his pickup truck. He often stayed out late; Jolene had no idea where he went. She had grown used to the banging of the back door, and his stumbling footsteps as he climbed the stairs.

Tonight, she happened to be up when he got home. The only light was from the moon coming through the window. The screen door creaked as Daddy entered. He saw her standing next to the sink, and walked slowly to where she stood with the glass of milk in her hand. As he grew closer she could smell his breath, which stank something awful. She tried to move away but he put his arm out, trapping her against the refrigerator. Then, Daddy ran his hand up her body and cupped one of her breasts.

She slapped his hand away and ran upstairs.

From then on, Jolene kept her distance. Finding a skeleton key in a bureau drawer, she started locking her bedroom door at night.

One morning Momma woke her up for chores. She fell back asleep, which angered Momma no end. "Sloth is a deadly sin," she intoned, jerking her daughter out of bed by the arm. Jolene was forced to kneel before the cross and pray for half an hour. After, she washed the dishes, swept the porch, and hung out the laundry. Only then did Momma give her permission to do as she pleased.

Jolene went into her bedroom and put on her favorite dress, special because it was yellow and buttoned up the front. Momma had bought it for her to wear to church, which she had done every Sunday. When her breasts blossomed, it became tight. Knowing her mother would never approve, she hid it in the closet and started wearing her sack-shaped dresses to services.

That morning Jolene put on the dress as an act of rebellion. It was the only thing she had that made her feel special. It was hot so she didn't wear a bra, and left the top two buttons open. She had to sneak out of the house, of course, but by now Jolene knew just how to do that.

Walking to the Handy-Mart, she bought a Slushie and went outside, sitting on the cinderblock wall at the side of the parking lot.

A boy pulled in on a motorcycle. He took off his helmet and ran his fingers through a mass of dark, curly hair. His muscled arms flexed beneath his white T-shirt. Jolene stared at him. She watched him cross the parking lot, open the door and his tight, denimed ass walked right inside.

In her romance novels, Jolene had often read of women who felt a fire raging within that could not be denied. She thought the writers made up things like that. To her, passion had been as fanciful as a unicorn. Now she felt herself falling apart inside.

The boy came out with a six-pack of beer. He was nothing like the kids at school. After putting his beer into a saddlebag, he looked up and locked eyes with her. They were dark brown and shot bolts of lightning.

Picking up his helmet, he prepared to put it on. Jolene couldn't let him leave.

"That's a nice bike," she blurted, feeling stupid for saying it.

"Thanks," he replied.

"I've never seen one that big before."

"It's a Harley."

Jolene felt like she'd fallen into the St. Johns River and couldn't swim. Not knowing what else to do she said again, "That sure is a nice bike."

The boy fiddled with the strap of his helmet. "You want to take a ride?"

Jolene heard an inner voice say *don't do this*, but something else spoke, too. It growled, drowning out the first voice, demanding to be set free. She heard herself answer, "Sure."

Her legs shaking, Jolene walked to him. The boy offered his hand. She took it, and a jolt passed through her fingers and up her arm. Stretching her leg over the other side, she tucked her dress between her legs, and searched for a place to put her hands.

"Hold on around my waist," he said. She did, pressing her breasts into his muscled back. He kicked his leg down and the engine started with a throaty rumble.

As they pulled out of the parking lot, Jolene glimpsed the woman in the Handy-Mart watching through the window. She hoped Momma wouldn't go to the store that day. The woman would tell and trouble would fall like hard rain.

The boy drove down the river road. Cypress trees lined the shore, their slender trunks stretching skyward, the knobby roots poking out of the shallows. The road plunged into a jungle-thick forest of mossy oaks, the river flashing silver through the shadows.

After a mile the boy slowed down. They had arrived at a place Jolene had never seen before. A dirty sign said: "Lakeside

Estates – Model Home," and "Imagine Yourself Living Here." Someone had planned lots and built roads, but there were no homes and the lots were overgrown with weeds. They turned onto the property, driving down an empty street that led to the river. One lonely house stood there, with broken out windows and walls covered with graffiti.

The boy pulled into the garage and killed the engine. "Saw this place when I drove in," he said. "Wondered what was back here."

He pulled the beer and a towel from his saddlebags, and walked into the house. Jolene followed him. The floor was littered with pieces of masonry. A crumbling flagstone fireplace was covered with black soot, and filled with the ashes of campfires.

"What's your name?" he asked. Jolene told him. "I'm Jimmy," he said, and then glanced away. "Sure is pretty here."

Jolene followed his gaze through the missing bay window. The St. Johns flowed its slow way north. Dark clouds gathered overhead.

Jimmy pulled a beer from its ring and handed it to her. Jolene took it, trying to act casual. Popping the top, foam sprayed from the can. They both laughed, and Jimmy opened another.

Jolene took a taste, and it was awful. *How could anyone drink this and like it?* Still, she raised the can to her lips again.

Jimmy kicked aside rubble and laid the towel on the floor. Sitting down, he offered her the space beside him.

"Where did you come from?" she asked, tucking her dress around her legs as she sat.

"Miami. Spent last night in Titusville. Ate in a restaurant that had beer in tin mugs."

Jolene listened in fascination as he described the meal. It was like he had dined with the Emperor of China and eaten monkey meat from golden bowls. She took another drink of beer and, deciding to act a little drunk, giggled at something that wasn't all that funny.

She felt his fingers in her hair. Her whole body stiffened. *What is he doing?*

"You got some leaves," he said.

She allowed him to pick them out. Then he stroked her ear, running his finger along the edge. Electricity shot through her heart to between her legs. She felt something wet down there.

Jimmy slid his arm around her waist. He continued to talk, not looking at her. They gazed out across the water. Jolene took another swallow of beer, slid sideways and rested in the crook of his arm. His hand felt nice on her waist. The sensations confused and excited her.

The clouds released a warm summer shower.

"What do you do?" he asked.

"I go to school. I hate it."

Jimmy said that the only thing he liked about school was working out in the gym. He made the football team but was kicked off for smoking. He got a job at a Burger King and saved every penny until he could buy his bike. He left the day after his eighteenth birthday.

Jolene asked, "Where are you going?"

"To Pensacola, to work with my cousin."

He moved his hand up and stroked her breast through her dress. Jolene caught her breath as he did. It was forbidden, yet felt good. Her nipples grew hard, and the warmth from his hand spread over her body. The slippery feeling between her legs grew more intense.

Taking her chin in his hand, Jimmy brought her mouth to his. Their lips met and she let him do as he liked. He sort of sucked on her mouth, and she tried sucking back. His tongue gently moved in and she felt it searching. Pushing her tongue forward, they swam together like two little fish. A sound rose from her throat with no effort on her part, an involuntary mew. Her hand squeezed his thigh because she didn't want to fall. How could she fall? She was sitting on the ground with his strong arm around her. Still, she felt herself falling and held on tighter.

They lay back on the towel. He ran his hands over her body, feeling her breasts, her buttocks and her legs through the fabric of her dress. Jolene relaxed and let the magic grow. Part of her knew the wrongness of it. Part of her felt frightened. Still, she did nothing to stop him.

The summer rain fell harder, dripping off the eaves of the broken house.

He lifted her dress. She felt his hands on her bare thighs. When he began tugging on her panties she lifted her hips and allowed him to take them off. Then Jimmy started to unbutton the top of her dress. She stopped him, grasping his hand, but her desire was stronger than her reluctance. When he pulled his hand free she let hers drop to the side of her head. His fingers opened buttons and she allowed it, her breasts now naked before his admiring eyes. Jimmy took one of her nipples between his lips. She closed her eyes as pleasure swept over her body.

The next thing she knew he had his knees between her legs, holding himself above her with his strong arms. His mouth moved to her neck. Jolene felt something like a warm chill, if that was possible, run the length of her body. A sound came from her throat again, breaking out like a wild animal from a cage.

He pulled away from her. *What happened? Did I do something wrong?*

Rising slightly on her elbows, her yellow church dress fell away from her shoulders. Looking into her eyes in the most intense way, Jimmy reached down, jerked his T-shirt over his head and tossed it aside. He had muscular shoulders and a strong, flat stomach. Falling back, he pulled off one boot and then the other, unbuckled his belt, and unzipped his jeans. His briefs were filled with a huge bulge. Jolene could not take her eyes off it. He took off his underwear and the thing stood naked before her.

She'd heard boys at school talk about their "dicks" and their "hard-ons." Nothing she had imagined compared to this. It was so ugly, and yet she could not look away. Fascinated, she wrapped her hand around it.

Jimmy gasped at the touch of her fingers. She quickly pulled her hand away. He grabbed her wrist and put her hand on it again. It felt hot. It felt hard. Jolene moved her hand up and down, and Jimmy sighed.

He kissed her again, running his hands down her body and between her legs. His fingers moved between the lips. She shuddered as a jolt shot up from her crotch into her brain.

The next thing she knew, Jolene felt his hard penis pushing into her. It hurt, and she clutched his shoulders, but did not stop him. Jimmy thrust in, ripping through something inside her. He pulled out a little and went back in again. Another spasm of pain assaulted her. Going in and out, faster and faster, it hurt less. Her hips began moving almost on their own.

Jimmy shuddered and cried out. Jolene felt a spasm inside, something shooting into her, warm and wet. He made the same sound again and again, eventually growing quieter. His thrusting slowed, his breath grew less frantic in her ear. He kissed her all over, her face, her neck, her breasts. Soft whispers of "Thank you" and "You're so beautiful" fell from his lips. She felt herself calming down as well.

And then he left, slipping out of her. She didn't want him to go.

His thing was smaller now, and covered in blood. Her vagina felt sore and she wondered if the blood had come from her. Looking down, she saw that it was so. It wasn't her time of the month, and yet she was bleeding. Jolene remembered overhearing some girls at school talking about sex, saying that it hurt and that there was blood. She supposed this is what they meant.

Jimmy glanced at his hand. His fingers had traces of blood. He looked at her, astonished.

"Are you all right?" he asked, concern in his brown eyes.

Besides feeling confused—and sore—there didn't seem to be anything wrong. She just nodded.

"Did you…" he started, and then asked, "Was this your first time?"

Jolene didn't fully understand what had happened, but knew she had never done anything like it before. "Yes," she said quietly.

Jimmy smiled. It wasn't like he was smiling at her, but to himself. He shook his head, then walked over to the broken window. Reaching out, he put his hand under a stream of rainwater falling from the eaves, washing the blood away. He scooped some up and rinsed off his thing. Then, he walked into the garage. Jolene panicked when he left, relaxing as he came back with a T-shirt. He held it under the stream of rainwater and then handed it to Jolene.

"Go on," he said. "Clean up."

The cool, damp T-shirt felt good between her legs. She wiped off the blood. Jimmy pulled up his jeans, put on his other T-shirt, and slid his feet into his boots.

Jolene buttoned up her dress. She drew her knees up to her chest, and hugged them with her arms. Jimmy opened another beer and offered it to her. She shook her head. He took a drink, found his cigarettes, drew one out and put it between his lips.

He held the pack out. Jolene carefully withdrew a cigarette. Jimmy struck the lighter. Hoping her awkwardness wouldn't show, she leaned in and inhaled.

Her body racked with coughing. Holding the cigarette to one side, she coughed and coughed. He took the cigarette from her fingers and she continued to hack and wheeze. Jimmy gave her the beer and she took a swallow.

"You don't smoke, do you?" he said.

Jolene shook her head. Everything she had done that day had been for the first time. He smiled, put his arm around her and pulled her close. She laid her head on his shoulder, and watched a wading bird inch its careful way through the shallows.

Speaking in whispers, Jolene told him things she had read about in her books, describing imaginary places as if they were real, making no distinction between Oregon and Oz. To her, Hollywood was a magical place where everyone was beautiful and always happy.

"Maybe you should go some day," he said.

"I don't know where it is."

"Straight across the country on I-10. It'd be a long drive, but I could do it."

"Will you take me?"

"I'm goin' to Pensacola. Got to make some money."

Jolene felt disappointed. She laid her head against Jimmy's shoulder. So much had happened that day. The sun hung low in the sky. Its rays slanted through the tall cypress—

The sun was going down! She had no idea how long they had been gone. Jolene sat up, searching frantically for her panties.

"Take me back! I got to go home right now!"

"Sure. Okay. Whatever you want."

"If I don't get back now my momma will kill me!"

"All right. Okay. I'll get you back."

Jimmy put on his helmet. Jolene climbed on behind him. She felt a sharp sting between her legs, and shifted backward to take her weight on her buttocks. Jimmy kicked the starter, and they zipped back into Enterprise. As they approached the convenience store Jolene pounded on his back. Jimmy pulled over, engine idling. She slipped off, standing on trembling legs.

Jolene knew she needed to get home quickly. Still, she couldn't just walk away. Anxiously she said, "Do you have a pen?"

Jimmy produced one. Jolene wrote her phone number on the palm of his hand. Grabbing him behind the neck, she gave him another kiss. He gunned the engine and rode off.

Jolene hurried home and entered through the back door. Momma was busy in the kitchen, and her father had not yet come home. Going upstairs, Jolene went into the bathroom, took off her dress and saw a huge bloodstain on the back.

Momma can't see this. She'll know.

Hiding her clothing under the sink, Jolene jumped in the shower. Then, wrapped in a towel, she hurried down the hall to her bedroom. Putting on one of her sack dresses, she pulled her hair into a ponytail and went back to the bathroom. Dumping the yellow dress in the sink, she ran cold water over it and began scrubbing.

"What are you doing?" said her mother.

"Jesus!" Jolene jumped a mile. She had forgotten to close the door.

Instantly she knew punishment would follow.

"In this house we honor the name of the Lord," Momma said coldly.

"I'm sorry. You scared me. Please don't make me pray."

Momma reached out and yanked Jolene by the ponytail, still damp from the shower.

"No, Momma, please!"

Jolene was dragged down the hallway. With a steely grip, Momma forced Jolene to her knees before the cross.

"Pray!" her mother commanded. "You sinful, wicked girl!"

"Our father, who art in heaven, hallowed be thy name . . ."

Momma produced a lighter and struck fire to a dozen candles on a makeshift altar. She never released her vice-like grip with her other hand.

"—and thine is the kingdom, and the power, and the glory forever. Amen."

"Again," Momma commanded.

"Our father, who art in heaven . . ."

After twenty or so times, she heard Daddy's voice.

"What's this?" he said.

Jolene turned to see him standing in the doorway holding her yellow, sodden dress, dripping bloody water on the floor.

"She is wicked and sinful," Momma answered. "She needs whipping."

"No, Momma!" Jolene cried.

Moments later she felt the sharp smack of Daddy's belt across her buttocks. She fell forward on all fours, sobbing. Through tear filled-eyes, Jolene glanced back to see something that chilled her soul.

Momma and Daddy had the same look on their faces. Jolene

had never seen it before, because she had never dared take her gaze off the tortured Jesus while being punished. It was an expression of pleasure. They enjoyed what they were doing to her.

She had sometimes wondered why her parents married, as they seemed to have nothing in common. Now she understood. Momma and Daddy had been drawn together by a passion fueled with punishment. Their eyes shone with it.

"Pray!" Momma commanded.

When they finished, Jolene was sent to her room where she wept into her pillow, on her stomach because her buttocks hurt so bad from the whipping.

Through her sobs, she could hear Momma and Daddy down the hall. She had heard those sounds before, in the night after they had beat her.

Momma and Daddy were doing what she and Jimmy had done.

Jolene hated them.

CHAPTER EIGHT

Silky

SITTING ON CHARLIE'S DECK, Silky took a break from reading to gaze out at the ocean. She wore a broad-brimmed hat and sunglasses, gifts from her host. Freshly squeezed lemonade waited on the table beside her, tiny drops of water on the cool glass.

She had been living with Charlie for two weeks. Each morning he would cook breakfast. After, Silky would go swimming, or sit on the deck to smoke and lose herself in the pages of *Seventeen*, *Star,* and *People*. The magazines and the cigarettes were the only things she had told Charlie she wanted. He didn't mention giving her more money and she decided to not ask.

Going back to the street was impossible now. She had been

away so long that Skunk would kill her if she showed up, and for real. It wouldn't be just a beating like the first time. She'd gambled on the man in the silver Porsche, and for once had hit the jackpot.

All Charlie wanted was to hear more about her life. So far, she had told him only about growing up in Enterprise, and school. Those things were so long ago it seemed like they had happened to a different person. Some of the more recent things were too horrible to remember.

The door slid open behind her. "Ready for lunch?" Charlie asked. Silky got up, put on a robe and took her lemonade inside. He had prepared a cucumber and tomato salad, and salmon served cold with a tangy sauce on top.

Every day at lunch, Charlie would ask her about what she had been reading in her magazines. She'd tell him about Julia Robert's latest boyfriend or whatever. He would listen, every now and then saying something like "I met him once and wasn't impressed," or "She sincerely is a nice person." Silky didn't know if he really knew those people or was just kidding.

Today he brought up something unexpected.

"When was the last time you went to a dentist," he asked carefully. "Or a doctor?"

"I don't know," Silky said. "Back in Enterprise."

"I could make appointments for you."

Dread welled up inside her. She had heard about AIDS, and although she had always made her clients use condoms the idea nagged at her: *What if I've caught some terrible disease?* She was afraid to know the answer.

"I can't," Silky said, in almost a whisper. "I don't have any makeup."

She had not even worn foundation since Charlie had thrown hers away. Not having it bothered her, like an itch in the middle of her back. She couldn't possibly be in public without it.

"I can take you to buy some," he said.

Silky picked at her salmon. It would mean going out into the world without her face. But there was no help for it. The itch had been driving her crazy.

"Okay," she said.

After lunch, Silky put on her old jeans and T-shirt. Glancing in the mirror, it simply didn't look right without makeup. She tried wearing the broad-brimmed hat and sunglasses, but they were ridiculous with her street clothes. So, she put on the summer dress Charlie had bought for her. The hat and glasses matched perfectly. It was a disguise. No one, not even Skunk, would recognize her.

The dress had no pockets, and she needed to take cigarettes and lighter. Her fringed bag didn't match the outfit, but it was the only thing she had. Opening it, Silky found the money-filled envelope still inside, along with Charlie's things she had stolen the first night. He must have noticed that his fancy pen and cuff links were missing, but had said nothing. There was no need to keep them, as she was never going back to the street. Silky returned everything where she found it. After a moment's hesitation, she also put the envelope filled with money in a dresser drawer. Better to leave it than lose it.

Charlie drove the SUV this time. Forty minutes later they arrived at a huge mall. Pulling into the garage, he gave the keys to a young man in a red jacket who drove the SUV away.

The mall sent Silky's mind reeling. There were people everywhere, buzzing around her like bees. She and Charlie walked past one fancy store after another. Mannequins wearing clothes like the ones in fashion magazines stared blankly at her through the windows.

Silky stopped in front of a place called "Eternity." It had a reception area with nice furniture and dim lighting. A lady dressed in black stood behind the counter. Beyond her were rows of chairs, where beauty parlor girls fixed women's hair or polished their nails.

"Would you like a makeover?" Charlie asked.

Silky gasped. Every magazine she had ever read had an article about makeovers. In Las Vegas she had gone to a nail salon, but it was nothing like this place called "Eternity."

Smiling, Charlie indicated that she should enter.

Charlie spoke to the lady behind the counter. "We don't have an appointment. Can you take her anyway?"

"Certainly," she answered. "Sandrine?"

A girl in her early twenties stepped forward, with cocoa skin, deep brown eyes, and long hair pulled back in a braid. She wore a white lab coat, open and showing a golden dress underneath.

"Enjoy yourself," Charlie said, smiling. "And be good. If anyone doesn't treat you nice, just tell me later."

Sandrine led her to a changing booth. The girl told her to take off the dress and put on a smock that tied in the back.

"Why?" she asked.

"You ordered a full body makeover," Sandrine said, as if that explained everything.

Hanging her dress in the booth, Silky put on the smock. When she came out, the girl had her lie back with her head on a padded sink. She rinsed Silky's hair and then massaged in some goo. Head wrapped in a towel, the girl led her to a flat table with a hole in it. Sandrine instructed her to lay on her stomach, face in the hole. For the next hour, another woman worked the kinks out of every muscle in her body.

After, Sandrine moved Silky back to the sink to rinse out her hair. She then went to another chair, where two women waited. One began working on her feet and the other her hands. They showed Silky color samples and she chose a light green polish. She hadn't had her nails done by someone else in ages.

Sandrine told her to close her eyes. "This will sting a bit," she said. The young woman plucked her eyebrows. As she worked, Sandrine asked, "Do you want a bikini wax or Brazilian?"

"I don't know," Silky said. "Maybe nothing." She had read about those things, but had never done them. It sounded like they hurt.

Sandrine seemed to understand. "You can schedule one for the next time," she answered.

The girl snipped and shaped Silky's hair, brushed it out using a blow-dryer and turned her toward the mirror. She looked like a different person. Her hair framed her face, full and golden.

The girl applied foundation, blush, mascara, eye shadow, and gloss. She then handed Silky a card listing the colors matched to her skin tone.

After getting dressed, she walked into the lobby. Charlie was waiting, reading a book. Looking up, his face took on an expression of wonder. "What a beautiful young woman you are," he said.

Sandrine handed him a tray with a slip of paper on it. Charlie signed it, and then turned to Silky. "I've made an appointment with a personal shopper." She got excited all over again. Personal shoppers were something else she had read about in her magazines.

As they walked, Silky saw a group of girls coming toward them. They looked like the kind who tormented her in middle school. She locked eyes with one of them and the girl smiled. It startled her. The girl had not looked on her with contempt or said anything cruel.

Charlie steered her into a boutique called Papillion. A woman greeted them, and led them to a private room where an attendant waited holding a tape measure. The woman lifted the measuring tape and tried to put her arms around her. Silky drew back, eyes flashing with alarm.

What was she doing?

"It's okay," Charlie said. "She won't hurt you."

Still uncomfortable, Silky let the lady do her work. She put the tape measure around her body, down her arms and legs, around her neck, wrists and ankles, calling numbers to the other woman who wrote them on a clipboard. When finished, both women left.

It had been hours since she'd had a cigarette and needed one badly. They walked out of the mall, into the warm afternoon air where she lit up and inhaled deeply.

"What are you getting out of this?" Silky asked.

"I want you to be happy."

"Yeah, right," she said, looking away. Silky thought she had figured out Charlie's game, but now she wasn't so sure. He was unlike any man she had ever known.

After smoking, Charlie led her to a store that sold only makeup. The size of it overwhelmed her. She usually bought or swiped stuff from Walgreens, which had a lot, but nothing like this. Charlie took the card Sandrine had given her and summoned a salesgirl. As the girl collected the cosmetics, Charlie picked up a bottle of perfume and sprayed it on Silky's wrist. A sweet smell filled her nose. She tried another one, and another.

"Which one do you like?" she asked.

"The first one," Charlie said. "It reminds me of someone I was in love with long ago." It was the only thing Charlie had ever told her about himself. He had heard the most intimate details of her life and she knew nothing but his name.

The salesgirl handed her a bag, and Charlie signed another slip of paper.

Returning to Papillion, Silky saw clothes, shoes, belts,

handbags, and jewelry everywhere. The woman took a black dress from a rack and had Silky try it on. It fit perfectly. Admiring herself in the dressing room's three-way mirror, Silky realized that she looked exactly like one of the beautiful actresses in the magazines.

Charlie's eyes lit up when she came out. "Gorgeous," he said.

This is his kink. He must be having a blast.

Silky tried on everything. There were pants, shorts, skirts, blouses, and shoes of every color and style. Each outfit made her look glamorous.

There was even underwear. Silky had never had a bra like the ones the ladies gave her at Papillion. They fit comfortably, without pinching at all.

When they were finally done, the women packed everything in bags. Charlie carried them to the garage, where an attendant retrieved the SUV. Silky fell asleep on the ride home.

Charlie woke her when they arrived. Taking a soda from the fridge, she walked out on the deck to light another cigarette. The sun hung low, a huge orange ball in the darkening blueness.

Maybe there is another Hollywood.

The neighborhood where she worked the streets was called Hollywood, but it was nothing like the place she knew from the magazines. Silky thought that maybe she had seen a glimpse of the real Hollywood at the mall.

Charlie came out on the deck carrying a tray with sandwiches.

As they ate he asked, "Would you feel comfortable going

to the dentist now, and the doctor? I just want to be sure you're healthy."

So that was it.

He was waiting to fuck her until she got checkups. No wonder. He was such a neat freak.

"Sure, Charlie," Silky replied. "Whatever you want."

After they had finished eating, when the sun had gone down and the lights from inside cast a soft glow through the glass wall and onto the deck, Charlie brought out a bottle of wine. Silky lit another cigarette and told him more of her story.

CHAPTER NINE

Jolene

JIMMY REMAINED in Jolene's mind for the rest of the summer. Each day she would walk to the Handy-Mart and linger in the parking lot, hoping to hear the low rumble of his Harley. At night, he appeared in her dreams where, like a wild horseman in one of her romance novels, he would ride in and rescue her. This was what all the books had been talking about when they said things like "a passion that could not be denied." Without question, she was in love with him.

Love!

The idea startled her. She had only seen him once, yet it had to be love, because she couldn't stop thinking about him. It was the most wonderful feeling in the world.

School began again, and once more Jolene kept a safe distance from the other kids. Autumn passed and winter came. When it was too cold to go out for Phys. Ed. the students stayed in the locker rooms for Health Class, which the girls took separately from the boys. Their teacher was a stocky woman with a blunt haircut named Ms. Beckon. They had lectures on hygiene, dental care, and exercise. They spent a week learning about illegal drugs, with a slide show displaying marijuana cigarettes, heroin needles, and pills of all kinds.

One day they watched a presentation entitled *Becoming a Woman*. "Many of you have noticed changes in your body," Ms. Beckon began. "This is called puberty. Your breasts will grow like Jolene's have—"

Jolene tried to disappear. She did not like being singled out.

"Once a month," Ms. Beckon continued, "you will experience several days of passing blood. This is called mensuration, or 'having a period.' It is a natural process."

The first few slides showed women's bodies, before and after puberty. Then sketches of men's bodies appeared. One slide had a drawing of a flaccid penis, and then an erection. Ms. Beckon described what would happen next: the man pushed into the woman's vagina and moved back and forth until he erupted inside her. She said it might hurt, and there would be blood. Jolene remembered every detail vividly.

She was completely unprepared for what Ms. Beckon said next: "The sperm meets an egg inside the woman's uterus and a baby begins to grow."

Jolene felt dizzy. Ms. Beckon kept talking, about "trimesters" and "labor," her voice sounding like it was coming down a long tunnel. Recovering, Jolene blurted out, "How long does it take for the baby to grow?"

Everyone looked at her in surprise. Ms. Beckon answered, "The woman delivers it nine months later."

Jolene counted back. Jimmy had come in August. Now it was February. Six months. She had a baby inside her, and would have it three months from now.

"What happens at six months?" she shouted. The girls all stared at her.

The teacher clicked back to find the image of a woman with a swollen belly, smiling happily. Jolene stared at the image. She didn't look like that.

Ms. Beckon skipped forward. Jolene sat back confused. She listened with half her mind as the teacher explained delivery, recovery, and breastfeeding. The other half of her mind raced.

Was she pregnant or not?

The bell rang. The other girls jumped up, talking about what they had heard. Jolene remained deep in thought as the room emptied around her.

Ms. Beckon noticed her and asked, "Are you all right?"

"I don't want to have a baby."

"You're already having periods, aren't you?"

Jolene nodded solemnly.

"Have you had sex, Jolene?"

Jolene couldn't tell Ms. Beckon. Momma could never find out. "No," she said.

"Then you can't have a baby. Even women who have sex don't always get pregnant. Some women have sex all the time and never get pregnant."

A huge fountain of relief sprang up inside her. "How do they know?"

"As long as you have your period, you can't be pregnant."

Jolene had gotten her period every month since having sex with Jimmy.

"Don't you have a class?" Ms. Beckon asked.

Gathering her things, Jolene hurried down the hall to Algebra. As the teacher droned on, Jolene thought about what she had done. Jimmy had made her feel good, but it could never, *ever* happen again. She could *not* get pregnant, could *not* have a baby.

When the bell rang, she hurried out of the room to catch the bus home. As always, she took the long way to avoid the other kids.

Turning into the alley between the two buildings, she was startled to see a group of five girls. One of them was Audrey, the brunette who took peculiar delight in tormenting her. Three of the others were in her Health class. No one else was around.

"You fucked somebody," Audrey stated.

"No," Jolene answered, trying to walk past. The other girls blocked her way.

"You're a slut," Audrey said.

"I am not. Leave me alone."

The girls surrounded her. Audrey punctuated her next words by poking Jolene in the chest with her finger. "You. Are. A. Slut. Everyone. Knows."

"Leave me alone!" Jolene tried to force her way through. The girls shoved her around, chanting "Slut! Slut! Slut!" One of the girls pulled the backpack off her shoulder, opened it, and dumped her books on the sidewalk.

"Hold her still," Audrey commanded. Jolene tried wiggle free, but with all four clutching her she couldn't get away. One of them clamped her hands on either side of Jolene's head so she couldn't turn it. Audrey took a marker and wrote something on Jolene's forehead.

"Let's go," Audrey said. They walked away, kicking her books as they left.

Jolene burst into tears. She had never done anything to Audrey or the other girls. Why were they so cruel to her? Jolene collected her things and sat for a while, sobbing. Recovering, she went back down the alley to the rear of the building.

In a restroom, Jolene looked in the mirror. Audrey had scrawled "WHORE" on her forehead. Taking a paper towel, soap and water, she scrubbed. The marker did not come off easily. Then she sat in a stall for a long time. She wanted to leave this stupid town, the awful girls, and her mean parents.

When she came out, the buses were long gone. Jolene had to walk seven miles home.

At dinner that night, she went to the table with her head

down, so that Momma wouldn't see her forehead, still red from the scrubbing.

Momma noticed anyway. "What happened to you?" she asked.

"I fell in gym class." Momma just granted and started spooning out creamed corn.

When finished, Jolene went to her room. The door banged shut as her father left, and the sounds of *Wheel of Fortune* began on the television downstairs.

Her brain raced. She thought about Jimmy, his handsome face, his motorcycle—his freedom. She pondered having sex, and babies. A lump rose in her throat as she thought about Audrey and her friends. Then her mind went back to Jimmy.

Eventually the television went silent. Down the hall, Jolene heard Momma's bedroom door close. Usually she went to sleep when her mother did, but tonight she couldn't. After another hour of restlessness, she went downstairs and poured a bowl of cereal. Daddy had not come home, and she listened for the sound of his truck to avoid him.

The black telephone on the wall jangled, startling her. It was past midnight. *Who could be calling at this hour?* She picked up the receiver and spoke a tentative "Hello."

"Jolene?" said a voice, as if from far away.

"Yes?" she asked, frightened.

"It's Jimmy."

Jolene's breath stuck in her throat. Recovering, she stammered, "Where are you?"

"Pensacola. It sucks. Really, really bad."

"I hate it here," Jolene said. "Please come and get me."

"Okay. I'm on my way."

"Who is that?" said a voice behind her.

Jolene turned to see Momma at the bottom of the stairs, hair in curlers, still half asleep.

"Wrong number," Jolene said, hanging up the phone.

Momma grunted and walked back upstairs.

Jolene's entire body trembled.

Had Jimmy really called her?

She had waited for so long, hoping to see his motorcycle rumbling down the street.

Now Jimmy was coming. He would ride in and take her away.

CHAPTER TEN

Jimmy

JIMMY HAD BEEN on an adventure of his own. After leaving Jolene he continued toward Pensacola. Checking into a motel at 11:00 p.m., he noticed her phone number on his hand. Ripping off the side of a cigarette pack, he copied the number and stuck the paper in his wallet.

He took a shower and headed out for dinner. His big brother had given him his old driver's license, which is what he used to buy beer. The picture looked a lot like him, and most cashiers didn't care enough to check the expiration date. He walked into the bar next to the hotel, but bartender noticed that the license was fake and refused to serve him. Jimmy ordered a burger and took it back to his room, where he ate while drinking the last two beers from his saddlebags.

He arrived at Pensacola the next afternoon. His cousin Doug and his cousin's wife Arlene were happy to see him. Doug had long red hair and a moustache that ended in bushy sideburns. Arlene, a fleshy woman, favored jeans and Def Leppard T-shirts.

She brought beer from the fridge as Doug called for pizza delivery. They talked and laughed until after midnight, and then Arlene showed Jimmy the spare room. He slept next to a pile of camping gear and old motorcycle parts.

The next morning, Doug took Jimmy to the construction site where he worked and convinced the foreman to hire him. Each day they would put up drywall together; each night Arlene had supper ready. After eating, the boys worked out with weights in the garage.

Jimmy got his first paycheck and opened a bank account, keeping two hundred dollars to celebrate. Doug suggested they visit The Booby Trap, a bar with neon signs boasting: "Girls, Girls, Girls." Inside, dancers writhed on brass poles. Jimmy and Doug drank tequila shots and tucked dollar bills into the girls' bikinis.

A dancer named Treasure took Jimmy into a back room. As the music pounded she writhed her nearly naked body against him. When the song ended, she asked if he wanted another dance. Of course he did.

Eventually Doug came in and said they needed to go. Treasure told Jimmy that he owed her a hundred dollars for five dances. He felt like an Arabian sheik, peeling off twenties.

The boys stumbled into the house. Arlene wordlessly placed reheated food on the table before them. They ate without her company. As Jimmy fell asleep, he heard muffled voices arguing down the hall.

Doug never went to The Booby Trap again, but Jimmy would go every payday, drinking beer and buying dances from Treasure.

The construction job lasted six months. Jimmy put most of his money in the bank. Doug never asked him to pay rent, although Arlene often suggested he should. She also hinted that Jimmy should bring home some groceries and pick up around the house, but Doug would say, "No, no, he's family."

When the job ended, Doug found work in a warehouse. They weren't hiring anyone else, so Jimmy decided to wait and see what would come up. Most days he sat in the living room watching TV. One afternoon, during a rerun of *The Andy Griffith Show,* he decided a cold beer would taste good. Arlene walked by carrying a load of laundry. He casually asked her bring him a Bud the next time she came through.

An ashtray flew across the room. It missed Jimmy by inches and smashed into a wall, scattering butts everywhere. Arlene stood over him, red-faced and snarling. "I am not your slave, you son-of-a-bitch! Get the fuck out of my house!"

Jimmy drove to the warehouse where Doug worked and waited. A buzzer sounded and men came pouring out., heading for a food truck. Jimmy found his cousin and told him what happened. Doug said he would talk to his wife.

Jimmy ate lunch and went to a movie, heading back to the

house in the early evening. Arriving, he saw two grocery bags on the front stoop containing his clothes. Doug came out and announced, "You can't stay here anymore."

Jimmy protested. They were family. He couldn't just throw him out. His cousin listened silently until Jimmy stopped.

"You have to leave," he said.

Jimmy drove off, wondering where he would sleep. He called some of the guys from the construction job, but none had room for him. Then The Booby Trap came to mind. Maybe Treasure would let him stay at her place. He had paid her plenty for lap dances. The least she could do is let him sleep on her sofa. She might even fuck him.

Treasure was not there. He drank one beer, and then another, watching the other girls dance. Going to pee, he glanced in the back room and saw Treasure there dancing for a sailor.

When he returned to his seat, the waitress came by offering two-for-one tequila shots. *Why not?* Jimmy thought. He downed both shots immediately. His head buzzed like it was filled with wasps. If Treasure did not come out soon he would go in and get her.

Jimmy lurched toward the men's room again. Passing the back room, he saw her talking to the sailor. Jimmy didn't like that, not at all. He peed and went back to his table, fuming.

Treasure finally emerged. She glanced around and her eyes landed on Jimmy.

"Hey, there," she said, dropping into a seat beside him.

"That guy somebody special?"

"He just wanted a lot of dances."

"I don't want you doing that anymore."

Treasure looked at him more closely. "Are you drunk?"

"Come on, let's get out of here," Jimmy grabbed her wrist.

"Stop it!" she said loudly. "You're hurting me!"

Jimmy felt steely hands grasp his shoulders. The bouncer had grabbed him, and escorted him outside. Jimmy had no place to sleep, no job, and no reason to be in Pensacola.

Taking out his wallet, he noticed the piece of cigarette pack with Jolene's number on it. The warm summer rain came to mind, and the broken house by the river where she had fucked him. He must have been crazy, leaving that sweet piece of ass behind.

Jimmy found a pay phone, managed to put a quarter in the slot and dialed Jolene's number. An operator told him it would cost a dollar eighty-five for the first three minutes. After he dropped in the change, the phone rang once and someone answered: "Hello?"

"Jolene?" he asked.

"Yes?" It was her voice. Nothing had ever sounded sweeter.

"It's Jimmy."

"Where are you?" said the distant girl.

"Pensacola. It sucks. Really, really bad."

"I hate it here," Jolene said. "Please come and get me."

"Okay. I'm on my way."

The phone went dead. No matter. Jolene had said to come and get her, probably wanted to fuck as badly as he did. It would be worth the trip.

Jimmy staggered back to his bike and kicked it to life. On Highway 10, he pushed the machine to seventy miles an hour, then eighty, then ninety. After two hours he turned south on 75. Pulling off to pee, he bought a cup of coffee. His arms ached from driving, but after a brief rest he continued on. The miles flew past. The cold night air stung his face and knuckles.

He left the highway near Ocala. His entire body hurt and he needed sleep. The lights of a Holiday Inn beckoned. The clerk didn't like being roused at nearly four in the morning, but he accepted thirty bucks for a room. Jimmy collapsed into bed without undressing.

The next morning, he felt like he had a machete buried in his skull. After taking a hot shower he dressed and set out again, stopping at a diner for breakfast and coffee.

Enterprise was another two hours. He had no idea where he would find Jolene, and had not even thought about what he would do except fuck her.

Pulling into town midafternoon, he drove toward the convenience store where he had first met the girl. He noticed her as soon as he pulled into the parking lot. She had a heavy winter coat because it was February, and a gray backpack.

She had been waiting for him.

CHAPTER ELEVEN

Skunk

SKUNK WOKE UP LATE IN THE MORNING. Beside him was a girl with curly hair and a rat-like face, which wouldn't matter to the men who stopped at the curb. He called her "Girlycue."

He finally had someone to replace Silky, who had been gone for over a month. There was no way to know what happened. Maybe someone had persuaded her to go to Covenant House, or the police had picked her up. Skunk doubted it. He had drilled it into each of his kids to avoid those people. "The priests at Covenant House are perverts," he said, "And the cops will throw you in jail for the things you've done."

There was always the possibility that she was dead. That

didn't seem likely. Of all his kids, Silky had been the smartest. She even read books.

Skunk shoved Girlycue awake. She saw Skunk and cowered.

"You did good last night," he said in a reassuring tone. The girl broke into a tentative smile. Only a little purple bruising remained below her left eye.

Skunk walked naked into the bathroom. He took a whiz, came out, pulled on pants, a T-shirt, and his leather jacket. November had come and there was a chill in the air.

"I'll be back," he said, tying his boots. "Don't do anything stupid." Leaving his apartment, he dead-bolted the door from the outside.

Breakfast was a cup of coffee and a pastry in an outdoor café. Across the street, he watched LightLight and Oxie making their way through the tourists, asking for change. He trained his kids well; Girlycue would soon be ready to join them.

CHAPTER TWELVE

Silky

SILKY STOOD IN the ocean, waiting for a wave. The water had turned cold, but going in every morning felt good once she got used to it.

A swell rose behind her and Silky caught it, driving her toward the shore. Reaching shallow water, she stood up and scanned the beach. People lay in the sun, and some surfers bobbed in the water, too far away to see how many.

Returning to her towel, she dried off and picked up her cigarettes. Only a few remained, and she decided to wait before lighting up. Eating Charlie's delicious meals every day had filled her out. Her boobs had grown large again, so much so that the new bras Charlie had bought for her were now too tight.

Her skin had cleared up; the tiny pimples gone and the bruises healed. Regular conditioning had turned her hair golden.

A few days after her first makeover, Charlie asked her if she was ready to visit the dentist. Silky agreed, still feeling nervous. Putting on makeup, she applied it thickly, as if going back to the street. Charlie gave her a strange look but didn't say anything.

He drove her to a dentist's office and helped her fill out some forms. She wrote "Holly McMillan" at the top, a name she had picked up in Las Vegas. Charlie told her use his address.

A woman led her to a room and spent what seemed like an hour scraping her teeth. Silky managed to remain calm by closing her eyes and sending her mind to another place, like she did when one of her clients was fucking her. After, a dentist examined her and took X-rays. "No serious damage," he said, "but you simply have to take better care of them."

The next day they went for a checkup. Charlie helped her fill out some forms again. A nurse weighed her, took her blood pressure, and drew blood from her arm. The doctor, a soft-spoken Asian woman, gently asked a few questions and then examined her. Once again Silky sent her mind to the other place, especially when the doctor prodded between her legs. The last thing the she said was, "We'll send the results in a few days."

That was a week ago. Silky had spent the time anxiously waiting. Swimming and watching television did not completely keep her mind off what she feared the doctor might say, that she was sick and did not know it.

She walked back to the deck to rinse off in the outside

shower. There were always clean towels and a couple of robes in the cabinet beside it. She put a on a robe and went into the house.

Charlie looked up from his computer as she came in. He held out an envelope.

"From the clinic," he said.

Silky tore it open. The pages inside made no sense to her. She gave them to Charlie, who studied the writing carefully.

"Everything's negative," he finally said. "You're perfectly healthy." A huge feeling of relief came over her, and she couldn't keep her face from breaking into a smile.

Charlie grinned back. "Congratulations," he said.

Silky's smile vanished, and her armor snapped into place. Now that Charlie knew she didn't have some disease, he would want to have sex with her. If they had done it the first night, it would have been just business. Things were different now.

What would happen after? Would he take her back to the street?

But he only said, "I'll start lunch," and disappeared into the kitchen.

His reaction startled her. Silky had been sure that he had been waiting for the results from the doctor. For the thousandth time, she wondered what kind of game he was playing.

Sitting on the sofa, she read and re-read the clinic report, trying to make sense of it. Charlie came out with tomato soup and grilled cheese sandwiches. As they ate, she told him what had been happening on a show called *All My Children* that she had started watching. After, Silky went upstairs to see it, but her mind wouldn't stay on the program.

I'm not sick. Not a bit. I'm fine!

When the show was over she felt restless. No longer worried about her health, her mind needed something to keep it occupied. Charlie had so many books. Maybe he had a romance novel, like the ones from the library back home.

Going downstairs, she found him busy at his computer.

"You got anything I can read?" she asked.

"Your choice," he said, pointing to the bookshelf beside the fireplace.

Silky scanned the titles. *Moby Dick*? *Pride and Prejudice*? *The Iliad*? She asked, "Is there anything that would be good on the beach?"

Charlie selected one saying, "This might do."

The books she liked usually had a woman in a long dress on the cover, her shoulders bare, and a handsome man with his shirt open. This had only the title: *Lady Chatterley's Lover*. Silky shrugged. "Lady Chatterley" sounded like someone who might get swept away by a masked horseman.

She sat on the deck to read. It wasn't easy. The people in the book talked so differently. After awhile, the general story began to fall into place. It was about an English lady who married a rich man. Her husband went off to war and came back in a wheelchair. He couldn't have sex anymore, but she stayed married to him. The set-up was familiar, so Silky continued reading.

That night at dinner she asked Charlie about the book. Silky grew fascinated as he explained the old English times. They had a queen who dressed all in black and didn't want anyone fucking except to have children. The English navy was the best in the world, and they had colonies everywhere. Silky listened to every word, because Charlie had a way of talking that made it all sound so interesting.

When he paused Silky said, "Well, the book needs bandits or pirates or something." Charlie laughed out loud, and then agreed that *Lady Chatterley's Lover* would indeed be better with pirates in it.

The next morning Silky read for several hours. The book kept talking about "the colliers striking," so at lunchtime she asked Charlie what a "collier" was. He explained it was someone who worked in a coal mine, and that Lady Chatterley's husband owned a coal company. The story made more sense once she knew that.

Each day after that Silky would read more. Each afternoon Charlie would explain what she had read. It was like a game, to figure out part of the story and then ask Charlie later to see if she was right. And at night after dinner, Silky would tell him more about her own life.

One day, while reading on the beach, she stopped and looked back toward the house. Through the glass wall she could see that Charlie was not at his computer. That usually meant he was cleaning. She would often go inside to find him vacuuming, or scouring the bathroom wearing rubber gloves. Once she found

Charlie on his knees scrubbing furiously at a spot on the carpet with a toothbrush.

Silky closed the book, rinsed off on the deck and walked up the outside stairs to her room. Taking a shower, she shampooed and conditioned her hair and then blow-dried it full.

Coming back down, she saw Charlie at his computer. He faced away from her, his eyes locked on the blue screen. The white letters looked like tiny clouds in a summer sky. Silky suddenly felt kindness for him. This man had given her food, a home, and peace of mind. In return he asked only for her story. An emotion came to her that she had not felt in a long time: gratitude. Crossing the room, she laid her hand on his shoulder.

Charlie shot up out of his chair as if touched with a thousand-volt cable. "Oh, my G-G-G-God, Susie," he said. "You sc-sc-scared the life out of me."

Silky's defensive armor snapped into place. Looking at him coldly she asked, "We gonna each lunch or what?"

Charlie's eyes grew sad. "Sure. I'll bring it out."

They ate in silence. Silky had started to feel comfortable with Charlie, but his reaction told her how shaky the situation was. All he wanted was hear her story. One day she would come to the end of it, and then what?

After lunch, Silky went upstairs and took a nap. The sun had dropped to the horizon when she awoke. Walking out on the deck, she had a smoke and watched the day fade away. When finished, she went downstairs to find Charlie cooking. They had beef with gravy, sautéed asparagus, and the roasted potatoes she liked so much.

Silky finally broke the silence and asked him a question about *Lady Chatterley's Lover*.

"What's a 'game-keeper'?"

"You mean Mellors, right?" Charlie asked. "He takes care of the animals that live on the property. There have hunting dogs, and deer in the forest."

As they ate, Charlie continued to tell her about the old English times. It seemed like everything was okay again.

The nights now got cold, so they sat in the living room after dinner. Silky would go on the deck to smoke, but most of the time they stayed inside where Charlie coaxed more of the story from her.

CHAPTER THIRTEEN

Jolene

AFTER JIMMY CALLED, Jolene could not sleep. He was coming, and Momma had accepted her lie that it was a wrong number. She would run away, and never again have to face Momma or the bullies at school. Jolene stuffed her backpack with clothes. There was nothing to do but lie in bed, stare at the ceiling and wait.

About 1:00 a.m., she heard Daddy's truck, and listened to the sound of his footsteps as he climbed the stairs. They stopped right outside her door. Jolene heard her doorknob rattle.

Daddy was trying to get in!

She knew what he wanted. He had tried before, that night in the kitchen. Jolene had locked herself in with the skeleton key, but Daddy might be able to open it anyway. She sat fixed in terror until the knob stopped rattling, and couldn't relax even after his footsteps faded away.

The next thing she knew Momma was telling her to get up. Jolene dressed and went downstairs for breakfast. Her hand shook as she lifted a forkful of scrambled eggs, and she prayed that Momma would not notice. After, she put on her winter coat, hat, and gloves, lifted her backpack, said "Good-bye, Momma," and headed for the door.

"Wait," Momma said.

Jolene froze.

Had Momma suspected? Would she say, "I know what you're up to you wicked girl?"

"Brush your teeth," Momma ordered. Relieved, Jolene bounded upstairs.

At the bus stop she hid behind some bushes. The bus came, waited a few moments, and then moved on. The driver must have assumed she would be absent that day.

Jolene walked to the convenience store. She felt certain that Jimmy would come to the place they first met. Her heart beat faster when she thought of him, and that they were going to Hollywood together. A cinderblock wall separated the parking lot from the woods beside the store. Jolene crouched down behind the wall, on the side away from the parking lot. No one going into the store would see her. There was nothing to do but wait.

Jimmy was coming!

Every now and then the sound of an engine quickened her

breath. She would peek over the wall, but each time it was only a car pulling into the lot. Around 11:00 a.m., she went inside to use the bathroom. Noon came, then 1:00 p.m. If Jimmy did not arrive, she would have to walk back at the time she would usually come home from school and try again the next day.

Midafternoon she heard a low rumble. Peering over the wall Jolene saw Jimmy in the distance, driving down the narrow street. Her heart beating madly, Jolene walked into the parking lot, not caring if everyone in Enterprise saw her.

Jimmy pulled up and stopped, engine idling. He took off his helmet, his hair a tangled mess. As if pulled toward him by a magnet, Jolene kissed him. They were together after long months apart, hours and hours of agonized waiting.

Jolene broke the kiss. "We have to go," she said. "Right now."

"Where?" Jimmy replied.

"Anywhere," she said. "I have to get out of here, as far as possible."

Jimmy slid forward and Jolene sat behind him, backpack on her shoulders. He put his helmet back on, gunned the engine and pulled out squealing.

They sped north. Jolene saw places that she recognized from trips in the pickup truck, when Momma took her shopping or to the dentist. She had to squint against the wind, and the cold air stung her face. She didn't care. Every mile took her farther from home. The pine forests turned to rolling hills. There were miles of white fences, and horses grazing in open fields.

After several hours, Jimmy pulled into the parking lot of a

Denny's. Jolene's whole body ached, and her bra straps bit into her shoulders.

"That's all the driving I can do right now," Jimmy said.

Those were the first words he had spoken since Enterprise. There was no way to have a conversation, speeding over the highway on a motorcycle.

Jimmy ordered a Grand Slam with eggs, hash browns, sausage, and pancakes. Jolene asked for a tuna melt. Her parents had never taken her to a restaurant, and even a meal in a diner seemed glamorous. When their dinner arrived, they ate ravenously.

Finished, she looked at Jimmy. There were dark circles under his eyes.

"Are you okay?" she asked.

"I drove a long way last night," he answered. "Gotta check into a motel soon."

"How long before we get to Hollywood?"

Jimmy looked startled. "What makes you think we're goin' there?"

His reaction shocked her. Jolene had worked it up in her mind that she and Jimmy were headed for the land of eternal sunshine, to walk with the beautiful people on red carpets.

"You said we could," she answered.

Jimmy's eyes wandered over her body and lingered on her breasts. Jolene felt uncomfortable under his gaze. For months she had thought of nothing but Jimmy, and how much she loved him. The man sitting across from her was a stranger.

"I thought we'd get a room," he said.

Jolene knew instantly what he had on his mind.

"We can't do that," she said. "I am goin' to Hollywood, and you're gonna take me."

He stared at her for a long time. She didn't look away. Jolene had never been more determined in her life.

Finally, Jimmy dropped his eyes. "I am so tired I can't even think," he said. "I don't know what I'm gonna do. I got no job in Pensacola, no place to stay. There's work out in Hollywood, I guess, but right now I'm gettin' a room."

Jolene didn't think he understood. But what else was there for her to do? She had left Enterprise and was never going back.

The sun had dropped when they got on the bike. Jolene couldn't handle a motorcycle; she didn't even have a license. Wherever they went, Jimmy would have to do all the driving.

They pulled into a motel. Jimmy went into the office and came out with a key. Once inside, he collapsed on a bed and fell asleep. Jolene undressed and showered. Her body was sore all over, but the hot water helped her relax. After, she put on her nightgown, crawled into bed, and fell into a deep sleep.

A dream came to her. She and Jimmy were in the abandoned house by the river, and he was kissing her. Suddenly there was weight on her body. She couldn't breathe.

Waking up gasping, Jimmy was on top of her, naked, his hard penis rubbing against her thigh. She tried to push him away. "Stop! What are you doing?"

Jimmy grabbed her wrists, pinned them to the bed. She

thrashed, screaming "No, no!" Her knee slammed into Jimmy's crotch. He cried out in pain and rolled off her.

"What's wrong with you?" he groaned.

"I told you, I ain't doin' that!" Jolene said. "I don't want to have a baby."

"You practically killed me."

"I'm sorry, but I ain't gonna."

"Jesus," he said, still breathing hard.

Jolene gasped at the word. If Momma heard it, she would be so mad. But Momma was not there and had no control over her anymore.

Jimmy caught his breath. "We did it before."

"I didn't know I could get pregnant then."

"If that's all you're worried about, there are other things we can do."

"Like what?" she asked warily.

"Gimme your hand."

Jimmy reached toward her. She pulled back.

"It's okay," he said. "I can't get any sperm in you this way."

Jolene remembered Ms. Beckon's lecture. Her teacher had said that the man had to put it inside her for a baby to come.

"Come on," Jimmy said. "Let me show you."

Jolene let him take her hand. He put it on his penis, which was hard again. She wrapped her fingers around it, like she did before in the house by the river.

"Move it up and down," he said. Shifting her body a little, she did as he asked.

"You can't squeeze it too tight," he explained. "Pull the skin up each time. Don't touch the head with your fingers."

Jolene saw his face in the dim light. His eyes were glassed over. "Faster," he gasped. She stroked harder, and Jimmy gave out a huge groan. His cock throbbed and began to spurt, flooding over her hand.

When his dick grew soft she let go, holding her hand away from her body.

"Go clean up," Jimmy said.

Jolene went in the bathroom, and washed off using hot water and soap. When she came out Jimmy went in and washed, too. Flicking off the light, he flopped down beside her.

"Was that so bad?" he asked.

"No," Jolene said. If that's all it took, she could do it.

Jimmy rolled over and fell asleep. Before long she did, too.

A bright shaft of sunlight through the curtains woke her. Jimmy lay asleep, looking sweet and innocent. Jolene felt filled with love for him. She got up, put on one of her dresses, and then her coat and hat.

Waiting for Jimmy to wake up, she thought about what might be happening at home. Momma and Daddy would have expected her to come back on the bus. When she didn't, what had they done? Maybe they called the police. She needed to get far away, and quickly.

Shaking Jimmy, he gasped and woke up.

"We got to get going," she said. "The sooner the better."

"All right." Jimmy rolled off the bed and went into the bathroom. Jolene heard the toilet flush, then the shower running. Soon he came out toweling off, looking so handsome. Every muscle in his body was taut and strong, with thick arms and stomach flat as a board.

"What are you wearing?" Jimmy asked as he pulled on his pants.

"A dress," she said.

"It's easier in Levi's. On the bike, I mean."

Jolene had longed to wear jeans, like the other girls at school. "Can I get some?" she asked. "I need a helmet, too. I can't even open my eyes."

Jimmy looked stunned. After a moment, he said, "We'll see."

They checked out of the motel and climbed on the bike. Jimmy drove to a convenience store, filled the tank with gas, and took Jolene inside for coffee and donuts. It was the first time she ever had coffee, and the taste shocked her.

"I been thinkin'," he said, after swallowing a bit of jelly donut. "New Orleans is just the other side of Pensacola. Always wanted to go."

Jolene waited, puzzled. *Wasn't the matter settled?*

"I'll get you a helmet," he continued. "But you got to come with me, and no fuss."

"And then what?" she asked.

"And then we'll see."

Jolene bit into her donut. She supposed it was the best she could hope for right then. Jimmy might have to be talked into it, but one way or another she was going to Hollywood.

After breakfast they continued driving. Passing Tallahassee, Jimmy pulled off the highway and into the parking lot of a Harley-Davidson store. Inside, Jolene marveled at the colorful gas tanks and chrome finishes. A burly salesman with a walrus mustache and tattoos came up to them. Jolene had never seen anyone like him, and clung nervously to Jimmy's arm. Jimmy explained that he needed a helmet "for his girl." Jolene heart beat faster when he said it.

He loves me, too!

The salesman took them to a wall, covered floor to ceiling with helmets. Jolene chose a blue one, with a clear plastic bubble that would cover her face.

They stopped again at a Target store, and Jimmy told her to get what she needed. First, she found jeans, and then boots, because her feet had been cold in just sneakers. She also got an orange and blue sweatshirt with a gator on it, a red T-shirt, and a plain white one. Momma never allowed her to wear makeup and she pick up mascara, blush, and lipstick.

They met at the register. Jimmy had been shopping for some things of his own.

A girl rang everything up, but when Jimmy saw how much the total he told her to put some of it back. Jolene insisted that she needed it all. They argued about it until the people in line started to complain. The checkout girl pointed out an ATM, where Jimmy withdrew more cash and paid for everything.

Jolene went into the store bathroom and put on the jeans, white T-shirt, and sweatshirt. The ugly dresses Momma had bought for her went in the trash. She would never have to wear those awful things again.

It was nearly sundown. Having a helmet with a face shield, Jolene could now see everything. They passed a sign reading, "Welcome to Alabama, The Heart of Dixie." An hour later they crossed another state line into Mississippi.

Jimmy pulled into a motel just past the Louisiana border. Jolene's body ached from riding all day. She had pulled her hair back to wear the helmet, and sat in the room brushing out the knots as Jimmy went for dinner. He came back with a sack of burgers and they feasted sitting on the bed.

After dinner Jolene took a shower. The water warmed her skin. She let her mind drift away —

Jimmy walked naked into the bathroom. Jolene sputtered, and tried to cover herself with her hands. He paid no mind and stepped into the shower. His cock stood up proudly between his legs. He guided her hand to it, and then reached out to caress her breasts. Running his thumb over her nipples, they began to grow hard. Jolene worked his cock up and down as they kissed, their lips nibbling, their tongues dancing one around the other.

How wonderful to be in love!

Then Jimmy dropped his hand between her legs. His finger slithered into her, creating delicious sensations. She kissed him harder and stroked his cock faster, the water running down over them both. Jimmy's fingers went deeper, sending her into a sort of trance. Then his penis jerked in her hand, and shot against her belly.

Jolene jumped back with a cry, brushing it off her body. Grabbing the washcloth, she wiped frantically. Jimmy stood back a bit, watching her like he was half asleep or something. She climbed out and grabbed a towel.

Back in the main room, Jolene put on her jeans and the white T-shirt, and then sat on the bed with her knees drawn up thinking about what they had just done.

Jimmy walked into the room with a towel around his waist. "You don't have to worry," he said. "You didn't get any inside you."

"We didn't even think about it. We just did it."

Jimmy smiled. "Let me show you somethin'."

He pulled out a box, took out a little packet and tore it open. He placed the thing in the palm of her hand.

"It's a rubber," he said. "I wear one and it keeps the sperm from getting inside you."

"Are you sure?" she asked.

"Sure, I'm sure."

Her curiosity overcame her caution. "How does it work?"

"Take off your clothes," Jimmy said, setting his towel aside. His penis hung heavy, not hard like before. Jolene stripped off her shirt, jeans, and underwear. Jimmy stretched out on the bed, his penis lying against his upper thigh.

"Why ain't it hard?" she asked.

"Cause I just shot. It might take a while."

Jolene took his soft thing in her hand. It had a head shaped like an army helmet. There were crinkles of skin underneath that, and the shaft felt thick and spongy. Below that, more crinkly skin with two round things inside. She touched them lightly.

"That's my balls," he said. "You can play with them if you want."

Jolene did. They rolled around inside their skin sacks.

"You can do something to get me hard quicker," he said. "Suck on it."

Jolene pulled back. *What sort of a suggestion was that?*

"You can't get a baby if the sperm gets in your mouth," he urged.

That seemed right from what Ms. Beckon said. Jolene bent down and took the head of his penis between her lips. It had a soft, velvety feel.

Jimmy let out a soft groan. "That's so good," he said.

Jolene felt his penis grow. Holding the shaft, she moved her hand up and down. Jimmy looked back at her with the faraway expression she had seen before. Then he started thrusting. His cock hit the back of her throat. It made her gag, and she pulled away coughing.

"You all right?" Jimmy asked.

"Don't jam it in like that," she replied, annoyed.

"Yeah, but look what you done," he said, grinning. His penis was hard again. He picked up the condom and rolled it over the head. Then, he pushed her back on the bed.

Jimmy kissed her, and their tongues swam together. He

moved down her neck to her breasts, and took one of her nipples in his lips. His fingers probed into her pussy. Jolene slipped into the magic place in her mind. Jimmy wrapped his arms under hers, grasping her shoulders. She felt the tip of his rubber-covered cock slip between her lower lips. He pushed harder. In a moment, he was inside her, moving back and forth. It hurt a little bit, but nothing like before. A sensation spread across her body, and she grasped Jimmy's strong arms.

He cried out, and she felt his penis twitching. Then he collapsed, his body heavy on hers.

"Jimmy," she said, "I can't breathe."

He rolled off, his penis slipping out with a wet plop. "That was great," he said.

"And you didn't get nothin' inside me?"

"Nope," he said. "Have a look."

His penis was soft, the rubber clinging to it. Jimmy slid the condom off, his goo trapped inside, and held it up for her to see.

"It's awful," she said. "Get rid of it."

Jimmy went into the bathroom. She heard the toilet flush, and then running water. He came back out wiping his penis with a towel.

"All clean," he said, and kissed her. Jolene felt the anxiousness well up inside. Her body was ready to do more, but Jimmy rolled away. "Get some sleep," he said, flicking off the light.

Jolene lay in the darkness beside him. She wanted to reach out, pull his body to hers, and finish what they started. In the books she read, the women were always reaching "heights of ecstasy." If what they had just done was everything, then what was the fuss about?

She rubbed Jimmy's back, trying to get him to turn over and kiss her again, to say soft words to her, to say he loved her, but he was snoring softly.

It took her a long time to fall asleep.

CHAPTER FOURTEEN

Jolene

JIMMY WOKE JOLENE with kisses. He had already put on a condom and started fucking her while she was still half-asleep. He finished and went to take a shower, leaving her breathing hard and wanting more. She also needed to pee, but couldn't with him in there. Jimmy finally came out naked, toweling his hair. Jolene dashed into the bathroom.

She could hardly wait to do her makeup. After a quick shower, she tore the mascara out of its package. It was hard to put on because her eye closed every time the brush came near it. She finally got some black clumps on her lashes. After rubbing blush on her cheeks, she finished with lipstick, blotting it using tissue like the women on TV.

Jimmy had already left the room. Jolene crammed her clothes into the backpack, put on her coat, and tied back her hair. Stepping into the sunlight, a cool breeze caressed her skin.

Jimmy was strapping his saddlebags to the bike. "What's wrong with your face?" he said.

"I put on makeup," she answered.

"It looks awful."

His words stung. Jimmy didn't understand what putting on makeup meant to her. Other girls wore it, and all the women in her magazines. Momma wouldn't like it at all, but she didn't have to do what Momma said anymore.

"I'm gonna wear it," she said.

"Fine," Jimmy answered, and put his helmet on his shaggy head.

They stopped at a Waffle House and, after eating, Jolene watched Jimmy light up in the parking lot. He held the cigarette casually, as if it belonged between his fingers. Finishing, he flicked the butt away by snapping out his thumb.

As the miles passed Jolene had time to think. In two days, she had become a different girl, one who wore jeans and makeup, and rode with a boy on a motorcycle. Momma always said girls like that were whores.

Maybe that's what I am now.

But she wasn't a whore. She was Jimmy's girlfriend. That's what he told the man at the motorcycle store. She loved him, and he loved her.

They crossed the longest bridge. Jolene never imagined

there could be so much water, miles and miles of it. On the other side, the signs had strange words on them like "Pontchartrain" and "Michoud." They had entered a foreign country.

They passed a place that had rows of little stone buildings. Jolene thought that maybe they were toolsheds. *But why would they have so many sheds in one place?* She realized with a shock that it was a cemetery. The little buildings were houses for the dead.

Jimmy got off the highway, and soon they were driving down narrow streets lined with old buildings. The walls were painted bright green, yellow, and blue, with wooden shutters over the windows. Many had balconies made of black iron that looked like twisting branches and vines. Finding parking spot, Jimmy unhooked his saddlebags and told her to take her backpack and helmet. They did not dare leave their valuables behind.

Now late morning, it was so warm that Jolene took off her coat. The air had a musty smell, which Jolene figured was from the horses that came *clop clopping* past pulling carriages.

They turned a corner to find a small band on the sidewalk. It was only three instruments: a trumpet, a big horn going "oom-pah," and a guy with a drum. Jolene stood listening, her body moving on its own to the music. She glanced over at Jimmy and he was watching her, a smile on his face. Dropping her backpack, coat, and helmet, she started dancing for real. Momma would never approve, and the girls at school would have made fun of her—

To hell with them. To hell with them all. I'm dancing!

The band finished the song. People broke into applause. The

horn player walked around holding out a battered hat and some of the others dropped money in.

Jolene picked up her things. A store window caught her eye. The display was filled with candles shaped like bunnies and mushrooms. Jimmy came up behind and kissed her neck.

"Jimmy, can we stay?" she asked. The words came out of her without thinking.

To her total surprise, he said, "Maybe we should. I been drivin' a long time."

Jolene squealed, threw her arms around Jimmy, and kissed him. They walked the streets hand in hand. Entering a large hotel, Jimmy asked the desk clerk how much a room cost.

"Three hundred and fifty dollars," she said.

"For one night?" Jimmy asked, astonished.

The clerk suggested they check into a hostel. She gave them an address and drew the route on a map. They walked back to the bike and went looking for it.

The map took them to a neighborhood with ordinary houses, old and run down. They passed the hostel twice before they saw the address. It was a squat building with bars on the windows, like a prison.

Inside, a chubby man with white hair sat at a desk watching television. Jimmy said, "Excuse me." The man raised a finger and kept it there until the program went to a commercial. Only then did he turn his attention to them.

"You're in luck," the man said. "We had a cancellation, a room for two." When Jimmy asked the price the man said

"Thirty-five dollars." He glanced at Jolene. "Each."

Jimmy hesitated. "It includes breakfast," the man said. That seemed to be good enough for Jimmy, who handed him four twenties. The man opened a drawer, unlocked a small metal box filled with money and handed Jimmy ten dollars change.

Jolene's spirits fell when they entered the room. It was barely big enough for the bed. There was no television, telephone, or any other furniture. There wasn't even a bathroom.

"Where are we supposed to pee?" she asked.

Jimmy stepped out of the room and returned moments later.

"Down the hall," he said. "One for men, one for women."

Jolene thought that strange. At the other hotels they at least had their own bathroom.

"We ain't gonna be here all that much," Jimmy explained. "Let's go back and get something to eat." They left their things in the room.

They went back to the other place, parked the bike and walked, stopping outside a café with a sign that said: "Po' Boy Sandwiches."

"This don't look expensive," Jimmy observed.

A waitress showed them to a table. Jolene noticed a woman drinking something red in a tall glass and asked her about it.

"A Hurricane," the waitress said. "Fruit juice and three kinds of rum."

"Bring two of those," Jimmy ordered.

The waitress asked for ID. Jimmy produced his brother's driver's license; the waitress glanced at it, handed it back, and turned to Jolene.

"I don't have one," she said.

"Then you have to have a virgin. It's the same thing with no rum."

She returned with two tall glasses. A little fire burned on top of Jimmy's. Jolene's eyes grew wide. *What kept it going?* He blew it out like a birthday candle.

The menu had so many choices! The waitress suggested the coconut shrimp and Jolene nodded. Jimmy ordered a "Catfish Po' Boy."

"Make sure they take off the paws," he said, and Jolene giggled.

Jimmy pushed his drink toward her. She stuck her straw in and sipped. It tasted a little like medicine. They shared it until Jimmy saw the waitress coming and pulled it back. She placed a huge piece of sourdough bread stuffed with fried fish in front of him. Jolene's shrimp came on lettuce. Jimmy ordered another drink, as his glass was almost empty.

The second Hurricane came and they shared it, too. Jolene felt light-headed. Jimmy picked up his sandwich and the piece of fish plopped out. They laughed until their eyes watered.

Halfway through the meal two musicians came in, one with a big horn and the other with an instrument that looked like a black stick. They strolled around the tables playing happy music as Jolene listened with delight.

"Let's get out of here," Jimmy said, putting money on the table. Jolene stood up. Her head spun, she lost her balance and sat down again. They stumbled out of the café laughing.

Wandering around, Jolene saw amazing things in store windows. One had crystals in all different colors, and another had paintings of clowns. They found a park bench and watched as the gas lamps came on, dotting the street with flickering flames.

Jimmy lit up and inhaled, pushing the smoke out through his nostrils.

"Can I have one?" Jolene asked.

He shook a cigarette up from the pack. Jolene drew it out carefully. Flicking his lighter he said, "Go easy."

Jolene sucked the smoke a little way in. It tasted bitter. She blew it out without taking it into her lungs. They sat in the twilight, Jolene taking little puffs and Jimmy inhaling deeply.

Momma would explode if she knew.

Jolene felt an unexpected pang of sorrow. Momma would be worried about her, and Daddy too. She would never see Enterprise again. She hated everyone there, but it was the only place she had ever lived, the only world she had ever known.

Jolene put the cigarette between her lips, inhaled deeply and felt a sharp pain in her lungs. She started coughing and couldn't stop.

"Too much," Jimmy said shaking his head, but the smoke had done its work. The coughing had driven all thoughts of Enterprise from her mind.

After their cigarettes, Jimmy took Jolene into a club. It was dark and spooky. They sat at a little table that wobbled on its base. Jimmy went to the bar and came back with two frosty glasses of beer. It tasted bitter, but she soon grew used to the strange flavor.

An old black man sat down at a piano and played a cheery tune. A drummer began setting up his kit, and another man came in with a trumpet. A fourth musician joined them, opened a case and put together a black stick like the one she had seen before. Finally, a man climbed onstage carrying a huge wooden instrument and began thwacking the strings with his fingers. The drummer started *tick-tick-ticking* and *thump-thump-thumping*. The horn player joined in. Before she knew it, they were all playing a jumbled-up version of "You Are My Sunshine."

People poured in from the street, ordered drinks, and started dancing. Happy voices and laughter mingled with the music. The bartenders threw strings of shiny beads into the crowd. Jimmy snagged several and put them around Jolene's neck. He went to the bar and returned with more beer. Jolene drank and her head filled with feathers.

Jimmy pulled her on to the dance floor, where they flung their bodies around in time to the music. The silver and purple beads bounced against her chest. Jimmy put his hands on her waist and pulled her to him. She laced her fingers behind his neck and kissed him. The bodies of others jostled around them and against them. The music boiled into their ears.

"I love you, Jimmy," she said. Even though the bar was noisy, he must have heard her because he smiled and kissed her again.

They returned to the table, and then Jimmy went to get more beer. They drank, and leaned across to kiss each other as the music played and the crowd frolicked around them.

Later, Jimmy pulled Jolene into the cold night air. They walked down the street, arms around each other. It took them some time to find the motorcycle, and longer to find their way to the hostel. Banging in, a young man behind the desk told them to be quiet. They shushed each other and stumbled giggling toward their room, stopping to use the toilet on the way.

Jolene couldn't wait for Jimmy to make love to her. He had been beside her all day, smelling so nice she could hardly stand it. Once inside the room, she threw her arms around him. He jumped with surprise. She tried to take off his T-shirt but could not get it past his muscled chest. Jimmy peeled it off as Jolene fumbled with his belt buckle. His penis was already rock hard. She got his pants open and struggled to pull them down over his hips, where they bunched at his thighs.

Jolene dropped to her knees. She wanted his cock inside her the quickest way, and so she put it in her mouth. He groaned with pleasure and sat down on the bed.

Barely thinking about what she was doing, Jolene savored his salty taste, the softness of the head, the raging hardness of the shaft. Her hand grasped his penis tightly, giving the top little nips with her lips. Her tongue flicked out and swirled around it. Without even trying, happy sounds came from deep in her throat. Jimmy groaned, which fueled her passion even more. Taking the head deep into her mouth she sucked hard, moving her hand faster.

Jimmy exploded. She held him between her lips as he shot off again and again. It tasted warm and salty. Some of his goo slipped down her throat and she began to choke. She pulled her head away still holding the shaft. A few more spurts landed in her hair and fell on her cheek.

Jimmy sat up. "That was incredible, Jo," he said. Jolene looked at him and smiled. He had given her a new name, to match the new person she had become.

Jimmy fumbled, trying to take off his pants. Seeing him struggle, Jolene untied his boots for him. She pulled them off his feet, and yanked his jeans from his legs.

Rising, Jolene stripped off her T-shirt. The effort caused her to stumble. Wearing only her bra and jeans she went down the hall and into the bathroom. Flicking on the light, she looked in the mirror. There was a smear of Jimmy's goo on her cheek and a glob in her hair. *How could there be so much of the stuff?* She ran water, took a paper towel, and wiped herself clean.

Returning to the room, she heard Jimmy snoring. *Why did he always fall asleep?* Jolene removed her own clothes and slipped into bed beside him.

Jolene lay there with the room spinning around her. Too excited to sleep, she ran her hands over her body and felt her nipples grow hard. Grasping them with the tips of her fingers, she pulled and felt delicious sensations. Keeping her left hand at her breast, she ran her right hand down her body. Spreading her legs, she touched herself *down there*. The slipperiness began to flow. She rubbed harder, faster. A sigh escaped her lips. Reaching the top, she found a hard, little nub. *What was that?* She stroked it and the sensations came more strongly. Deep moans of pleasure emerged from her throat. She could not control them. Rubbing herself faster and harder, her moans grew louder and—

Bam! Bam! Bam! Someone pounded on the wall. "Hold it down!" a muffled voice called. "We're trying to sleep!"

Jolene froze. She lay still for a long time, one hand on her breast, the other between her legs. She didn't dare move. The passion vanished. After a while she relaxed, pulled down the T-shirt and covered herself with the blanket. Jimmy snored softly on the other side of the bed. Her head spun from all the beer, and she felt a sick in her stomach. Still, she smiled a thinking about all the things they had done that day. Drifting off to sleep, she expected the morning would bring more wonders.

CHAPTER FIFTEEN

Silky

THE WATER WAS NOW too cold for swimming. Silky sat on the deck dressed in a sweater and jeans. She had a new book called *Les Misérables*. It was about people in France in the olden times, and she had just finished reading about a girl named Fantine. The girl fell in love with a rich boy who got her pregnant and left her. After she had the baby, Fantine became a whore.

That's when Silky put down the book. The girl's story was too much like her own. She had never intended to turn tricks, it just happened. In Vegas, she and Jimmy were desperate for money. Then she came to Hollywood, where Skunk forced her to work for him.

She could never go back to whoring. No way, not after living like this. Yet Silky knew that she couldn't stay with Charlie forever.

Someday it had to end, and then what? Her whole life she had dreamed of living in Hollywood. When she got there, it was nothing like she imagined. The only place anything like it was the mall. Maybe she could get a job there, when he was done with her.

I have to go back and find out.

Charlie called her in for lunch. She picked at her shrimp-stuffed tomato and asked, "Can we go back to that place where I had the makeover?"

"Eternity?" he said. "Any particular reason?"

"My makeup," she said. "They put it on better." Silky thought it best not to tell Charlie she was thinking of finding work.

After lunch, Silky picked up the book again. In the next chapter, Fantine died without ever seeing her daughter again. It made her sad.

At dinner, Charlie told her that he'd made an appointment for the next day. It cheered her up a bit, but he seemed to sense something was different and didn't press her for more of her story that night. They watched a movie on TV instead.

Silky woke up excited about going back to Eternity. Selecting one of the nicer dresses Charlie had bought for her, for the first time she put on a pair of heels. Silky had taught herself how to wear them in Las Vegas. Charlie had not yet heard about that part of her life. Things happened in Vegas that she would just as soon not remember.

Charlie was working at his computer. He turned when he heard the click of her stilettos on the stairs, and his face took on a strange expression.

"What's wrong?" she said.

"I . . . I've never seen you like that," he stammered. "You look like a different person."

After breakfast, they went to Eternity. Silky relaxed as Sandrine and her assistants worked their magic. She paid careful attention when the cosmetician applied the makeup, and noticed she used only a little foundation and the barest amount of blush and eyeliner. Silky decided that she had been putting on too much all along.

Charlie greeted her with admiration. Walking back to the garage he said, "I need to run an errand. Would you mind coming with me?"

They drove down a street with elegant shops, that had names like Gucci, Prada, and Chanel. There was also a building that she remembered from a movie.

"Is this the real Hollywood?" Silky asked in awe.

Charlie chuckled. "It's Rodeo Drive."

They pulled into a garage so clean the floor squeaked under the tires.

"My meeting's at three," Charlie explained. "We have time for lunch."

They took an elevator upstairs to an open-air mall. Silky saw her reflection in a window. In her outfit she looked exactly like everyone else there.

Charlie led her to a fancy restaurant. The menu was in another language. "Would you like me to order for you?" he asked, and Silky nodded.

"Is this where you work?" she asked, meaning the neighborhood.

"Most of my work I do on the computer."

"What is your job?" It was the first time that question had crossed her mind.

"I tell stories," he said.

"You make money doing that?"

"Amazing, isn't it?" he said. "I write stories, other people turn them into movies and we all make lots of money."

The waitress placed a dish of pasta in front of her. It had red sauce and chunks of soft, white meat that melted on her tongue. She had never tasted anything so delicious.

"What is this?" she asked.

"Haven't you had lobster before?"

Silky suddenly felt out of place. Fear gripped her by the throat. She had left the safety of Charlie's house and entered the real world. Skunk might even be here. Silky imagined she saw him walking up the stairs with his stripe of yellow hair and a scowl on his face.

"It's okay, Susie," Charlie said. "I never had lobster until I moved to Los Angeles either."

Halfway through their meal, a good-looking black man and an attractive white woman passed their table. The man stopped suddenly. "Charlie?" he asked.

"Stanley," Charlie replied, with a smile. He rose and shook the man's hand.

"Where have you been hiding?" Stanley asked.

"Working on a new project."

"Do you know Angelica?" Stanley indicated the woman.

"We haven't met," said Charlie. "But I've seen *Top Floor.*"

"Thank you," the young woman beamed. "I loved *The Consignation.*"

The man Charlie had called "Stanley" was looking at Silky. He was handsome, with brown eyes and a neatly trimmed beard. When he smiled, dimples appeared.

Charlie introduced her: "This is Susie, my research assistant."

Research assistant? What was that?

"Good to meet you," Stanley said, and shook her hand.

If Daddy had seen that, he'd be so angry. He didn't like black people, not at all, and wouldn't have stayed quiet if one touched his daughter. But Silky had met lots of them since leaving home, and they were just like everybody else. Stanley seemed particularly nice.

"We should get together," Stanley said to Charlie.

"I plan to have everyone out to the house one of these days," Charlie replied.

"I'll look forward to it," Angelica said, inviting herself.

"Come, dear," Stanley said, steering her away.

"What's a research assistant?" Silky asked once they had left.

"I had to tell him something," Charlie answered.

"Does a research assistant get paid?"

Charlie looked stunned. "I have been taking care of you for weeks."

"I'm just asking," Silky said. Her street sense had kicked in. If there was money to be made, she should be getting it.

"I've never needed one," Charlie said, "But other writers have them." His eyes grew serious. "I don't know what you are to me. When I picked you up, it was with the intention of taking you back the next day."

"But you didn't."

"I suppose I could say you are a house guest."

"I'd rather be a research assistant," she offered. "If it pays something."

Charlie chuckled softly, his eyes twinkling. "Perhaps we need to define this relationship. Very well, you're hired. I'll give you three hundred dollars a week, plus room and board."

"Five hundred a week and nothing else changes," she said.

Charlie looked surprised again. "Four hundred," he countered.

Silky thought it was a good deal, as long as he didn't try to have sex with her. It would cost him a lot more if he wanted to add fucking.

"Cash only," she said.

Charlie nodded in agreement. "Starting this Friday." He stuck out his hand and Silky shook it. She knew all about negotiation. Hollywood Boulevard or Rodeo Drive, striking a bargain never changed.

As they ate their lunch, Charlie explained that Stanley was

an agent and Angelica an actress. Stanley had worked with Charlie on a movie called *The Consignation*. Silky remembered the billboards, but had not seen it.

After lunch, they walked out of the restaurant, down the sidewalk, and entered an office building. At the elevator, Charlie pressed a button for the 12th floor.

The doors opened on a desk with a receptionist. Charlie called her "Debbie." Going into an office, a large woman greeted them. She wore a billowy black dress, and had a face surrounded by mass of dark hair. Her eyes peered at Silky through black-framed glasses.

"Charlie," she beamed as they walked in. "How's my favorite scribe?"

"Couldn't be better," Charlie answered. "You look fantastic." They hugged, and the woman turned to Silky. Before Charlie could speak, she did.

"I'm Susie, Charlie's research assistant."

The woman held out her hand. "I'm Melinda, Charlie's agent." Then she looked at Charlie, as if needing further explanation. He just shrugged.

They sat. Melinda and Charlie shot sentences back and forth like gunfire.

"They're anxious to see something," Melinda said.

"The treatment's almost ready."

"What can I tell them?"

"Character driven, woman on a journey of self-discovery, lots of sex."

Melinda mentioned somebody named "Abby," and that she might be able to persuade "Leo" to "come onboard." Silky didn't think she meant they were going anywhere on a boat. She also mentioned somebody named "Gabe" who was at a place called "Warners."

Eventually Charlie stood up. The agent turned to Silky.

"Nice to meet you, Susie. Research assistants take notes in meetings. Bring a pen and pad if you want to keep up the pretense."

Charlie looked embarrassed. "Thanks, Melinda. You're the best."

As they waited for the elevator Silky asked, "What did she mean by that?"

"Melinda is astonishingly perceptive," he replied. "It's one of the things that makes her a good agent. And she's right. I'll give you a notebook to take when we go out."

They walked to the garage, where a young man brought up the SUV. Once they were in traffic Silky asked, "How did you meet her?"

Charlie told her that he wrote a script many years ago. A director he met in college made it into a movie. Nobody had any money so they shot it on Charlie's parents' farm in North Carolina. The director put it in a contest and it won a prize. Charlie wrote to people trying to sell his other scripts. When a producer wanted to buy the screenplay for *The Consignation*, Charlie asked Melinda to "handle the deal." She had been his agent ever since.

They inched along slowly through heavy traffic. "Why do they call it a freeway when everyone's locked up?" Charlie groused. They didn't get home until the sun had gone down.

Silky went upstairs and changed out of the nice dress. Putting on a terrycloth robe, she turned on the TV and clicked through the channels.

Charlie knocked on the door. "Come in," Silky said, muting the sound.

He entered and stopped short, turning his eyes to the ground.

"What's wrong?" she asked.

"You're not dressed."

Silky saw that the robe had slipped off one shoulder, leaving her breast exposed. She covered up and said, "It's okay, Charlie."

He raised his eyes cautiously. The only light was from the television, giving the room a magical glow. "I wanted to know if you're hungry," he said.

Silky knew that Charlie liked it when she put on new clothes. Maybe he really wanted to see her naked. That was something she could give him, having done it many times before. Untying the robe, Silky let the top fall, shoulders and breasts exposed. Charlie stood motionless, his eyes not moving away this time. She stood and the robe dropped to her feet.

In that moment, she wanted Charlie to put his hands on her. He didn't, and she wasn't going to ask. Charlie needed to make the move.

The air conditioner kicked in, breaking the suspense. Feeling its cold stream on her body, she walked to the dresser, took out a pair of panties and slipped them on. As Charlie watched she donned a pair of jeans and slid a T-shirt over her head. Stepping into sandals, she turned toward him and said, "Dinner sounds good."

Taking her cigarettes, Silky went onto the deck. Lighting up, she stood in the chilly ocean breeze.

Silky realized she wanted to sleep with Charlie. The idea surprised her. Jimmy was the only boy she had ever wanted to do it with. After coming to Los Angeles, she sold sex like slices of pizza. It was a relief to not be screwing all the time.

But things had changed that afternoon. Charlie had hired her as his research assistant. It was a job for a normal person. She wasn't a whore any more. Sex, on her own terms, could be part of her life again.

But with Charlie? He was a lot older than her, and there was something going on in his head that she didn't understand. This was a good thing, living at his house. Having sex might screw it up. Better to just give him what he wanted most: more of her story.

Silky stabbed out her cigarette. Walking downstairs, she saw Charlie through the glass wall setting the table.

"Can I have some wine?" she asked, entering. He opened a bottle, and after two glasses Silky began telling him what happened after she and Jimmy left New Orleans.

CHAPTER SIXTEEN

Jolene

JOLENE AWOKE IN the tiny hostel feeling sick. Jimmy lay beside her like he was dead. She hurried barefoot to the bathroom, getting to the toilet seconds before throwing up. Lying on the cool tile floor, she waited until her stomach calmed down.

Some of the vomit had splashed onto her shirt. Returning to their room, she searched in vain for a clean one. Putting on the gator sweatshirt, she went to find a laundry.

The white-haired man in the lobby was watching television. Before Jolene said a word, he raised a finger, and did not look up until a commercial came on.

"Is there any place I can wash some clothes?" she asked.

"Out back," he said. "If you need quarters, I have them."

"Yes, please." The man reached into a drawer, took out the small metal lockbox and opened it. He looked at her, waiting.

"You have to give me something to change," he said.

"I guess later," she replied.

The man locked the box and put it away. "Breakfast ends at ten," he said.

Jolene found the dining room. There were about twenty people eating, most of them around her own age. The food was laid out like a cafeteria, served by a woman who didn't look black or white but like something in between. Filling a plate with eggs and biscuits Jolene ate, feeling better afterward. She noticed the woman putting things away, and grabbed a couple of biscuits and some packets of jam for Jimmy.

Back in the room, he was still asleep. Jolene stuffed their clothes into her backpack. Taking a five-dollar bill from Jimmy's wallet, she returned to the desk. The man gave her quarters, which she took to the laundry room. Laundry was one of her chores back home, and it didn't take her long to figure out how to start a load.

Jolene decided to go back to their room. Jimmy wasn't there. *What was he wearing? His jeans were in the wash.* In the hall, she saw him coming out of the bathroom wrapped in the blanket from the bed.

"Jo!" he said. "Somebody stole our clothes!"

"I'm washing them. We didn't have nothin' clean."

Entering the room, Jimmy sat on the edge of the bed and put his head in his hands. "I got to get some breakfast," he groaned.

"Breakfast is over," she said. "They put it away already."

"Damn! Shit!" Jimmy snapped. "Why didn't you wake me up, you stupid bitch?"

Jolene felt as if he had slapped her across the face. "I got you some biscuits," she said. "They're on the dresser."

"Fine."

"I took money for the laundry."

Jimmy looked inside his wallet. "I had a hundred dollars in here."

"You had seven. I took five."

"What happened to the rest?"

"You bought a lot of beer last night."

"Don't ever take my money again," he snarled.

Jolene walked out burning with anger. It wasn't her fault they stopped serving breakfast. He wasn't even grateful that she was washing their clothes.

Passing through the lobby the man behind the desk said, "Check out's at noon."

Jolene put their clothes in the dryer and thought about her situation. What if they had a real fight, and Jimmy left her? She didn't know anyone in New Orleans, or anywhere else. She didn't want to ever see Enterprise again. With nothing except the quarters in her pocket, she would be stuck wherever she was.

The man at the desk had a whole box full of money. Most of the time he paid no attention to it. If she took it, he might not even miss it.

Jolene couldn't believe that thought had come into her mind.

It was stealing, and Momma said that stealing was a sin. But so was wearing jeans and makeup. Jolene needed money desperately. *But could she just take it?*

When the machine stopped, she folded her clothes, put them in her backpack, and balled Jimmy's under her arm. Passing through the lobby, she saw other guests leaving.

Jimmy lay on the bed, the blanket wrapped around his waist. Jolene plopped the pile of clothes on the mattress beside him.

"Get dressed," she said. "We gotta check out."

Jimmy groaned and put on his jeans. "We're going through my money pretty fast."

Jolene strapped on her backpack and picked up her helmet. Jimmy jammed his things into his saddlebags. They walked to the lobby, where the white-haired man sat with his eyes glued to the TV screen. When a commercial came on he looked up.

"Which way to the interstate?" Jimmy asked.

The man got up and walked to the door. "See that billboard? Go past it, turn left on Napoleon, then right on Claiborne Avenue. You'll see the 10."

The man was distracted, and there was no time to think twice. Jolene set down her helmet and opened the drawer that held the lockbox. Slipping the box into her coat, Jolene closed the drawer and picked up her helmet. When the man finished talking, he immediately started watching television. He did not look at Jolene, or open the drawer.

Outside, while Jimmy put on his helmet, Jolene slipped the lockbox into her backpack. They were on the road moments later.

The highway was a low bridge over swampland as far as they could see. An hour passed before the regular roads returned.

What was happening back at the hostel?

The first time the white-haired man opened the drawer to make change he would notice his lockbox missing and call the police. Jolene needed to get rid of it. Without it, there was no way anyone could prove the money wasn't hers.

They sailed through Baton Rouge, and then Lafayette. About an hour later Jimmy pulled into a truck stop.

"Gotta pee," he said. "You'd better go, too."

They went inside, where a dozen truckers sat at a lunch counter. They wore a kind of uniform: plaid shirts and baseball caps. They all looked up as Jolene entered, swallowing her with their eyes.

In the ladies' room, she used the toilet and then examined the lockbox. It was shut tight. Banging it against the sink did nothing. She put it under her coat and went into the restaurant again. Jimmy was working the ATM in the gift shop. She handed him her backpack and helmet, saying she needed to walk around.

Outside, Jolene stepped over a cinderblock wall and walked behind the building. Lifting the lockbox high, she threw it to the ground. The box bounced on the concrete slab, but didn't open. She picked up a broken piece of cinderblock and hammered at the lock.

"What are you doing?" said a voice behind her.

Jolene turned to see a man standing in a doorway wearing a

cap with a Confederate flag. He had a red beard sprinkled with gray and eyes that burned fierce blue.

She held up the lockbox. "I lost the key."

The man gazed at her intensely. "Bring it inside," he said.

The garage was dark and smelled like grease. Two big trucks had their hoods open, with parts scattered around. Coming to a workbench, the man fitted the lockbox into a vise. Selecting a hefty screwdriver, he placed the blade above the lock and gave the handle three sharp blows with a hammer. The lock shattered. The man opened the vise and set the box on the workbench.

Jolene shoved the bills and coins into her coat pockets. Looking up, her eyes met the intense gaze of the stranger.

"Thank you," she said, and headed toward the door.

"Don't you want your box?"

Jolene turned to see the man holding it out, the top dented, the lock shattered.

"You keep it," she said. "Fix it or throw it out."

"That's all I get, a broken box?"

Jolene pulled out the wad of money. Peeling off a one-dollar bill, she held it out for him and stuffed the rest back in her pocket.

"That ain't gonna do it, girly." He grabbed her wrist and pulled her toward him.

What was he doing?

"Stop it!" she cried.

The man pressed her against the workbench. Jolene could feel his stiff dick through his jeans. Suddenly she knew what he wanted. His face was beside her hers, his breath hot in her ear. His hand yanked down the zipper of her coat.

"No! No!" she screamed. "Stop it! Help! Help!"

The man slapped his hand over her mouth. "This is gonna happen, girly. Just relax and enjoy it." His blue eyes burned into hers.

Jolene thrashed and tried to scream. Scrambling frantically, her hand found the screwdriver. Picking it up by the metal part, she swung it as hard as she could. It hit the man on the ear. He cried out and clapped one hand to the side of his head. Letting go of her wrist, he slapped her hard across the face. The force spun her around. Jolene saw a heavy wrench on the workbench. Taking it in both hands, she turned and slammed it against the side of the man's head. He went down shouting a string of curses.

Jolene dropped the wrench and ran toward daylight. Stumbling over the cinderblock wall, she hurried into the restaurant. Jimmy sat at the end of the counter with a menu.

"We gotta get out of here," she whispered harshly.

"Might as well eat," Jimmy replied.

"No. Let's go. Right now!"

"I didn't have a real breakfast."

"Get your ass up!"

The men along the counter fell silent, staring at her. Jimmy looked up, shocked. Jolene lifted her backpack from where it sat near Jimmy's feet and walked out. Jimmy followed. When he emerged, Jolene was beside the bike, helmet on her head, and backpack on her shoulders.

"What's wrong with you?" he asked.

"I'll tell you later. Let's go!"

Jimmy climbed on without another word.

They drove for over an hour. Jolene's cheek felt hot where the man had slapped her. She wrestled with how to explain what happened.

What would he do? Go back and beat the guy up? Maybe nothing at all?

After crossing the Texas state line, they pulled into a Burger King. Jimmy asked, "What got into you back there?"

Jolene walked into the restaurant without answering, and went into the bathroom. In the mirror, she could see that her face was still a little pink.

Jimmy was in line when she came out. They ordered, and took their food to a booth.

"You gonna tell me what happened?" Jimmy asked.

She didn't know how. "The men kept staring at me," she said.

"Guys do that," he said. "Get used to it." He picked up his hamburger.

Jolene couldn't believe her ears. Jimmy didn't give a damn. If she told him about the red-bearded man he would probably think it was her fault. She was traveling with a scarecrow—a man who could drive a motorcycle and fuck her but had nothing in his head but straw.

"You should be nicer to me," she said.

Jimmy looked up with an expression of bewilderment. An uncomfortable silence hung between them. Never taking his eyes from hers, he just bit into his burger. Jolene realized that saying anything more would be pointless, and turned her attention to her meal.

After lunch, Jimmy stopped at a convenience store to fill the tank. Jolene walked inside. There was nothing she wanted except to feel in control of her destiny. One way was teaching herself to smoke. For that, she needed her own cigarettes. Approaching the clerk, she asked for a pack of Camels.

"Got to see some ID," he said.

"I left it at home."

The clerk stared at her in a way that was becoming familiar. The boys at school, her male teachers, and even Daddy made that same expression. The red-bearded man had it, and thought that he could screw her just for opening the lockbox. The realization hit her like lightning:

They all want to fuck me.

It was a kind of power she had. It wasn't much, but it was something. Smiling at the clerk, she used a little-girl voice and said, "Please?"

He pulled down a pack and slid them across the counter.

"And a lighter." Jolene paid in nickels, dimes, and quarters.

They drove into Houston, where traffic grew thick. Jolene's arms ached and her neck felt stiff. Jimmy must have been exhausted and yet they didn't stop. He continued driving through San Antonio. Around midnight he finally pulled off the freeway. The lonely interchange had only a gas station and a small motel.

Their room was dark and cold. Jimmy stripped off his clothes. The weariness of the road showed on his face.

"Maybe we should stop for the day again," she suggested.

"Need to get there. We're running out of money." Jimmy walked into the bathroom and closed the door. Jolene heard the shower running.

"I'm going for a walk," she shouted, and stepped outside.

The night was bitter cold, the land around the motel flat and empty. The eastern sky was a glowing dome created by the lights of San Antonio. The rest was filled with stars.

Taking the cigarettes out of her pocket she opened the pack, struck the lighter, and pulled the smoke deep into her lungs. Her body fought back with violent coughing. Inhaling again, she forced her lungs to behave.

Back in the room, she found Jimmy already asleep. After showering, Jolene lay down beside him.

He woke her in the middle of the night. This time she knew what he wanted.

Might as well make the best of it.

Returning his kisses, Jolene slid her hand down to his erection and grasped it. That spurred him on, and he moved between her legs.

"No!" she commanded. "Get a rubber."

Jimmy put on a condom and was at her again, thrusting until he shuddered and lay still. Before Jolene could catch her breath, he was snoring.

Leaving late the next morning, they drove across the

emptiness of western Texas. Occasional outcroppings of rock and scrubby trees did little to relieve the boredom. Jimmy stopped for a lunch break midafternoon, and again for dinner when the sun grew dim.

He looked more tired than before. "Maybe we'd better get a motel," Jolene suggested.

"Can't," Jimmy answered. "The sooner we get there, the better."

After dinner, they drove on. Jolene's mind wandered toward the future. Once they arrived in Los Angeles she would need to find work, too. *What could she do? Maybe be a clerk in a store, or even get a job in the movies—*

Something appeared in the road in front of them, maybe a chunk of tire. Jimmy jerked the bike to one side, and the next thing she knew they were going down. The tires squealed and Jolene could smell burning rubber. A scream of terror burst from her throat, and she dug her fingers into Jimmy's shoulders.

He somehow managed to keep the motorcycle upright. A car zipped past them, horn blaring. Slowing to a crawl, they took the next exit.

Jolene slid from her seat like a jellyfish. Jimmy removed his helmet, and his face was white as a ghost.

"You okay, Jo?" he managed to utter. She nodded.

"I been pushing too hard," he continued. "We need to stop soon."

Jimmy rested a few minutes, and they climbed on the bike again. He drove more slowly into El Paso. The first hotel they came to looked expensive, but Jimmy didn't seem to care. He walked into the office and came out a few minutes later holding a key.

The room was fit for a king. The carpet was new, the furniture spotless, the lights soft and calming. The air smelled like flowers.

"Jimmy, can we afford this?" she asked.

"Can't drive anymore," he answered.

Jolene went into the bathroom. Thick, fluffy towels hung on the racks. Tiny bottles stood near the sink. Jolene picked up each one: shampoo, conditioner, lotion, and bubble bath.

Bubble bath.

Turning on the tap, steaming water began filling the tub. Dumping in the liquid, the foam rose as she slipped off her clothes. Sinking into the soapy goodness, her skin tingled and her muscles begin to unravel.

A rattling of the knob followed by knocking invaded her daydream.

"I need to get in there," Jimmy said.

"Give me a minute, okay?"

"I really have to use it."

Sighing, Jolene rose. Holding a towel to her body, she unlocked the door. There was time to slide below the foam before Jimmy discovered it was open. He came in and peed, and she tried to not listen.

Pulling back the curtain, he looked down on her with weary happiness.

She pleaded, "Jimmy, let me do this by myself, okay?"

Paying no mind, he took of his clothes and entered the tub.

His penis, half hard, lay against his thigh. They stayed in the warm, fragrant water for long minutes, his arm around her, Jolene listening to Jimmy's soft breathing, her head against his chest. He made no move to fuck her and she felt grateful.

If only we could do more things like this.

The bubbles faded, the water grew cold. Jolene stepped out of the tub. Grabbing one of the thick towels, she went into the other room and dried off. Jimmy came out a few minutes later. He was fast asleep in seconds.

Jolene woke before him the next morning. Dressing, she gathered her cigarettes and lighter. Going into the parking lot, she coughed her way through another smoke. Then, she went into the lobby looking for breakfast.

At the front desk, she bought a road atlas for three dollars. There was a buffet, and the attendant told her that it was included with the room. Jolene ate looking at her map. Finding El Paso, she saw they were far from New Orleans and close to Los Angeles. They had completed most of the trip already.

Excited, Jolene hurried back to the room. Clicking on a light, she shook Jimmy's shoulder to wake him.

"What time is it?" he asked.

"Morning. Look at this." Jolene spread her map out on the bed.

"We're in El Paso," she said. "Here's Los Angeles. If you can drive that far, we can be there tonight!"

"Where did you get this?" he asked.

What did it matter? Didn't he see how close they were?

"They gave it to me at the desk," she said.

Jimmy studied the map. After a few moments, he jumped up and dressed.

"I need breakfast," he said.

"It's free downstairs. Good one, with eggs."

Jimmy went to eat and Jolene stayed in the room. It gave her time to take a shower and shampoo her hair. There was also a bottle of conditioner, with instructions on the back. Using the blow-dryer, she experimented until she got the hang of it.

Jimmy returned to the room, and his eyes grew wide.

"Wow," he said, and started kissing her.

Jolene knew what he wanted. "We ain't got time," she said, but it didn't stop him. He pulled up her T-shirt, whispering "Come on, Jo. You look so hot. Let's do it."

There was one thing she could do to get it over with quickly. Jolene dropped to her knees, opened his pants, and put his hard dick in her mouth. She pumped his cock, sucking on the head until Jimmy's penis throbbed, and she tasted his salty goo. The last time Jimmy shot his stuff in her hair, so she kept her lips around his penis. When he finished, she had his stuff in her mouth.

What should I do with it?

Jolene swallowed. The spunk slid down her throat like Jell-O. It was gone in an instant.

"Come on," she said. "Let's go."

Walking down the hotel hallway, they passed a housekeeper's cart filled with tiny bottles of shampoo and conditioner.

Jolene stuffed a handful of each into her backpack.

They drove across New Mexico, seeing one wonder after another — open desert dotted with low bushes and cactuses. They stopped for lunch in Phoenix, and as they ate Jolene asked, "Can you keep going?"

"Sure," Jimmy said. He now seemed excited too.

Driving was Jimmy's job, and Jolene had never paid attention to where they were. She thought it strange that the road out of Phoenix had only two lanes because they had always been on the freeway. Then again, a lot of things were different around there.

They stopped at a diner in a town called Kingman just as the sun was going down. Jimmy stretched out in the parking lot, doing push-ups and sit-ups to work the kinks out of his muscles. He didn't say much as they ate. Jolene chattered on, excited because they were almost there.

"How far are we now? Can we get a hotel in Hollywood? I bet they got nice ones, like the one we were in last night."

Jolene pulled the map out of her backpack to see if she could find Kingman on it. Before she could unfold it, Jimmy snatched it away.

"You don't need to look at that now," he said, and put it inside his jacket. Jolene felt a pang of anger. It was her map! But their destination was so close, and she thought it would be better not to make trouble.

They drove on in darkness. The road stretched in a straight line across the empty desert—no streetlamps, no houses, nothing. Occasionally a big truck came toward them and passed, but most of the time the only light was from the headlamp on Jimmy's motorcycle.

The road to Hollywood should have more on it than this.

Billboards began to appear. "Stay at the Stardust," one said, and "$5 Steak Dinner" another. The road went up into some mountains and the air turned cold. Jolene felt its bite through her coat.

They crossed another bridge with a sign that said, "Welcome to Nevada."

Nevada? Why were they in Nevada?

She began pounding on Jimmy's back, shouting "Stop! Stop!" He only drove faster.

The road wound down through the hills. They passed a hotel with "Casino" on its sign. They passed billboards screaming things like "Loosest Slots" and "$20 a night."

Jimmy got off on a ramp marked "Las Vegas Boulevard." Down the street, she could see huge hotels with flashing signs that said, "Tropicana," and "Aladdin."

They pulled into a convenience store. Jimmy went straight inside without taking off his helmet. Jolene followed him in, relieved by the warmth. Jimmy poured a cup of coffee sat on a vinyl-covered chair in front of some machines.

Jolene sat beside him. "Jimmy, what are we doing here?"

"I'm almost out of money, Jo. I need to make some fast."

"I thought we were gonna get jobs in Los Angeles."

"I can win the money we need." He nodded toward the machines.

Jolene frowned. Jimmy never mentioned going to Las Vegas.

"I have to," he continued. "We'll have no place to sleep, no food to eat, nothing."

Maybe Jimmy could win some money. He had gotten them this far. Why doubt him now?

Jolene looked at the machine in front of them. It had three little windows, and a lever on the side. On the top was the picture of a smiling leprechaun dancing beside a pot of gold, and the words: "Luck O' The Irish. Jackpot $10,000."

We can live a long time on ten thousand dollars.

Jolene reached into her coat pocket, filled with change from the lockbox, and held some of it out to Jimmy. He took two quarters, put them in the machine and pulled the lever.

The first wheel clicked on an empty space. The second clicked on an empty space. The third clicked on the word "Bar." The machine fell silent.

"What happened?" Jolene asked.

"We didn't win," Jimmy said. He took two more quarters, put them in and pulled. The first wheel said "Bar," the second wheel "Bar," the third wheel clicked on a blank space.

Jimmy put in two more quarters. When he pulled the lever, the first wheel stopped on "Bar." The second one stopped on "Bar." The third one—

Stopped on "Bar."

The machine came alive with lights and music. Jimmy and Jolene burst out laughing. They hugged each other. They had won. Jimmy pressed a button that said, "Cash Out." Quarters fell from the machine, clanging joyously into a metal tray at the bottom.

Jimmy scooped them up. The total was three dollars.

"Come on," he said, smiling. "Let's find a place to stay."

CHAPTER SEVENTEEN

Charlie

THE SECRET TO CHARLIE'S STUFFING was sun-dried tomatoes. He started with a loaf of whole wheat bread from the bakery, not off the shelf and never from a box. After browning garlic, onions, and mushrooms, he mixed everything with a stick of melted butter. Rosemary, black pepper, and a hint of cayenne were the only spices. The tomatoes gave the dish its predominant flavor.

As the aroma of roasting turkey filled the kitchen, Charlie wondered if the surprise would please his houseguest-turned-research assistant. Food could be a powerful stimulus, and a traditional meal might bring back unpleasant memories. He had felt great empathy when Susie had told him about her mother and father beating her. An abusive relationship deeply affects a person's character. He knew from personal experience.

Charlie was not aware how much he needed feminine influence until he stumbled upon Susie. Even in the early days, when she behaved like a feral animal, Charlie felt alive in a way he had not for a long time. She scared the hell of out him, but he forced himself to face the fear—always maintaining a careful distance. As time passed and Susie's attitude softened, he grew to like having a woman around.

At first, the thought of making love to her was as distant as China. His insistence on appointments with a doctor and dentist were purely altruistic—at least, that's what Charlie told himself. Then one day she came down the stairs wearing a nice dress and high heels. Her breasts bounced enticingly beneath the fabric, and her hips rolled with a jeweled movement that could make a Swiss watchmaker weep. For the first time in years, Charlie felt desire.

He suppressed it. She was his guest, and much too young for him. Even later that evening, when he accidently walked in while she was half naked, he was incapable of touching her. He *wanted* to, but stood frozen on the spot, and was relieved when she put on some clothes.

Susie was Eurydice to his Orpheus, an inspiration that he dared not turn his gaze upon.

How does anyone find his way out of hell?

"That smells wonderful," she said, behind him. He turned to see her wearing one of his robes, her blonde hair tousled from sleep.

"It'll be a couple of hours before it's ready," he advised.

She sat watching a parade on television. Charlie basted the turkey, whipped the potatoes, and prepared green beans with almonds. When they feasted, she told him that having turkey reminded her of Uncle Paul, Aunt Ouida, and their two boys Owen and Joe, who always came from Jacksonville for the holiday. It was, she said, the only time in her childhood when she remembered being happy.

"I usually don't go home at Thanksgiving," Charlie mused. "It's a long trip for just a few days. But I always visit at Christmas. What would you do if I went?"

"Stay here, I guess," Susie answered.

The idea made Charlie uncomfortable. Although nominally his "research assistant," there was much about Susie that remained an unanswered question. They had built a wary trust between them, but he might return to find his house ransacked.

"I wouldn't want to leave you alone for the holidays. I'll tell my parents I have to work this year. They'll be disappointed, but will understand."

Later, Charlie made notes on his computer about her Uncle Paul and Aunt Ouida. He kept a running journal of everything she told him, although very little of it would go into the project he was drafting. He had finished a treatment, and was now writing the script itself. The ending was ambiguous, because Susie hadn't told him everything yet. For the thousandth time, he felt immense gratitude that she had come into his life.

A few days after Thanksgiving Charlie heard Susie coming down the stairs behind him.

"Ready for dinner?" he asked.

"Let's go to a restaurant," she suggested.

Laughing a little in surprise, Charlie said, "Okay. Go get ready."

She bounded up the stairs. He opened the Yellow Pages, chose an intimate place on the ocean, and called to make a reservation.

Susie came down wearing a slinky black dress with a plunging neckline. Glossy high heels and dangling onyx earrings complimented it perfectly. She had applied her makeup lightly, unlike the horrible mask she wore when he met her. The brassy street whore she had once been had vanished. In her place stood an elegant young lady.

Once again Charlie felt the urge to make love to her. That would change everything between them, and he dared not take the chance. He stood up and said: "Is this the face that launched a thousand ships and burnt the topless towers of Ilium?"

Susie looked confused, but there was no time to explain Marlowe's *Doctor Faustus*. Compared to her, he was underdressed.

"Wait," he said. "I'll be right back."

In the downstairs bedroom he slapped on shaving lotion, chose a fresh shirt, and then donned tie and jacket. Coming out, he found Susie reading the last chapter in *Anne of Green Gables*. She glanced up, her lips curling into a slight smile.

"You look nice, Charlie," she said.

Offering his arm, Susie slipped her hand into the bend of his elbow. It was the first time they had touched, and it was a very big deal.

They took the Porsche, and Charlie slipped a cassette of Stanley Turrentine's *Sugar* into the player.

"It's like one of your books, isn't it?" Susie asked. "The music. You're not supposed to understand it right away."

"It's not about understanding at all," he explained. "Jazz is something you feel."

They pulled up to the restaurant. Two eager valet parking boys approached. As Charlie gave his keys to one of them, he noticed the other opening the passenger side door. The valet offered his hand to Susie, whose dress rode up a bit as she got out exposing her beautiful legs. The boy watched her every move.

A waiter led them to a table overlooking the sea. Through the window, the rolling waves reflected the light of a yellow half-moon, large and low.

"Would you like me to order for you?" Charlie asked. Susie nodded, and he selected Salmon with Parmesan Crust for her, Sole *En Papillote* for himself.

A server brought a basket of rolls. Charlie watched as Susie tore off a piece to nibble.

"I'm almost done with *Anne*," Susie offered. "What's next?"

"You might like *Moll Flanders*."

"Is there any reason you pick these books for me?"

"The women in them are like you. They live extraordinary lives."

Susie frowned. "I'm not all that special."

"Few have been through what you have, and so young."

She shrugged and said, "I just did what I had to do."

The waiter presented Susie's salmon on a cedar plank. Charlie explained that the wood enhanced the flavor of the fish. Then their server cut open the pastry paper in which Charlie's dinner had been cooked.

He ordered tiramisu for dessert. "I used to make this myself," Charlie said, when the coffee-soaked confection arrived. "I worked my way through college in a restaurant."

"Where did you go?" she asked.

"Greensboro," he replied.

"Where is that?"

"North Carolina."

"Did you grow up there?"

Why is she pestering me with questions?

Susie had never pried into his life before. He found her inquisitiveness intrusive.

"I don't like talking about myself," he admonished.

"Me neither," she replied.

Charlie considered that he was being unfair. Susie had told him a great deal about her life, and he had said next to nothing about himself. Before he could offer any insight, she asked:

"You're writing a screenplay about me, aren't you?"

Susie had inspired him; that was uncontestable. But not everything in the rough draft he was assembling was something she had told him.

"No," Charlie replied. "It's about another girl, named Zoe. No one who sees the movie will think it's you."

"Can I read it?"

"There's nothing to read. I haven't even gotten notes from the studio on the treatment. That might change everything."

Charlie raised his hand to summon the waiter. "It's late," he said. "We'd better go."

Susie was quiet for a long time on the ride home. They listened to the music, without a word between them, until she finally asked:

"Why haven't you ever tried to fuck me?"

It was a simple, honest question that deserved a response. He waited before answering, choosing his words carefully.

"That's not why I picked you up."

"I know, but still—"

Charlie glanced over. Susie was staring out the window into the dark night as if searching for something she couldn't quite see.

"I haven't had much luck with women," he said, hoping that would be enough.

"Why not?"

Charlie hesitated. He didn't want to revisit unpleasant memories.

"I don't know," he said slowly, measuring his response. "I

dated a couple of women in college. The first one dropped out, moved to New York. I never saw her again."

"And the other one?"

Long suppressed memories of Clarissa gushed into his mind. She was bright, funny—and had a violent temper. They had known each other for only a few months before she moved into his apartment. One evening, in the middle of an argument, she flung a cereal bowl that struck him on the head. She apologized later and promised to never let such a thing happen again, and yet it had—more than once. Charlie sometimes went to classes with bruises under his clothing.

"She wasn't very nice to me," was all he could manage to say. He was grateful that Susie did not press him further.

"I'm tired," he said, when they entered the house. "Turn the lights out when you go."

Charlie looked back before disappearing into his bedroom. Susie had gone onto the deck, and he watched through the glass as she lit a cigarette. The glow at the end floated in the air like a tiny star, and he could see her silhouette through the soft haze of smoke around her.

Over the next few days Charlie noticed a change in Susie. She was more available to him when telling her story. In earlier sessions, she talked about her time in Las Vegas in a superficial way. And no matter how gently he asked, Susie avoided telling him anything about the punk kid she called "Skunk." One night, after she had drunk more than the usual amount of wine, he learned what happened that made her so brutally defensive.

CHAPTER EIGHTEEN

Jolene

AFTER WINNING THREE DOLLARS on the slot machine, Jolene and Jimmy rode down Las Vegas Boulevard. They passed hotels like "Caesar's Palace," "Flamingo," and "Desert Inn." Farther down, the street was lined with pawnshops, gun stores, and tattoo parlors.

Jimmy stopped at a place called the Inca Inn. A sign advertised: "Studio apartments $80 per week." Jimmy went in a door below a neon sign that said "ffice," because the "O" had burned out. He returned with a key that had a plastic tag.

The room had a double bed with a thin spread and sheets that didn't look too clean. The carpet was worn and stained, the curtains faded. There was a nightstand with a lamp, and a desk with a folding chair. One wall had cabinets, a sink, and a small refrigerator. There was nothing in the cabinets but a plastic bucket for ice. Jimmy said it was a "kitchenette," which was why the place was a "studio apartment."

Taking off his boots, Jimmy lay on the bed and stared at the ceiling. Jolene looked at him a long time. This wasn't what she wanted, leaving Enterprise. She had expected to go straight to Hollywood, but had wound up here.

Jimmy noticed her, and held out his hand. She took it and he pulled her onto the bed. Snuggling against him, Jimmy put his arm around her. His hard, muscled chest was comforting.

He stroked the skin on Jolene's forearm. It tickled and she giggled a little. He continued to run his fingertips over her skin and she began to feel a different sensation. Moving her hand to his thigh, she caressed it through his jeans.

They kissed tenderly. Running her hand up his leg, Jolene stopped at his hard cock. Squeezing it through the denim brought a moan from Jimmy's lips. His hands roamed over her body and up to her breasts. She began working his belt buckle loose.

Jimmy slid his hands under her T-shirt. The slickness grew between her legs, and she breathed harder. Jimmy's fingers unsnapped the clasp of her bra, and then pulled off her T-shirt and bra together. A gasp came from Jolene's throat as she felt his lips on her nipple.

Jimmy already had his boots off and began pushing his jeans down over his hips. Jolene pulled back and removed her own boots. Jimmy's jeans landed on the floor. He pushed her back on the bed, which sagged and groaned under them. She let him pull the jeans off her legs.

Jimmy's eyes roamed over her body, and then locked into hers. She sent back the silent message: "Do it." His penis raged, and yet he paused.

Why was he waiting?

Jimmy caressed her neck, breasts, and stomach, and then pressed his fingers into the softness between her legs. He plunged in deep and then came back out, his fingertip rolling across a spot on the top of the tunnel inside her. She gasped, and waited for him to touch it again.

Jimmy plunged his finger in like before. He pulled it out slowly, and when he hit the spot she moaned. He plunged in again and slowly pulled out. She grasped his wrist when he hit the spot and said in a husky whisper, "There." A delicious feeling shot through her body, and the little nub at the top of her vagina grew hard. Jolene slipped further into the place that cried, "Now, now."

Withdrawing his finger, Jimmy was up off the bed and scrambling through his saddlebags. She realized was getting a condom, hated that he had to stop, but glad that he did. She wanted him inside her, touching that spot with his penis the way he had touched it with his finger. Jimmy found the packet, dropped it and scrambled around on the floor. Jolene put her finger inside her vagina, searching for that spot Jimmy had found.

Crawling onto the bed, Jimmy sat back on his legs, his hard cock ready, and struggled to put the rubber on. Jolene lay there waiting and wanting, her finger caressing the wonderful spot inside her. He managed to pull the condom over his hardness. She raised her knees, wrapping her arms around his body as he positioned himself between her legs.

The delicate touch that got her so excited was replaced by a hammering that did not bring on the same feelings. Moments later, Jimmy exploded and collapsed. She knew to expect no more. Hugging his body, she drew in his musty smell. Looking at his handsome face, Jolene felt grateful for Jimmy. He had done so much for her, taking her away from a place she hated. Even though they never said it, she loved him and knew that he loved her.

Jimmy suddenly said, "I'm hungry."

Jolene drew back in surprise. She had been having such sweet feelings for him, but apparently he wasn't thinking about her at all.

Pulling the condom off with a wet snap, Jimmy strolled into the tiny bathroom. The shower came on. Jolene sat in bed hugging her knees, waiting for him to finish.

Coming out Jimmy groused, "This place has lousy towels." He rummaged in his saddlebags and found the one he had laid on the floor in the broken house by the St. Johns River. Wiping his body, he said, "Go on, Jo. Get cleaned up."

In the bathroom, she discovered that Jimmy was right — the towels were thin, the soap a sliver. A weak stream of warm water was all she could get. Jolene lathered up as best she could with her hands, and washed the stickiness from the sex off her skin.

Jimmy was already dressed when she came out of the bathroom. "We got nothin' clean," he said. "You need to do laundry tomorrow."

Outside, the air was biting cold. Taking the motorcycle, they drove until they found a street with signs that said "Casino" and "Glitter Gulch." A giant, neon cowboy smiled at them; across the street sat a sexy cowgirl. Jimmy found an open space at a meter and parked the bike.

They strolled down the sidewalk, looking wide-eyed at everything. Inside every door were rows and rows of slot machines that winked with light and tinkled with sound.

Jimmy stopped to read a faded banner across a window: "Prime Rib Dinner $5.00." It showed a steak with potatoes and green beans. Going inside, they passed a long row of slot machines. People sat at tables, playing cards and throwing dice.

Going into the restaurant, Jimmy ordered two of the five-dollar dinners. When they came, the food didn't look anything like on the banner. The meat was fatty, the baked potato small, and the broccoli soggy. Neither of them felt satisfied.

Walking back into the casino, Jimmy sat at a bar and ordered a beer. The bartender asked for his ID, glanced at it, and handed it back. He then turned to Jolene.

"How old are you?" he asked, his eyes drinking her in.

"Eighteen," Jimmy answered.

"She can't sit here," the bartender replied. "She's not twenty-one. She shouldn't be in the casino at all."

"Go on, look around," Jimmy said. "Just don't go far."

Jolene went into the street. Music blared from unseen speakers. Shop windows displayed T-shirts and souvenirs. It seemed like only a few minutes had passed when Jimmy found her.

They walked with arms around each other to the motorcycle. Back in the room, they undressed and fell asleep right away.

Jolene woke up first the next morning. After dressing she shoved their dirty clothes into her backpack. Outside, she smoked one of her own cigarettes and waited for Jimmy to wake up. When he did, they drove to a small restaurant called Dinky's Diner for breakfast.

"I'll drop you off at a Laundromat," Jimmy said as they ate. "While you're washin' the clothes I'll go win the money we need to get to Los Angeles."

They found a laundry near their hotel, close enough that she could walk back to their room. Jimmy handed her the key and drove off.

CHAPTER NINETEEN

Jimmy

AT AN ATM, Jimmy withdrew more money. The receipt told him he had less than a hundred dollars left.

We got here just in time.

Parking the bike, he walked to the casino where they had eaten the night before. While Jo had been outside, the bartender showed him how to play the video poker machines. Jimmy quickly lost twenty dollars. The only upside was that his beer had been free.

He stopped to watch one of the table games. It had a wheel at one end, and a grid with numbers. It seemed simple enough. Put money on a number. When the ball lands on the number you win. Jimmy sat down and took a twenty from his wallet.

"Lay yo' money on the table," said the woman spinning the wheel. Jimmy did. She handed him a small stack of blue chips. Jimmy put one chip each on ten numbers.

The woman spun the wheel. The ball clattered around and stopped on 34. A man beside him had a chip square in the middle of the number, but Jimmy had nothing. The woman swept all the chips off the table, and pushed a stack of purple chips toward the man.

Jimmy had ten more chips. He placed some directly on numbers, and some on the lines around the numbers. The women spun the wheel and the ball stopped on number 22. Jimmy had a chip on 22, and two on either side of it. He had won! The woman counted out a huge stack of blue chips and pushed them his way.

This is more like it.

"Cocktails?" someone said. He turned to see a waitress holding a tray.

"Scotch," Jimmy said. All the rich people on TV drank scotch.

When the waitress left, Jimmy placed more bets. The ball landed on 14. Jimmy had two chips on it. The woman pushed a huge pile of chips his way.

"Jesus!" the man beside him said. "I ought to be betting with you."

The wheel spun, the ball clattered and landed on a green "00." Jimmy saw "00" at the top of the grid for the first time. There were no chips on it. The black lady swept everything away.

Jimmy thought maybe he should stop. He had already won a lot of money.

Where was that damned waitress?

The man beside him was putting down chips again. So what if he lost one spin? Jimmy spread his chips around the table.

The waitress returned with his drink. It was just liquor in a glass. Jimmy swallowed it and put more chips around the table.

Jimmy stayed over an hour. He ordered more scotches and kept shooting them down. The spinning lady left and a skinny guy took her place. Jimmy put a stack of ten chips on number 12. The ball landed on 12. Jimmy gave out a whoop and everyone looked at him.

Skinny-guy handed Jimmy three black chips on top of a pile of blue ones.

"What's this?" he asked, holding up a black chip.

"One hundred," the spinner explained.

Jimmy had won over three hundred dollars on one spin.

Was it enough for Los Angeles?

One black chip on one number would be more than enough. If he put all three down, they could live like kings. Jimmy placed the three one-hundred-dollar chips on number 22.

"Three hundred bet," the spinner said. A man wearing a suit turned to watch. The ball ran round and round, bounced into 22, out again, and landed on 34.

Jimmy felt awful. He looked up to see the man in the suit watching him carefully.

"Place your bets!"

Jimmy didn't want to play anymore. His head spun and he felt sick in his stomach. The ball clattered around the wheel. When the turn finished, the spinner said, "You can't sit here if you're not playing. You have to bet or cash out."

"Cash out," Jimmy said, the words thick in his mouth. The man pulled Jimmy's chips toward him, counted them carefully, and gave him others.

"Take them to the cage," he instructed, pointing across the room.

Jimmy stumbled to the cashier, who counted out two hundred and forty dollars.

That was more money than when he started! So what if he had lost three hundred on one spin? He was still a winner. Maybe he should get a beer and think about whether to play the wheel game again, or try something else.

I'm not going to pay for a beer when I can get one free.

He sat down at the bar, gave the bartender a twenty-dollar bill, asked for two rolls of quarters and a cold one. Dropping a full roll into the slot, Jimmy pressed the "Max Bet" button and began to play.

In ten minutes both rolls of quarters had disappeared into the machine. Jimmy asked the bartender for another roll and kept playing. Ordering more beer, he played game after game.

Two hours later he pulled out his wallet. There were only two twenties in it.

Jesus, what had happened to it all?

He still had five dollars in the machine. Pressing "Max Bet," the screen displayed the ten, queen, king, and ace of spades along with the three of hearts. That meant he had four cards of a royal flush, the biggest win in the game. He needed only the jack of spades, and he would win four thousand dollars. This is what he had been waiting for. The machine owed it to him.

He saved the spades and pressed "draw." The three of hearts disappeared, and in its place, the six of clubs.

The six of clubs meant nothing. The machine had betrayed him. It owed him four thousand dollars. Four thousand dollars. Four thousand dollars. The sum bounced around in his head like the little ball rattling in the wheel.

Jimmy got up, stumbled, fell and hit his knee hard. A spike of pain shot through his leg. He tried to stand, his knee buckled and he caught the edge of the bar. He began pounding on the machine shouting, "Damn you, motherfucker! Damn you! Fuck! Fuck!"

A security guard came out of nowhere and caught Jimmy in a headlock. He thrashed and cursed. Another guard arrived and they carried him, twisting and wailing, to the front door. The guards pushed him outside, where he fell on his hurt knee. Jimmy screamed in agony. He spewed curses at the guards and limped away. Lightning shot up his leg with every step.

Jimmy staggered through an intersection against the light. Cars whizzed past blowing their horns. One painful step at a time, he hobbled to the spot where he had parked his bike.

It wasn't there.

A man wearing a faded camouflage jacket leaned against

the wall. "My bike," Jimmy asked. "Did you see who stole it?"

"Got towed," the man replied. He pointed to a sign that said *One-Hour Parking.* "Station's on Ninth."

Jimmy limped off. After forty minutes, every step in agony, he found the precinct office. Inside, an officer asked for his driver's license, registration, and proof of insurance. Jimmy handed his real license and the other documents to him. The officer made a call and said yes, his bike had been impounded. The fine was four hundred dollars.

Jimmy had forty bucks in his pocket and less than a hundred in the bank. The officer said he had sixty days to pay. If not, his beloved bike would be sold at auction.

The waiting room had a bank of phones, the wall behind them covered with flyers for lawyers, bail bondsmen, and taxi companies. Jimmy called a cab. The ride back to the Inca Inn cost twenty-three dollars.

Jo didn't answer when he pounded on the door. Limping to the office, Jimmy asked the clerk to let him in. The laundered clothes were there, his shirts folded on the desk, but no Jo.

Taking the plastic bucket, Jimmy went to the ice machine. Back in the room, he managed to pull off his boots and pants, which wasn't easy because his knee had swollen to twice its normal size. Wrapping the ice in a towel, he balanced it on his leg and drifted into fitful sleep.

CHAPTER TWENTY

Jolene

AFTER DOING LAUNDRY, JOLENE carried their clothes back to the Inca Inn. She hung their shirts in the closet, and put their socks and underwear in the drawer. That took ten minutes.

With nothing else to do, Jolene went for a walk and found a 7-Eleven. She bought beef jerky, a two-liter bottle of soda, and a copy of *People*. Returning to the motel, she put the soda into the fridge, ate the jerky, and read her magazine.

Crazy with boredom, Jolene took a second walk around, passing strip malls where most of the signs were in Spanish, and headed home just as the sun was going down. Unlocking the door, she flicked on the light and gasped.

Jimmy lay on the bed. He wore his shirt and jacket but no

pants. A sodden towel lay over one knee, the sheets beneath it sopping wet. Jolene shook his arm and called, "Jimmy. Jimmy." He stirred and moaned, and then sat up with a shriek. His eyes were bloodshot.

"Jimmy, what happened?"

Reaching down, he carefully lifted the towel from his leg. The knee was swollen twice its normal size and purple.

Jolene gasped, "Oh, my god."

He looked at her like a dog that knew it was going to be whipped.

"How did you do this?" she asked.

Jimmy rose shakily. Placing his hand against the wall, he used it as a crutch to inch toward the bathroom. He didn't make it. Grabbing his stomach, Jimmy vomited on the floor. Jolene pulled back in disgust. When he stopped retching, Jimmy went into the bathroom and threw up again. Then he rinsed his mouth, limped back and flopped onto the bed.

"Jo, could you get more ice?" His voice was a hoarse whisper.

Jolene took the plastic bucket down the hall to the machine. Returning to the room, the sharp odor of Jimmy's vomit caused her to recoil.

"You threw up," Jolene said, pointlessly.

"Clean it up," he said without opening his eyes.

"I ain't touchin' it.

"I can't kneel down," Jimmy said.

Using the cheap motel towels, Jolene mopped up the mess.

"You want some soda?" she asked.

"Yes," Jimmy replied weakly.

She took the two-liter bottle from the tiny refrigerator. There were no cups, so she held the bottle for him as he drank.

"What happened?" she asked.

"Lost a lot of money. Fell and hurt my leg."

"You lost?" she said. "Jimmy, you were gonna win enough to get us to Los Angeles."

He looked at her with bleary eyes. "Need ice," he said.

Jolene wrapped some in the sodden towel and placed it over his knee.

"Cops took my bike," he said. "Can't pay the fine. I'm sorry, Jo. I'm so sorry."

He started to cry. Jolene had no idea what to do. She had never seen him like this.

"You're just gonna have to pay it," she said.

"Fine's four hundred. I got less than a hundred left."

"What?!" Jolene blurted, astonished. "Where did it all go?"

"Spent most of it getting here. Lost the rest today."

"What are we gonna do?" she asked.

"Get a job," he replied. "When my leg gets better."

Jolene looked at his bruised knee. Getting better wasn't going to happen any time soon.

How would they buy food? How would they pay the rent?

She would have to get a job herself. Jimmy told her several times that they would both need to work in LA. She had actually been looking forward to it.

"I'm going out," Jolene said.

She walked back to the 7-Eleven and went inside. A clerk stood idly behind the register.

"I need a job," Jolene announced.

The man eyed her up and down. Jolene had opened her coat, as the walking had made her warm, and his eyes lingered on her breasts. She didn't like it, but let him look.

The clerk took a pad from under the counter. "Fill out an application," he said. Jolene took the pad and asked to borrow his pen.

The first line was easy enough, her name. The second one posed a problem: an address.

What would she put there?

Scanning down the rest of the application, there were other problems. Previous employment? She never had a job before. Education? She hadn't finished middle school. She turned back to the clerk. "Can I do it at home?"

"Bring it in whenever you're ready."

Jolene's mind buzzed on the walk back to the Inca Inn. The address of the motel could be her residence, and she'd write in the name of her middle school. As for previous employment, she'd tell the truth. It would be her first job.

The man in the motel office told her the address, and allowed her to fill in the office phone number as her own. With the application complete, she walked back to the 7-Eleven. The clerk took it, and put it under the counter.

"I don't know if we're even hiring," he said. "They'll call you."

Jolene walked into the night. She needed a job right now.

The street where they had eaten the five-dollar steak dinners had been lined with T-shirt shops and souvenir stands. She headed that way. Walking into the first store she found, Jolene approached a girl behind the counter.

"I need a job," she said. "Can I get one here?"

The girl fixed her with dead eyes and said, "Shit, you don't want to work for Tee-Time."

"I need to make some money."

"You won't make any here."

"You work for free?" Jolene asked, astonished.

"No, just the pay sucks."

"It would be something," Jolene pressed.

"Okay, well, the manager isn't here tonight. He won't be back until tomorrow."

Jolene moved on to the next place. That salesgirl also said the manager wasn't there. She went from one store to store, but it was the same everywhere—either the manager wasn't there or they weren't hiring.

The last shop sold shot glasses and ashtrays that said "Las Vegas." A man stood behind the counter, strips of graying hair pasted across his balding head. Jolene went into a speech that had become familiar: She needed a job, could start right away, and would work very hard.

"How old are you?" the man asked.

"Eighteen," she said.

"How much really?"

"Sixteen," Jolene answered. The man didn't need to know the truth. He certainly wouldn't hire someone only fourteen.

"Don't ever lie to me again," the man said. "I've had plenty of sixteen-year-olds work for me. I have no problem with sixteen, but I'm not going to hire someone who lies."

"I'm sorry," Jolene said. "I really need the job."

"You go to Las Vegas High? Clark? Valley?"

"We just moved here," Jolene said. "I'm not in school right now." Both of those statements were the absolute truth.

"Okay," the man said, taking a pad from under the counter. He ripped off a form almost exactly like one the 7-Eleven clerk had given her.

Jolene moved to the end of the counter and filled in the spaces. Giving it back to the man he asked, "What is your social security number?"

"What's that?"

"I can't hire you without one."

Jolene felt her spirits fall. She had looked so long for a job, and this man was ready to give her one. Seeing her expression, he said, "Go to the Social Security office and register. Come back with your card."

Jolene went out and sat on a bench. She felt lost and helpless. Jimmy couldn't work. He couldn't even walk. What little money she had might buy them food for a while. Then they would have nothing. *Nothing!*

"You're too pretty to look so sad," someone said.

Jolene turned to see a man on the bench beside her, a cup of coffee in his hand. He was about thirty, dressed in a baseball cap, plaid jacket, and jeans.

"I can't get a job," she said. "I've been tryin' but nobody will hire me."

Tears started to flow. She couldn't help it; they just came out of her. Jolene wiped her eyes on her sleeve.

"God, I've been there," the man said, handing her a napkin. "I got laid off once. I had rent, and car payments—"

"What did you do?"

"I got through it. You will, too."

The man told her he worked for an oil company in some place called Bakersfield. He came to Vegas to play in poker tournaments.

"My name's Barry," he said. "What's yours?"

Why does he want to know my name?

"Audrey," she said. It was the name of the girl who tormented her in school. Jolene didn't know why that came to mind, but it was better than telling a stranger her real one.

He asked, "You want to go to my room?"

Why did he want her to go to his room?

"We can order room service," Barry explained. "You look hungry."

Jolene was ravenous. The only thing she'd eat all day was beef jerky.

"Where?" she asked.

"Right over there," he said, pointing to a brightly lit hotel.

She followed him inside, past the slot machines, to an elevator. Getting off on the eighth floor, they walked down the hall without speaking a word. Barry unlocked the door and they entered. Through the window, Jolene could see a million lights twinkling.

The man picked up the phone. "What do you drink?" he asked.

"Coke's fine."

Barry talked to someone on the phone, and then turned on the TV. He found a sports program and stretched out on the bed. Jolene took off her coat and sat in a chair. They watched until waiter came bringing a little cart with two thick sandwiches on it.

Jolene attacked her meal, and then took a big swallow of her Coke. It had a medicine taste, like the drink in New Orleans. She was so hungry she didn't care.

"Slow down," Barry laughed. "It's not going anywhere."

When they had finished eating, the man lay back on the bed. With the remote control, he turned the television to a station that played music, and flicked off the lamp.

"Why did you do that?" she asked.

"To make it nicer," he said. "Come here."

Jolene suddenly realized he expected her to have sex with hem. The idea had not crossed her mind. Barry had been so nice, more like a friend than some guy who wanted to do *that*.

"I'll give you a hundred dollars," he said from the gloom.

Jolene's mind reeled. Barry would pay her one hundred dollars. She had over three hundred from the lockbox. It would be enough to get Jimmy's motorcycle back.

"Okay, three hundred," Barry said from the darkness. "I know that's the going rate."

Jolene, still trying to understand what was happening, found herself shocked again. Three hundred dollars plus what she had might be enough to get them to Los Angeles.

Jolene thought she could do it, if she didn't really have to touch him.

"You got a rubber?" she asked.

Barry took one from his wallet. He also counted out three hundred dollars in twenties. Jolene folded them and stuck them into her pocket.

Now what? Was she supposed to just open his pants?

"Take off your shirt," Barry said. "I want to see your boobs." Peeling off her T-shirt, Jolene reached around and unsnapped her bra. Her breasts fell free.

"Jesus," Barry said. "You're magnificent." He opened his jeans and slid them off. His penis was already hard.

"Put on the rubber," she said.

Barry slid the condom over his penis. Jimmy had always lost interest after she sucked him off, so she took Barry's rubber-covered cock into her mouth. Barry fondled her breasts, which had no effect. She didn't feel the golden glow. There was no slickness between her legs.

It didn't take long for him to come. Jolene pulled away, and put her bra and shirt back on. There didn't seem to be anything else she needed to do.

"Thanks for the sandwich," she said, and went out without another word.

Walking back to the Inca Inn, Jolene thought about what

she would say to Jimmy. There was now enough money to pay his fine. He would be so grateful.

Would he be grateful?

She had been with another man. It wasn't really sex, because she had only done it to get the money. Still, it was best to not tell him. She could say that she got it from the lockbox. He wouldn't know the difference.

In their room, Jimmy was fast asleep. The ice had melted, so Jolene got more to wrap in the towel, and placed it over his knee. After taking a shower, she put on a freshly laundered T-shirt, slid into bed, and fell asleep in seconds.

Morning came, and Jimmy had not moved at all. Getting ice again, she put it on his knee. Jolene then went to the 7-Eleven, where she bought two coffees and a box of muffins, carrying everything home in a cardboard container. Shaking Jimmy by the shoulder, he woke up bleary and disheveled. He accepted one of the coffees gratefully.

"How is your knee?" she asked. Jimmy pulled back the blanket to show that the swelling had gone down. He tried flexing and winced in pain.

"I don't know what we're going to do," he muttered.

Jolene dug into the pocket of her coat and pulled out a wad of bills. Jimmy's eyes grew wide with astonishment.

"Jo, where did you get this?"

"Remember the place we stayed in New Orleans? When you were talking to the guy I took his lockbox."

Jimmy looked stunned. "They had a lockbox?" he asked. "And you stole it?"

Jolene nodded, afraid he might get mad.

"I'm glad," he said, looking relieved. "We need it."

They counted the money: six hundred and forty-three dollars. Jimmy told her he had eighty or so in the bank, and seventeen in his wallet. It came to a little over seven hundred.

Jimmy sighed as if a stone had been lifted from his chest. "Come here," he said. Jolene crawled in under his arm. He bent down and kissed her.

"I'd be lost without you," Jimmy whispered. It was the nicest thing he had ever said.

"I tried to get a job last night," Jolene told him. "I almost had one, but I didn't have a Social Security number."

"I'll be back on my feet soon," he said.

"But I want to get a job," she pressed. "What's a Social Security number?"

Jimmy showed her his Social Security card, explaining that he had gotten one so he could apply for the job at Burger King.

"But what's it for?" Jolene asked.

"Taxes," Jimmy answered.

Jimmy rested his leg for the next few days. Jolene walked to the 7-Eleven where she bought food, cigarettes, and a towel that said "Fabulous Las Vegas," because they really needed a good one. At a drugstore, she got toothpaste, and big bottles of shampoo and conditioner; the little bottles from the hotel in El Paso were gone.

On the fourth day, Jolene came home to find Jimmy sitting outside their room smoking a cigarette, drinking soda from a paper coffee cup they had rinsed out and saved. As she approached, he stood up and took a few steps toward her. They kissed, and Jolene felt his penis grow hard against her belly. A few moments later they were in the room, with Jimmy lying on his back and Jolene sucking on his cock. He stopped her and put on a condom.

"You're gonna have to get on top this time," he said.

Jolene had never done that before. Sex had always been with her lying on her back and Jimmy pounding.

"Guide my dick into your pussy," he instructed.

Taking his boner in her hand, Jolene pressed herself down. She had never felt anything so nice. Being on top, she could adjust her position. The little nub at the top of her pussy had grown hard, and as she moved back and forth it rubbed against Jimmy's skin. It felt like music filling her body, low bass tones that came from deep inside.

Jimmy began thrusting up. She could no longer rub herself against him. The now-familiar groan burst from his lips as he came.

When they made love before, Jimmy would simply roll off when he was done. This time he couldn't with the weight of her body on his. She tried rubbing against him again, but his penis had grown soft and slid out of her with sticky plop.

The next morning Jimmy was able to walk to the diner, where they enjoyed their first hot meal in days. Then they took a cab to the police station, where he paid the fine. The desk officer gave him a receipt and told Jimmy he could pick up his ride at the impound lot. They had to take a cab again, but soon they were back on the bike.

The following day he set out to look for a job. Jolene stayed in their room, anxiously waiting to hear what would happen.

CHAPTER TWENTY-ONE

Jimmy

JIMMY DROVE TO A CONSTRUCTION SITE and found the contractor's trailer. The foreman, a big guy with a sunburned face, talked to him from the doorway.

"I know the men who work for me," he said. "Some of them for twenty years."

Jimmy went to the next site. The foreman asked if he had any welding experience. Jimmy said he didn't, but was willing to learn. The man just shook his head and wished him luck.

Nobody was hiring. By the end of the day he was thirsty and frustrated. About a mile from the Inca Inn, he stopped at a place called "Double Jacks." The bartender handed him a roll of quarters and a beer.

The machine gave Jimmy three twos, a six, and an ace. He held the three twos. The machine turned over the other two. Jimmy looked at the screen, disbelieving. On his first bet, he had won $125! It was enough to cover groceries and gas for another week.

Waving the bartender over Jimmy bragged, "Hit four of a kind."

"Your lucky day," he responded, handing Jimmy a plastic bucket.

"Didn't feel like it earlier," Jimmy said. He pressed "Cash Out" and quarters began spilling into the tray. Jimmy raised his voice over the noise: "I been trying to find work but nobody will hire me."

The bartender dumped the bucket of quarters into a machine that counted them, and then handed Jimmy his winnings. "We need a dishwasher here," he said.

Jimmy couldn't believe it. The bartender had offered him a job! He filled out an application using the address at the hotel, including the construction work in Pensacola and his high-school employment at Burger King.

The manager, Mr. McQueen, came out of the office to interview him. A small man with dark-rimmed glasses and a mous-tache, McQueen asked Jimmy if he knew how to run a dish-washing machine. Then he said, "How much time you done?"

Jimmy looked at him. "I worked at Burger King for three years."

McQueen smiled wryly. "I mean how much prison time?"

"None," Jimmy said, puzzled. *Why would he ask a thing like that?*

McQueen looked at him with suspicion, and then explained he had a shift from midnight until 8:30 a.m. If he wanted, he could start that night.

Jimmy thanked him over and over. He drove to the hotel, stopping to pick up a sack of burgers. He burst into the room where Jo sat reading a magazine. He told her about the job, and how he won at video poker. His luck had finally changed. Jo laughed, and he laughed because she laughed, and they pulled out the burgers and ate them.

Then they had sex. After he came, Jo held on to him like she didn't ever want to let go. He had to pry her arms loose to snap off the condom and take a shower.

Jimmy went back to Double Jacks at 11:30. The place was crowded with locals: maids and maintenance men, black jack dealers and change makers. McQueen took him into the kitchen, gave him an apron, and had him fill out a timecard.

Then he introduced Jimmy to Otis Fender, a skinny fellow about forty years old with sandy blonde hair and beard. His forearms were covered with tattoos. He was the cook for the graveyard shift.

"McQueen calls me Otis," he said. "But most call me Hammerhead."

"Why?"

The cook shrugged. "Maybe 'cause I can take a beating."

Hammerhead chattered endlessly. He told Jimmy that he

had learned to cook at Lovelock Correctional Center in upstate Nevada. Having been sent up for possession of methamphetamine; three years without drugs had straightened him out. Now he was on parole.

Jimmy spent the shift bussing tables, cleaning spills, and running things through the dishwasher. He got a half-hour break with a meal at 4:00 a.m. Jimmy mentioned how tight money was, and Hammerhead fixed an extra sandwich saying, "Just don't tell the boss."

The cook left when the morning shift came on. Jimmy helped load in deliveries with the day manager, a crusty Irishwoman named Demorra. By the time 8:30 rolled around he felt ready to collapse. After clocking out, Jimmy went into the bar where he saw Hammerhead drinking.

"When you work graveyard, 8:00 a.m. is happy hour," the man explained.

Jimmy drove home, found Jo still sleep, and slipped into the shower. When he came out she was awake, bleary-eyed but smiling.

"How did it go?" she asked.

"Feels good to be working." He kissed her and then lay on his back with a sigh.

A loud banging woke him up. Jo was not in the room. He opened the door to find the hotel manager demanding another week's rent. Jimmy gave him eighty dollars he had from hitting four of a kind. The manager left, and Jimmy fell once more into slumber.

CHAPTER TWENTY-TWO

Jolene

JOLENE WATCHED JIMMY SLEEP. She was ready to do *something*, yet there was nothing to do. Hungry for breakfast, she walked to the 7-Eleven for a muffin and coffee. Then she went to Fremont Street. At ten o'clock in the morning, it already buzzed with life.

Jolene saw a building with letters spelling: B-U-S. Inside, the station was filled with people. Passengers waited in line to buy tickets. A schedule showed the times busses left for Phoenix, San Diego, Los Angeles—

Los Angeles! That's where she was going. For ages, she had wanted nothing else. A one-way ticket cost $42. She could leave right now, with the money in her pocket.

I can't leave Jimmy.

It wasn't his fault that they hadn't reached LA. They'd had one lousy break after another. She loved him, and he loved her. They would finish the trip together.

Wandering into a different neighborhood, she came across a branch of the Las Vegas Public Library. Inside, Jolene found a romance novel. Taking it to a comfy chair she curled up and started to read, stopping only to use the bathroom and get a drink of water.

Late in the afternoon, she felt hungry again. Jimmy would be waking up, and they could go to dinner. She hadn't finished the book, and wanted to take it for when he was at work.

At the desk, a woman with glasses on a chain looked up and said, "Yes?"

"I want to check out this book."

"Your card?" asked the librarian.

"I don't have one."

The woman handed her a blank form. "Fill this out."

Jolene took the form, filled in her name and the address of the Inca Inn. Handing it back to the librarian, the woman said, "I need to see your ID."

"I don't have any," Jolene answered.

"Your parents can sign for you."

"All I want is to check out a book," Jolene said. "What's the big deal?"

The librarian slapped her hand on the novel and pulled it away.

Fuming with resentment, Jolene walked back to the Inca Inn. It was bad enough that she couldn't get a job. Now the library wouldn't even let her check out a book!

Arriving at the room, she found Jimmy doing push-ups on the floor. "I got to get some ID," she said abruptly.

"Don't worry about it," he said. "I have a job." Flipping over, he started doing crunches.

"No!" she said. "I need it now! If we left tomorrow, I got to get a job there, too."

"Okay," he said. "Let me think about it."

He tried to kiss her. She pushed him away. "Jimmy, stop. What are we going to do?"

"I said I'd think about it," he said and tried to kiss her again.

She shoved harder. "We got to figure something out."

"Come on, let's fuck," he replied, grabbing her breasts. She knocked his hands away.

"No," she said. "Not until we think of something."

He grabbed her face and tried kissing her again.

"Stop it," she protested, trying to squirm away. "I said no. No!"

Jimmy pushed her violently onto the bed. The fall almost knocked the breath out of her.

"Bitch," Jimmy spat, and left slamming the door.

Jolene heard the roar of his motorcycle, and went outside to see him driving away. Her mind burned with anger and confusion. *Why didn't he understand? Does he think I'll have sex any time he wants?*

Jolene walked to Dinky's Diner alone. They had been there many times before, and people there knew them a little. Betty, a waitress with hair dyed blonde, greeted her saying, "Where's the stud, hon?"

"He was shitty to me," Jolene said.

"Can't live with 'em, and can't shoot 'em," Betty answered with a chuckle.

Jolene ordered meatloaf. After eating, she walked back to Fremont Street, browsed the shop windows, and then sat on a bench to people-watch. It was the same place she met the man in the plaid shirt and baseball cap, who had given her three hundred dollars for a blowjob.

Jolene thought about doing that again. It had been such a little thing, easy and quick. And the man had given her so much money! Jimmy never knew she had done it. Of course, women who had sex for money were whores, but Momma always said that girls who wore jeans and makeup were whores, too. Jolene had already accepted the fact that she was now a fallen woman.

But how could I do it again?

She couldn't imagine asking a man on the street if he wanted a blowjob for money.

There was nothing to do but go back to the Inca Inn. Jimmy was not there when she returned. Lying on the bed, her mind still churning, she eventually fell asleep.

CHAPTER TWENTY-THREE

Jimmy

AFTER HIS FIGHT WITH JO, Jimmy drove to Double Jacks still angry.

Didn't she see how hard he was working? How dare she not have sex with him!

He got there a little after 9:00 p.m., sat at the bar and ordered a beer and a sandwich, asking for a roll of quarters. He began playing, waiting for his dinner to arrive. At one point he had doubled his money, but by 11:30 he was forty dollars down.

Going into the kitchen he found Hammerhead already at work, burgers sizzling on the grill. "How's the Midnight Rider?" the cook asked.

"Okay," he answered, still miffed at Jo. Hammerhead kept

a steady stream of patter but Jimmy responded only in grunts, stacking dishes, hosing them off, pushing everything into the dishwasher, and hoisting them onto the drying rack.

"What's going on with you?" Hammerhead finally asked.

"My girlfriend's a bitch."

"Better off without 'em, that's what I say. Got an ex-wife in Reno. Even after the divorce she kept askin' for money. Haven't heard from her since I went to Lovelock. Only good thing about bein' in prison is the cunt finally left me alone."

"Jo needs ID," Jimmy said. "Nobody will hire her without it."

"Hell, I can help you with that," Hammerhead offered. "Guy I met inside does fake ID's. He's out now, and here in Vegas."

Hammerhead explained that the fellow's name was Prudome. The man had once worked for some big corporation. A master forger, he skimmed off "about a million dollars," according to Hammerhead, before the company noticed. Prudome had pled guilty to a lesser charge, got a reduced sentence, and was out in six months.

"I'll call him tomorrow," Hammerhead said. "Soon your troubles will be over, my friend."

Jimmy drove home at the end of his shift. Waking Jo, he explained Hammerhead's offer. Turning aside her questions he collapsed into bed, falling asleep despite her voice in his ears.

He woke in the afternoon, and started doing exercises on the floor. It wasn't as good as a gym, but it was something. Jo came in an hour later. She had spent the day at the library reading, with some librarian watching. "What did she think, I would steal the book?" she complained.

The two of them walked to Fremont Street for dinner. They found a couple of plastic souvenir mugs in a trash can and took them back to the Inca Inn, where Jo washed them out in the sink. Jimmy left her in their room and drove back to the Double Jacks.

Hammerhead greeted him as he punched in. "Prudome wants to meet the both of you. A lot depends on what your girl looks like."

Jimmy wasn't sure why that mattered, but said he would bring her.

"Come here tomorrow at ten," Hammerhead instructed. "We'll talk before the shift."

Jimmy went home in the morning and woke Jo with the news. She bounded out of bed, laughing and chatting. Jimmy shared her joy, but soon fell into exhausted sleep.

Waking in the afternoon as he had before, Jimmy exercised until Jo returned. Excited about getting her ID, she had walked to look at the big hotels and then back again.

That night Jimmy took her to Double Jacks. They sat at a booth to order dinner. Hammerhead came in just after 10:00, accompanied by a small man in a p-coat and a black knit cap.

"Wait here," he told Jo, and went over to meet them. The man in the p-coat was thin, with a bald head, light blue eyes, and pale skin. Jimmy thought he looked like a skeleton.

"Otis tells me you need identification," he said.

"Hammerhead," the cook corrected. Prudome paid no attention.

"My girl does," Jimmy answered.

Jimmy took them to the booth where Jo waited. He slid in beside her, and the two men sat across from them. Prudome looked Jo up and down. Jimmy felt her pull closer to him, as if trying to hide from the man's penetrating stare.

Prudome turned to Jimmy. "She's fourteen, fifteen tops."

"She's eighteen," Jimmy insisted.

"Fourteen, fifteen at most. If she tries to say she's twenty-one, nobody will believe her. Eighteen they'll accept. I can give you ID for that. She can work any place that doesn't serve booze, which is what my buddy Otis says you want."

"Hammerhead," Otis corrected.

"She'll make the most dancing in an all-nude club," Prudome continued. "They don't sell liquor, so they can hire eighteen-year-olds."

Prudome turned his gaze toward Jo. "You'd make a fortune," he said, giving her a toothy grin. Jimmy felt her squirm closer to him.

"She'd be awesome!" Hammerhead proclaimed.

"If all you needed was a fake driver's license I could set you up for about two hundred dollars," Prudome continued. "But since you want to work, they'll check into your background. That makes it more complicated."

"How much?" Jimmy asked. He had no idea where he'd get even two hundred dollars.

"Five thousand," Prudome said.

"Five thousand?!" Jo blurted out beside him. "What do you think, we're rich?"

"Lower your voice," Prudome ordered, and did so with such ice that Jo shut up. "Listen to me," he continued. "You will be getting a driver's license, birth certificate, and Social Security card. They are the real thing." He paused to let that sink in, then continued: "Say you get stopped by a cop. The officer will find a clean record. To all eyes, you are the person the ID says you are."

"How do we know it's that good?" Jo asked.

"You're buying the identity of someone who no longer exists," Prudome answered. "That's hard to come by, which is why it's so expensive."

Jimmy said, "We don't have five thousand dollars."

"She can earn it," Prudome said. "Men with money like to spend it on sexy girls. They will drown her in cash." He flashed his teeth at Jo.

"But she needs the ID to get the job," Prudome continued. "That costs money, which you don't have. What to do, what to do?"

Jimmy felt awful. Jo had been counting on him to solve the problem, but five thousand might as well be five million. They didn't have it.

Prudome said, "Otis, why don't you take the girl outside for a smoke?"

"All right," said Hammerhead. "Come on, let's let these boys talk."

Jo clutched Jimmy's arm. Prudome ignored her, staring at Jimmy, not moving. Jimmy stared back, but the man's eyes were like ice.

"Go on," Jimmy mumbled. "Go outside with Hammerhead."

"But—" she protested.

"Get out!"

Jo released his arm and slid away. She glanced back at Jimmy before going out the door.

"I will create the identity for her," Prudome said, once they were alone. "She can use it to earn the five thousand. I will give you six months to raise it."

Jimmy considered the deal. Jo wanted so badly to go to work. It's all she talked about. Maybe they could raise that much money. They had no other choice. Jimmy nodded.

"Then you agree," Prudome pressed. "I will provide your girlfriend with a new identity, and you will pay me five thousand dollars in six months."

Jimmy nodded again.

"Say it," Prudome urged.

"I'll do it."

"Say what the agreement is," Prudome insisted. "Articulate it."

"You'll give her ID and I'll pay you five thousand dollars."

"In six months," Prudome prodded.

"Six months," Jimmy said.

"There's one more thing. I want a show of faith. Something

that tells me you're serious about this."

What did he mean, "show of faith"?

"I want to fuck your girlfriend."

What the hell?

"I will not give you the I. D. until I do," Prudome said. "You will deliver her to me, to do as I want, and afterward I'll give her back to you."

Jimmy felt his anger rise. "You're a sick fuck," he said.

"Oh, yes. Very sick." He laughed, and a shiver went up Jimmy's back.

"She won't do it," he protested.

"Convince her," Prudome continued. "You're in no position to turn down this offer. You work as a dishwasher. You live in a hole. The only thing you own is a motorcycle that might disappear again any moment."

Was he threatening to steal my bike? How did he know it had been towed?

"But the girl—" Prudome continued. "Men will pay money to look at her naked. She is the only asset you have. What an asset she is."

Jimmy didn't know what he meant by "asset."

Prudome continued: "With the identification I give her she will produce cash, like a machine. The work she does will make you rich."

Jimmy tried to make sense of things. Jo needed the ID, and this man has offered the only way to get it. But she would never agree to the sex thing.

"It don't matter," Jimmy said. "She won't do it anyway."

"Talk her into it," Prudome replied, and stood up. "Otis knows how to find me."

The man went out the front door. Jimmy sat alone, looking at the hamburger plates smeared with ketchup. Soon, he would be washing those dishes.

Jo and Hammerhead returned. She slid into the booth and crawled under his arm. Jimmy continued to stare at the plates.

"What did he say?" Jo asked.

"Nothin," Jimmy answered. "We can't afford it."

"He'll come through,'" Hammerhead said. "He's the best of the best."

Jimmy said nothing.

"His work is awesome," the cook continued. "You can't tell the difference between what he makes and what you get at the DMV."

"I need ID, Jimmy," Jo added.

"Almost time to punch in," Hammerhead said. "Got time for one last eyeball washer." He ambled to the bar.

"Jimmy?" Jo asked. The single-word question roused him from his trance.

"Come on," he said. "I'll take you home."

Jo slid out of the booth, with Jimmy following. They climbed on his bike and drove through the dark streets back to the Inca Inn.

Jo got off and asked, "What did he want?"

"I'll tell you tomorrow," Jimmy answered. Before she could say anything else, he put the bike in gear and drove away.

For most of the shift Jimmy remained sullen and withdrawn.

Hammerhead noticed and didn't ask until business slowed.

"What did he say to you?" Hammerhead demanded.

"Don't matter."

"Whatever he wants just give it to him. His word is good. Prudome is gonna set you up for life, man. For life!"

"I'll talk to her about it."

"Good," Hammerhead answered. "I went to a lot of trouble to put you and Prudome together. He won't ever trust me again if you don't come through."

Jimmy stayed quiet the rest of the evening. Hammerhead tried to cheer him up with stories of his adventures. 3:00 a.m. came and Jimmy mopped the floor. At 4:00 a.m., Hammerhead made him a turkey sandwich.

"What's that place he said she could work?" Jimmy asked.

"You been to a strip club?"

Jimmy nodded. "But they weren't all nude. They wore bikinis."

"Not in Vegas," Hammerhead said. "They dance onstage naked, and for a lot more money they get naked in the back room."

"Do they fuck there?"

"No, no," Hammerhead said. "They can get arrested for that."

"Where are these clubs?" Jimmy asked.

"Sweethearts is right downtown here," Hammerhead replied. "There's Déjà Vu, the Diamond. Shit, your girl would kick ass in a place like that. Hell, I'd want to see 'er myself."

Jimmy shot a glance that knocked Hammerhead back three paces.

"I mean, with you there," the cook added.

The bartender appeared at the window with an order. Hammerhead turned his attention to fixing the customer's meal.

When Jimmy's shift was over he went home, showered and came out to find Jolene sleepy-eyed but awake. He assured her that he would explain everything later. Getting into bed, he turned away from her and closed his eyes. He never heard the door snap shut as she left.

CHAPTER TWENTY-FOUR

Jolene

AT THE LIBRARY Jolene tried to read, but her mind buzzed with questions.

What did the scary man say to Jimmy? Was he going to give them the identification?

After reading the same page three times, she decided to walk again. Jolene ate lunch in a café, and on the way home picked up more soda at the 7-11.

Jimmy was still asleep when she came in. Unable to stand the suspense any longer, she shook his shoulder and called his name.

"I got to have ID, Jimmy," she said "How are we going to get the money?"

Jimmy looked at her with a cloud in his eyes that she had never seen before.

"Just say it," she urged.

"Prudome says he'll give you the ID if you fuck him."

Jolene wasn't sure she heard him right. "He me wants to have sex with him?"

"Yeah. He'll do it if you fuck him."

Men were all alike.

The boys at school, the guy who tried to rape her at the truck stop, and the man who paid her for the blowjob. They didn't even *know* her, yet they wanted to have sex with her.

"I ain't gonna do that," she said.

"That's what I told him. But he won't help us any other way."

"Well, you can forget it."

"I know," Jimmy said. "I'll just keep working as many hours as I can."

"You ain't gonna make five thousand dollars." She didn't know how much he would bring home, but it certainly wouldn't be *that* much.

"If you did it—" Jimmy said.

"Jesus, Jimmy, how can you say that? I'm your girl!"

"I know."

"How can you even ask me?" Jolene thought for a moment about Prudome, his faded skin, his pale eyes, and shuddered.

"You'd only have to do it once," Jimmy added.

Jolene couldn't believe he'd said that. She wanted out, away from Jimmy, away from their sad little room, away from Las Vegas, everything.

"I'm going for a walk," she said, grabbing her coat.

The sunlight was fading, the streets growing dark. Men sitting in the shadows turned their heads to watch her pass, their eyes stabbing through the gloom. Jolene pulled out a cigarette and struck her lighter. She walked quickly, going nowhere.

Everywhere she went someone wanted to fuck her. The boys at school behaved like animals, smacking and drooling. In the darkness of the family kitchen, her father fondled her breast. Men at truck stops, and clerks in stores —

Damn them! Damn them all and damn Jimmy, too!

Jimmy. Her only pleasure had been with him. He had set her free and shown her wonders. Now he worked at a job that wore him down; she could see it on his face. If Jimmy asked her to do this, there was no other way.

She had done it before, with the man in the plaid shirt. That hadn't been so bad. She had even thought about doing it again.

But Prudome gave her the creeps. He looked like a skeleton. But what else could she do? The library wouldn't even let her check out a book. It was do this, or spend the rest of her life wandering the streets. Once it was done they would be back on the road to Hollywood.

Hollywood — the city filled with beautiful women in long dresses, walking on red carpets. Smiling men in handsome suits looked at them sweetly. They gave interviews, the microphones inches from their perfect lips. They lived wonderful lives.

Jolene sat on a cinderblock wall across from the Lucky Seven motel, flicked her cigarette away, and watched it roll away.

She would do it. Not because Jimmy wanted her to, but for herself.

Back in their room, she found her so-called boyfriend lying on the bed staring at the ceiling. Jolene fixed her eyes on his face until he turned to look at her.

"He's got to wear a rubber," she said. "I won't do it unless he wears a rubber."

Jimmy turned his eyes back to the ceiling. Jolene crawled in beside him, lifted his arm around her. He pulled her close, held her tight.

She would do it. Then she would forget it and go on.

CHAPTER TWENTY-FIVE

Jimmy

JIMMY STAYED WITH JO, holding her close, hoping it would make her feel better. Later, they ate the sandwich he had brought home from the night before, saying nothing because there was nothing to say. At 11:30 p.m. he left for work, arriving a few minutes before midnight.

Walking in , Jimmy saw a brown-skinned man working the dishwasher. Hammerhead stood at the grill, poking a couple of burgers with his spatula.

"Who is this?" Jimmy asked.

"Filipe," the cook answered. "I thought you had the night off."

Jimmy had never asked about the schedule. He found a calendar tacked to a bulletin board. There was his name, dates marked "12-8:30" and the word OFF on Thursday.

Hammerhead came up beside him. "What about Prudome?"

"We're gonna do it," Jimmy said.

Hammerhead broke into a grin. "That's my boy," he said, slapping Jimmy on the shoulder. "I'll call him tomorrow. Your girl is gonna make a fortune."

Jimmy had been thinking about Jo dancing. He had better check out one of the clubs to see what she would be getting into.

"See you tomorrow," Jimmy said.

He drove around until he found a place. It had a neon sign of a pink heart with the word "Sweethearts" written across it. He could hear music pounding. A man at the door said it cost twenty dollars to get in.

The place was dark except for a brightly lighted stage with a brass pole at the far end. The the room had small tables and there were padded booths along the walls. Women lounged in skimpy outfits, some chatting with men.

Could Jo really make thousands of dollars here?

A dancer came onstage, the DJ's voice announcing, "Glory." She wore a cropped top that barely covered small, firm breasts, and a scarf-like skirt wrapped around her waist. Hauling herself to the top of the pole, she slid down holding it with her legs, thighs bulging with muscle. She flipped, grabbed the pole with her hands, and circled slowly to the floor.

It wouldn't be so bad for Jo to work there. Not all the girls had to dance nude; Glory wore her skimpy costume the entire time.

Then a new song began. The girl's skirt melted away, her top fluttered to the stage. Totally naked, she hardly touched the earth during the second song, as if she lived on the pole.

Men threw bills at Glory's feet. Jimmy took out his wallet and removed a few ones. He walked to the stage and set them down. Glory looked straight into his eyes. The song ended, and a moment later she was gone.

The DJ announced, "Cherry," and another girl appeared onstage.

"Would you like a private dance?" said a soft voice. Jimmy turned to see Glory standing beside him, dressed in her filmy skirt and top. Her nipples stood at attention like tiny soldiers under the sheer fabric.

Jimmy somehow found his voice. "Is it twenty dollars?"

"Twenty out here," the girl said. "Thirty for a private dance in the back. In the Champagne Room, it's a hundred dollars for fifteen minutes."

"The Champagne Room?"

"There's a bed in the Champagne Room," Glory said. She leaned in and whispered in Jimmy's ear. "We can have a lot of fun in there."

She took Jimmy's earlobe between her teeth and bit it. Instantly, his dick became hard as steel. He could think of nothing else but fucking Glory. Looking in his wallet, Jimmy saw a hundred and thirty dollars. It was all the money he had left.

"Okay, let's go," he blurted.

Glory led him to the back room through a curtained door.

A muscled black man in a suit sat just inside.

"Did you want the Champagne Room?" Glory asked. Jimmy nodded and took out five twenties, which the man counted carefully.

"Is that all you want, fifteen minutes?" Glory asked.

"That's all I got," Jimmy declared.

She led him down a dimly lit hallway. They passed a bunch of little rooms with padded seats inside. In one of them, Jimmy saw a man with a naked girl wiggling on his lap.

The Champagne Room was the largest, with a low, flat couch. Jimmy sat on it, and Glory dropped her clothes. He started to unbuckle his pants.

"No," Glory said, grabbing his wrist. "You have to stay dressed."

How could he fuck her with his pants on?

"Lie back," she commanded.

Glory straddled his hips. Her vagina looked like a little flower. His cock grew harder, straining to break through his jeans. The girl began moving her body against him. She breathed in his ear. Jimmy tried to kiss her but she pulled back, avoiding his lips. Sitting upright, she continued to grind against his penis through his pants. Whipping her head side to side, Glory sent her long hair flying. Her hips kept working against his body, her crotch rubbing his hard cock.

Jimmy placed his hands on her legs. She didn't stop him. He caressed Glory's muscled thighs, feeling her soft skin. He looked up and noticed Glory looking back at him. Eyes locked on hers, Jimmy ran his hands up and touched her breasts, like little cupcakes with nipples hard as gumdrops. He pulled them with his fingers. She gasped with pleasure.

Jimmy wondered how much the girl would let him do. He let one hand wander down her body until his fingers probed between her legs. She pulled away and turned around, dancing with her back to him. His eyes watched her round buttocks, her dark hair flicking about her creamy shoulders.

Glory turned and stretched against his body, her face only inches from his. Unbuttoning his shirt, she ran her hands over his chest. Her fingertips pinched one of his nipples, driving him crazy. Jimmy grabbed her hand and put it on his erection. She gave it a squeeze.

"I can't," she whispered. "But there's nothing stopping you."

He unzipped his pants, released his hard cock and began pumping. Glory sat back and kept her eyes locked on his. She ran her hands over her naked body, fondling her breasts and making sounds of pleasure.

"Fifteen," a voice said, just outside the curtain.

"It's another hundred dollars for fifteen more minutes," Glory said.

"I ain't got it," Jimmy said.

"Then you have to stop."

Stop?! He looked at her desperately.

"You can finish if you do it quick," she said. Scooping up her clothes, Glory disappeared through the curtain.

Jimmy pumped his hard cock furiously. He came moments

later. Taking tissues from a box beside him, he wiped off and pulled up his pants. His cock, still half hard, didn't go back easily. He dropped the used tissues into a wastebasket and staggered into the showroom.

He still felt charged and ready to go. Leaving the club, Jimmy drove straight to the Inca Inn. Banging open the door, waking up Jo.

"Jimmy, what are you doing here?" she said, in near darkness.

He did not answer. Grabbing the bottom of her T-shirt, he yanked it up, trying to pull it over her head.

"Slow down," Jo said, but he could not. Seizing her arms, he jerked them over her head and stripped off her T-shirt. She wasn't wearing a bra; his lips found a nipple and sucked on it hungrily. Jo gasped. He stripped off her panties and she lifted her hips to help him.

Ripping off his jeans, Jimmy lunged between her legs. Jolene fell back and he crushed his mouth against hers. Their tongues swirled together. His erect penis found the entrance to her vagina, already slick, and he entered her without a condom. It felt so good.

He heard Jo's voice like it was far away. "Jimmy, stop! Put on a rubber! Stop!"

She yanked her body backward. The motion pulled her vagina off his cock, which need her so badly it hurt.

Jimmy grabbed Jo's legs and pulled her toward him. She was saying something, he wasn't sure what, because he could think of nothing but being inside her again.

Her hand came out of the darkness and slapped him across the face.

Jimmy stopped dead. Jo's wide eyes stared back at him, frightened and confused.

"You have to put on a rubber," she said.

What had he been thinking? What would they do if she got pregnant?

"Get one," Jimmy commanded. "Quick!"

Jo climbed off the bed, found one and tore the packet open. Grabbing his raging penis, she fit the condom over the head and rolled it down the shaft. Jimmy threw himself on her. He brought his arms up under her back, grasped her shoulders, and entered her smoothly. A moan of pleasure sprang from her lips. Moments later, Jimmy felt the sensation swell in his balls. He kept thrusting until he could thrust no more. His passion spent, he rolled off and lay panting.

"Jimmy?" Jo asked. "Why aren't you at work?"

"They made me take a night off," he said, his breath slowly returning to normal.

Jo put her arm across his chest and snuggled against him. In a few minutes, she fell back to sleep. Jimmy tossed fitfully. Each time he managed to drift off, he dreamed of Glory.

The next morning, they went to the diner to have breakfast. Betty greeted them at their table. "Haven't seen you kids in a while."

"He's been working a lot," Jo answered.

Jimmy didn't listen to the other things Jo and Betty said. It had finally sunk in that Glory had taken most of his money.

"We can't eat here after this," Jimmy said, after Betty left. "I only got thirty dollars left." Jo counted her money. Together, they had sixty-four dollars and change.

"Filled the bike with gas yesterday," he said, "And paid the rent for the week. If we're careful, we can make it until I get my paycheck."

After breakfast, Jo took him to a grocery store she had seen. They bought a bag of apples, a loaf of bread, and some baloney. They would make breakfast of the fruit and have baloney sandwiches for lunch. Jimmy would eat at work and bring back whatever he could.

That night the Double Jacks was packed with customers. Hammerhead could hardly keep up. When it slowed, Jimmy asked, "Did you call him?"

"Yup," he said. "We didn't talk, but I left a message."

At 3:00 Jimmy went to get the mop and bucket. He was surprised to see Prudome, in his p-coat and black knit cap, standing in the back doorway.

"Otis tells me your girlfriend has agreed," he said.

"You have to wear a condom," Jimmy said. "She won't do it if you don't."

"Of course," the man said. "I have no idea who she's fucked."

Jimmy wanted to bash in Prudome's thin skull, but controlled himself.

The man handed Jimmy a card. "Bring her at ten tomorrow night. You can pick her up the next morning."

The card had an address on it. When he glanced up, Prudome was gone.

Jimmy returned to the Inca Inn at dawn. He told Jo the plan. She nodded, but said nothing. He then took a shower, and when he came out Jo wasn't there.

He awoke hours later, and worked out on the floor until Jo came back. They shared another sandwich that Hammerhead had given him, and then sat outside smoking, not saying much at all.

Nine o'clock came. Jimmy said, "Better get ready."

Jo went into the bathroom and closed the door. When she came out Jimmy saw that she had showered and shaved. She put on bra and panties, a plain white T-shirt and jeans. Instead of boots she wore sneakers.

The address was a high-rise apartment building. Through a glass wall Jimmy could see a fancy lobby. A uniformed guard sat behind a desk.

He considered calling the whole thing off. All they had to do was drive away. But Jo lifted herself from the seat, took off her helmet and handed it to him.

He watched as she entered the lobby. Jo spoke to the guard, who pointed her toward some elevators. Jimmy sat hoping that she would turn back. Hammerhead would be mad, and Prudome would never give them a second chance. Jimmy didn't care.

An elevator opened and Jo stepped inside.

Jimmy headed off for Double Jacks. He hoped it would be as busy like the night before, to keep his imagination from going wild.

CHAPTER TWENTY-SIX

Jolene

JOLENE RODE THE ELEVATOR in silence. She could hardly feel it moving. She was scared, but also excited. The idea of doing something forbidden, even something disgusting, made her tingle all over.

The elevator opened on a smaller lobby with four doors. One of the doors stood open. Dim light glowed inside, and music playing quietly. She walked in, and down a hallway. At the far end was a stylish living room. The couch was a long, flat slab, with two matching chairs. Lamps like glass bubbles glowed softly. Most of the light came through a giant floor-to-ceiling window with a view of the Las Vegas strip in the distance.

"Welcome to my party palace," said a voice behind her.

Jolene turned to see Prudome, in a charcoal-gray shirt buttoned at the sleeves and dark slacks. Barefoot, his white feet stood out against the dark carpet. Although she was a taller than him, she felt terrified by his presence.

"Never tell anyone that you were here," he said, taking a few steps closer. "If you do, I will find you." The way he said it froze her blood.

"Your coat," Prudome continued.

Jolene unbuttoned it — slowly, to delay whatever might come next for at least a few seconds. Slipping it off, Prudome's eyes fell to her breasts. Her T-shirt did little to hide them.

He laid her coat across the back of a chair, and then gestured to the far side of the room where a camera stood on a tripod. "Sit there," he said.

There was a single stool. Lights were pointed toward it. Jolene sat down.

Maybe Jimmy had misunderstood. Perhaps Prudome didn't want to fuck her after all.

What if he just liked taking pictures of pretty girls? This could be fun.

"Do you want me to smile?" she asked.

"No," he said.

Prudome turned his attention to the camera. The room filled with a blast of white light. Jolene flinched and squinted. He whipped a cassette out of the camera. "This will take a few minutes," he said. "Fix yourself a drink." He disappeared into another room.

Jolene slid off the stool, a blue blob from the flash floating in front of her eyes. When it cleared, she wandered the room. There were paintings on the walls that didn't look like anything, just swirls of color. There were statues too, carved shapes that looked like an arm thrown over a head or the curve of a woman's bottom. Her eyes fell on the bar.

Fix yourself a drink.

Prudome had bottles in all shapes and sizes. One looked like a little man dressed in a robe, except where his head should be was a black screw cap. Jolene lifted it, but could not read the fancy writing in the dim light. Opening it, she smelled a heavenly aroma. She put the cap back on and returned the bottle to its place.

There was a television. Finding a remote control, Jolene hit the red "power" button. The screen lit up, showing a black and white movie.

About twenty minutes later she heard Prudome's voice behind her: "I have finished your identification." She turned to see him standing like a ghost in the shadows. "You can take it with you in the morning." He came over, picked up the remote, and muted the movie.

"What's this?" Jolene asked, pointing to the man-shaped bottle on the bar.

"Hazelnut liquor."

Prudome selected a glass that looked like a fishbowl and poured the drink into it.

"Like this." Prudome slid his bony fingers under the bowl.

"Let your hand warm the liquor." Jolene took the glass and raised it to her lips. The delicious aroma stunned her nose.

"Drink," Prudome said. He pressed his fingers against her hand, forcing the rim to her lips. Jolene took a big swallow. It tasted like cough syrup. He continued to push the glass toward her mouth and she drank all of it.

"Do you know what will happen here tonight?" he asked.

"You want to fuck me," Jolene said.

"You will do everything I say, the way I want it. You will never tell me no."

His statement disgusted and excited her. She didn't want to have sex with him, but the idea that that he would take whatever he wanted aroused her.

Prudome pressed buttons on the remote. The television showed naked people, their bodies covered with oil. Jolene watched as the men in the movie tied the women's hands behind their backs, put blindfolds over their eyes, and force a ball on a strap into their mouths.

She felt Prudome behind her. He ran his hands over her body, and she had no choice but to allow his touch.

The men on the television forced the women over, their faces on the floor and their bottoms in the air. One of the men grasped a woman by the ropes around her wrists and plunged his hard penis into her. He had a huge dick, much larger than Jimmy's.

Prudome pulled up her shirt. She raised her arms and let him remove it. He then unhooked her bra and slipped it off her shoulders. His hands squeezed her nipples between his fingers.

In mingled disgust and excitement, her pussy grew moist.

His fingers undid the button of her jeans, lowered her zipper and worked her pants down. She still wore her sneakers and the jeans bunched up at her ankles. Prudome grabbed her shoulders and pushed her onto the sofa. The man yanked off her shoes and then pulled her pants from her legs. She lay naked before him.

"Get on your knees," he commanded. "Put your hands on your head."

Jolene did as she was told. Prudome grabbed one wrist and closed a metal ring around it. He pulled her hand down behind her back, and then forced her other arm down. A ring closed on the other wrist. The man came around in front, standing with his crotch inches from her face. Lowering his zipper, he reached in and pulled out his hard penis.

Wow. For a little guy, he sure has a big cock.

"Open your mouth," he ordered. Having had some experience with Jimmy, she tried to relax and take his penis down as far as possible. The man grabbed her head and thrust into her throat again and again. She gagged and tried to pull away. He wouldn't let her, jamming into her again and again.

He pulled his cock from her mouth. Grasping her jaw in his hand, he forced her face to look up at him. Spit dribbled down her chin; she was unable to wipe it away.

"Do you like that?" he asked.

"No."

His slapped her across the cheek.

"You will like it if I say so. Do you understand?"

Jolene's eyes filled with tears. A lump came her throat, and a sound something between a sob and a choke burst out of her.

"Did. You. Like. It?" the man demanded. He lifted her face, forcing her to look into his pale blue eyes. She saw them through the blur of tears, and remembered what he said:

You will never tell me no.

"Yes," she managed to utter. "I liked it."

"You will call me sir, or master."

What the hell?

"Sir or master," he repeated. "Do you understand?"

"Yes, sir," she said. "Yes, sir, I liked it."

"Now thank me for giving it to you like that."

Jolene saw him raise his hand.

"Thank you, sir. I liked it, sir."

She saw a look of satisfaction come into his eyes. "That's a good girl," he said.

Jolene felt him come up behind her. He yanked her hair hard. It scared her more than hurt, and she yelped in surprise. Prudome put a leather collar around her neck. She stayed perfectly still as he pulled it tight. A leash in his hand led to the collar.

"This way," he said, tugging on the leash. "On your knees."

Jolene looked at him, confused. He glared back, his blue eyes like razors. When he tugged on the leash, she followed walking on her knees. It wasn't easy with her hands cuffed.

"Come on," he said. "We've only just begun."

They passed through the door into a bedroom. Prudome

pulled her until they reached the side of the bed. Jerking her up by her arms, he threw her face down on it.

"You've been a bad girl, haven't you?" Prudome whispered harshly in her ear.

"No."

"No *what*?" he demanded again. Jolene lay there confused, her arms locked behind her.

"By what name do you call me?" he insisted.

"Sir," she said, realizing what he wanted. "No, sir," she said. "I haven't been bad."

"Oh, yes, you have. You've been very bad. What do you have to say?"

"I haven't been bad," she answered.

"You haven't been bad *what*?"

"Sir," she said. "I haven't been bad, sir."

"That's better," he said. "But you're wrong. You have been bad."

"No, sir."

"You tease men," he said. "You walk around with that sexy body, in those tight jeans. You know they want you, but you won't give it to any of them. You will give it to me tonight."

"Yes, sir."

"Isn't that right?"

She had already told him he was right. Confused, she said nothing.

"Answer me!" he commanded, pulling on the cuffs. Pain shot through Jolene's shoulders.

"Ah!" she cried. "That hurts!"

"And you don't like that, do you?"

"No."

"Well, I don't like it when little girls tease me."

"Yes, sir," Jolene said, not wanting him to pull on the cuffs again.

"You will have to be punished," he continued.

"Please don't," Jolene pleaded.

"You still haven't learned," he responded. Prudome brought his open palm down on her bare buttock. She felt dull pain.

"Ow!" she cried.

"What do you call me?"

"Sir," she remembered. "Please don't hurt me, sir."

"That's better," he said. "But still, you must be punished."

His open palm came down on her bottom again. He spanked her slowly, taking his time between each slap. Each whack stung terribly. She remembered the times when her father had spanked her with his belt as she knelt before Momma's makeshift shrine. This was not as bad, but it still hurt. She cried out, and tears streamed from her eyes. She pleaded with him to stop.

Jolene's bottom felt like it was on fire. Prudome reached around to fondle her breasts and pinched her hard nipples. Jolene moaned and felt her vagina gush. The man ran his hands between her legs, and fingered her sopping pussy. Jolene gasped as pleasure shot through her.

"You're aroused," he said.

"Yes, sir," she said, her face pressed into the mattress.

"Then there is only one thing to do about that," Prudome rasped. "Daddy is going to have to fuck you."

Why did he say that? Did he know that his spanking had made her think of her father?

"Yes, sir," she said.

"Would you like that?" he said.

Jolene thought she had better agree. And in a way she didn't understand, she did want him to fuck her.

"Yes, sir," she said.

"Ask me."

"Will you please fuck me, sir?"

"Stay right there while I put on a condom. Don't you dare move."

She lay perfectly still, thankful that he remembered the rubber.

Moments later she felt his body behind her. She lay face down, her bottom exposed. What was he doing back there? She expected him to turn her over, because if he was going to fuck her they had to be face-to-face. That's the way Jimmy had always done it.

The man rubbed her vagina up and down, opening her with his fingers. He pulled her legs open and moved between them. Jolene could feel soft fabric. He had not undressed. The blunt end of his rubber-covered erection pressed into her. He slid inside with one quick move.

A wave of pleasure shot through her. This was the first man other than Jimmy who had fucked her. She shouldn't like it, but she did. Now that she had surrendered to the act, she became more aroused, and began to move her hips backward, meeting his thrust.

"You like this, don't you?" he said. "You like it when I fuck you."

"Yes, sir," she answered. It was the truth.

"Say it, then. Tell me how much you like this."

"I like this, sir."

"What do you like?"

"I like it when you fuck me. Please fuck me, sir. Please fuck me."

Prudome pounded into her. Jolene felt sensations rising like a wave. Jimmy would have been done by now, but Prudome kept hammering into her. Then, just as the wave swelled to its greatest point, just as it was about to break, he pulled out.

"Don't stop!" she gasped.

"Naughty little girl wants more, does she?"

"Please, sir," she said. "Please keep going."

He had moved away from her. Jolene turned to see what he was doing. Prudome held a small object. It looked like a toothpaste tube. He opened it and squirted a gob of goo onto his fingers. He noticed her watching him.

"Don't look at me," he said.

Jolene turned her face back to the mattress. She waited for what was coming next. She had not liked the spanking, but it had made her more excited than she had ever been.

His fingers, now slick with goo, rubbed her vagina. It felt

cool and nice. His fingers slid down to the bone at the top of her vagina and then up to her asshole. Then, he tried to push his finger inside. Jolene squirmed and tried to get away.

"Stop that!" she cried. "What are you doing?"

"Lie still," he commanded, "Or I'll punish you again."

Jolene didn't want to be spanked. She lay still. The man pressed into her bottom hole. It hurt, but not too much because his finger was covered in goo.

"This will be easier if you relax."

Jolene didn't know how.

"Come on," the man said. "Relax your ass."

"Don't do that," she said. "It's not right."

"Shut up!" he ordered. "You're going to take it."

Jolene lay face down. The man held her neck with one hand, and a finger of the other kept pressing into her asshole. She managed to relax a bit, and his finger slid inside her.

"Ow!" she cried. "Stop it. That really hurts."

"You have no choice," he said. "I am going to fuck your ass." He spoke slowly, with less anger. "It will hurt less if you submit. You might even like it."

Jolene let her muscles go limp, and sent her mind to a faraway place. She thought about riding on the back of Jimmy's motorcycle crossing long stretches of causeway over the Louisiana waters. The trees whipped past. The sun flashed golden through the branches.

Jolene felt the blunt end of his cock press against her asshole. Her vagina was swollen and hot. That's where she really wanted him.

"No," she pleaded.

His cock pressed relentlessly against her.

"No, no!" she cried. She squirmed and thrashed with her legs. Her hands were still cuffed, the leather collar tight around her throat. The man grabbed the leash and gave it a yank. The motion choked her. He released the pressure immediately.

"Stop it!" he ordered. "Lie still. If you don't, you will be punished like never before."

Jolene did as she was told. "Please, sir, don't," she begged. "Please don't fuck me there." Her pleading seemed to spur him on. He kept pushing until he had his hard dick up her ass.

He moved it in and out. She pleaded for him to stop, but he kept hammering into her backside. She had no choice but to allow it. He groaned, and his penis throbbed. Even with the condom Jolene could feel his orgasm. He shot off again and again. She knew what that meant. He would be done soon.

The man stopped plunging. The sensation of fullness in her asshole diminished as his penis went soft. After a few moments, he slid away. She felt a wave of relief pass through her body. Her ass still stung, but he had finished.

Jolene lay face down on the bed with her legs over the side. Her wrists were still shackled behind her back. It was hard to breathe, so she rolled over. Her breathing slowed and her heart calmed in her chest.

Prudome sat in a chair across from her. She could see him through tangled hair that had fallen over her eyes. He had removed his condom and zipped up.

"You've been a good girl," he said.

Jolene did not respond.

"I have paid you a compliment. What do you say?"

"Thank you, sir." She had her hands cuffed behind her back. The collar chafed her neck.

"Would you like something?" he asked.

"My arms hurt," she said. "Can you unlock me?"

"When will you learn how to speak to me?"

"Please, sir," she said.

He walked over to the bed. "You can have what you want if you ask properly."

Jolene felt his fingers working behind her, and heard the *snick* of the locks opening. She was soon able to massage her wrists. She felt his hands remove the collar and leash. He brushed her hair back from her face.

"Sir," she said. "May I please have some water?'

"Of course, when you ask properly."

Prudome walked out. Although the room was warm, Jolene felt chilled in her nakedness, and pulled the sheet across her body. He came back with a bottle of water. She gulped it down.

Later that night Prudome ordered her to suck his cock. Once she had gotten him hard, he slipped on a rubber and fucked her pussy from behind. He didn't shackle her, spank her, or take her in the ass again. Then he left her alone.

The sun shining in through the window woke her up. Her mouth felt dry and icky, her wrists were swollen and her ass hurt.

Jolene went into the bathroom and took a shower. Her wrists

bore red marks from the handcuffs and her neck felt raw from the collar. Returning to the bedroom, she found her clothes on the bed, neatly folded. She dressed.

In the main room, Prudome was gazing out the window sipping a mug of coffee. She wanted some badly, and also needed a cigarette. But Prudome might be angry if she asked, so she just stood there.

"There's coffee in the kitchen," he said without looking back.

Jolene poured herself a mug. Going back into the living room, she saw her coat over a chair and put it on, buttoning it up to the collar so that covered the marks on her wrists and neck.

"Come," Prudome said. Jolene walked to the table where he sat. There was a manila envelope in front of him. Picking it up, he poured out the contents.

"Driver's License, State of Nevada," Prudome announced. It had the picture he had taken of her, and the name Holly Susan McMillan. "Social Security card," he continued. "You'll need this to get a job." He then handed her a document with blue trim. One corner had a raised and bumpy circle. "Birth certificate from the State of Minnesota, Pine County. If anyone checks, he will find records in the County Clerk's office."

"You have to get another permit from the police," he continued, "if you want to work in a club. You can do that with the driver's license and the birth certificate."

Prudome looked at her with his fierce gaze. "You were never here. Do you understand? If you tell the police, I will have you killed."

"Yes, sir," she managed to reply.

Prudome dropped the documents into the envelope. He pushed it across the table and turned away. "Go now," he said. "Your boyfriend will be coming for you. Remind him he has six months."

Jolene had no idea what that meant. She picked up the envelope, walked out of the apartment, and rode the elevator down to the lobby.

Jimmy waited on his motorcycle in the parking lot.

"I want to go home," she said.

CHAPTER TWENTY-SEVEN

Charlie

CHARLIE DID NOT ASK SUSIE to tell more of her story after hearing about Prudome. He knew it had been difficult for her to expose that part of her life. It had been hard for him to hear. It made him sad and angry.

"I'm sorry that happened to you," he said softly. They sat in his darkened living room, Susie with her head lowered, an empty wineglass beside her. Charlie could not imagine anyone enjoying brutal sex, although he knew such things existed.

He considered calling the police. Prudome had raped Susie, when she was still only fourteen years old. The man had an ongoing practice as a blackmailer and forger, and deserved to be in jail. After careful thought, he decided against it. The police needed evidence of a specific crime to make an arrest. He had nothing to give them. They might investigate Prudome on his word alone, but they would also investigate Susie. She had been involved in criminal acts. Charlie did not want to lose her.

He might be in danger himself. Susie was really only seventeen, not eighteen as she had told him. Although they never had sex, there would be questions. He had done nothing illegal, but it still wasn't right. The desire he felt for her that day she came down the stairs, the thoughts and feelings he had since then—he would suppress them forever. In many ways, she was still a child, one that had been wounded, perhaps beyond repair. Susie needed a mentor and a friend, and Charlie resolved to be that person.

He had gained so much since Susie arrived. Not only had he been unable to work, he had also lost touch with humanity. Now he went out among people, taking her to the mall and restaurants. Caring for Susie brought him into the world again.

He continued to give her $400 per week, in cash, on the premise that she was his research assistant. She kept her money in the fringed bag she had the night he met her, hanging in the back of the upstairs closet. They discussed opening a bank account, but the problem that she faced in Las Vegas was still with her: no documentation. Prudome's false ID, which she had paid so dearly to obtain, was no longer in her possession. She lost it when she met her pimp, Skunk—a part of her life she was still reluctant to discuss. Her own birth certificate was somewhere in Enterprise, but Susie absolutely refused to go back there for any reason. The mere suggestion was met with snarls of anger.

They spent the holidays together. Charlie put up a small tree and Susie surprised him with a wrapped present on Christmas morning. She gave him a gold pen, purchased on one of her weekly visits to the mall.

Charlie noticed how much Susie enjoyed those outings, and they became a regular activity. He would drive her in the SUV and leave her there for most of the day. After a makeover at Eternity, for which Charlie paid, she would go to lunch with one of the beauticians. He knew it was necessary for her to have associations apart from him. Someday she would leave his house to make her way in the world.

He continued to recommend books. After she told him about Prudome he had given her *The Story of O*. It was about a young woman who became a sex slave. Susie read it, and then asked Charlie if it was true. He told her that nobody knew for sure but the woman who wrote it may have lived such a life. He also told her about the Marquis de Sade, a French nobleman who wrote about hurting other people for sexual pleasure.

"Would you like to read that next?" he asked.

Susie shook her head. "Can I have a book like the ones I used to read?"

Charlie balked at the thought of getting her a romance novel. She didn't need to pollute her mind with more twaddle. He suggested *To Kill a Mockingbird*. She enjoyed it immensely, and their discussions taught him more about her life growing up in a small southern town. Although she had dropped out of middle school, Susie grasped the novel's implications quickly. The girl had a keen mind. Charlie believed that Susie could become an extraordinary person with the proper education.

He sent away for materials so that she could take the GED exams. With his help, she could at least earn her high school equivalency. Reading the instructions, however, brought him up short. They also required identification. Charlie would have to find some way she could obtain valid documentation. Until then, his home would be Susie's safe haven.

He did not press her for more of her story, but one evening, after dinner and several glasses of wine, she began talking about what happened during the rest of her time in Las Vegas.

CHAPTER TWENTY-EIGHT

Jolene

AFTER HER NIGHT WITH PRUDOME, Jolene and Jimmy returned to the Inca Inn. Starving, she grabbed the sandwich he had brought home without taking off her coat. Swallowing a huge bite, Jolene asked: "He said to remind you about six months. What did that mean?"

"I got to pay him then," he said.

"Jesus!" Jolene blurted. "Wasn't what I did enough?"

"What did you do?"

Jolene stopped, the sandwich halfway to her mouth. She remembered being on her knees, her hands cuffed behind her back, the leather collar, the smack of his hand on her buttocks, his penis forcing its way into her ass.

"I don't want to talk about it," she said.

"Was it bad?"

Jolene exploded. "I don't want to talk! Not ever! So shut up! Shut up, shut up, shut up!"

Jimmy stared at her, shocked. She glared back, hot all over. If he said one more word—

He looked away. Jolene tore into the sandwich, chewing in angry silence.

Nobody will EVER know!

After eating she lay back, staring at the ceiling. Jimmy lied down beside her and fell asleep.

Going into the bathroom, Jolene opened her coat. The marks on her neck weren't too bad. Her wrists were turning purple. She needed to buy a long-sleeved shirt.

Taking money from Jimmy's wallet, Jolene picked up the envelope with her identification. There were stores on Fremont Street, but first she would have her triumph.

She walked straight to the library. Once there, she announced, "I want a library card."

The librarian recognized her. "Do you have identification?"

Jolene spilled the contents of the envelope. "Which one do you want?"

The librarian looked astonished. "Your license is enough."

Jolene handed it to her. The woman wrote on a card and said, "Sign here." She had written "Holly Susan McMillan." Jolene signed that name, and selected a book to take with her.

Next, Fremont Street. The stores there mostly sold T-shirts, but one had a rack of regular clothes. Jolene chose a long-sleeved blouse in rainbow colors like a hippie girl would wear, and a white shirt that buttoned at the wrists.

Back at the Inca Inn, she put on the colorful blouse. Sitting outside, she smoked and read until Jimmy woke up.

He came out holding the white shirt. "Where did this come from?" he asked.

"I took some money."

"How much?" Jimmy asked.

Jolene didn't like his tone. All she had done was buy a couple of goddamned shirts. Pushing up her sleeves, she showed him her bruised wrists.

Jimmy just looked at the ground.

"What's this place you were talking about?" she asked. "Where I can make so much money?"

Jimmy drove her Sweethearts. Jolene heard pounding music as they approached the entrance. A large man stopped them at the door.

"She's here to dance," Jimmy announced.

Dance?

Jolene had never danced in her life. Then she remembered frolicking in the New Orleans bar. She had also seen people on television dancing in matching costumes. Maybe that's the kind of job Jimmy had in mind. It sounded like fun.

The big man disappeared inside and returned with an older man. "I'm Amos, the manager," he said. "I understand you want to apply."

"She sure does," Jimmy replied.

Amos looked at Jolene. "Do you have any experience?"

"No," Jolene answered.

"That's okay," Jimmy said. "She'll learn fast."

Amos ignored him. "Are you eighteen?" he asked.

Jolene handed him the driver's license. Amos glanced at it. "Do you have your work permit and business license?"

"Ain't that enough?" she asked.

"Wait here," the man said, and disappeared inside.

"Jimmy, he took my ID," she said urgently.

"He'll bring it back," said the big man.

When Amos returned, he handed Jolene her license and a blank form. "Fill this out," he said. "Then go to the police department to get your work permit."

"Why does she need that?" Jimmy asked.

"Anyone who works for a casino or a club has to register with the police. You also need to go to the tax office for the business license. It will cost about a hundred dollars."

Jolene and Jimmy went back to the Inca Inn where they ate baloney sandwiches.

"We ain't got a hundred bucks," Jolene pointed out.

"Let me think about it."

When Jimmy left for work Jolene picked up the novel and lost herself in the adventure, falling asleep with the book across her chest.

Jimmy woke her the next morning and showed her two hundred dollars. "Hammerhead loaned it to me," he said. "Get dressed."

Jolene showered. The red marks on her neck had almost disappeared, but there were still bruises on her wrists. She put on the white shirt, buttoning the cuffs.

They drove to the police station, where Jimmy paid the fees. They waited in the lobby over an hour before an officer called out "Holly McMillan." Jolene didn't respond. The officer called "Holly McMillan" a second time. Jolene realized it meant her. She jumped up, jostling Jimmy awake.

The next stop was the tax office. Jimmy paid again and the clerk took Jolene's identification for copying. When the clerk called out "Holly McMillan," she was ready, and collected her business license.

They drove directly to Sweethearts. Amos came out, remembered her, and saw that her paper work was in order.

"You ready to audition?" he asked.

"Can we go in?" Jimmy asked. "She needs to see the kind of dancing the girls do here."

Amos looked at them suspiciously. "You can watch for a few minutes," he said.

It was dark inside. Music pounded from hidden speakers. The whole place made her afraid, until Jolene remembered Prudome.

What could happen here that could be worse?

They sat in front of a stage. A woman walked into the bright lights, wearing a schoolgirl costume and platform shoes. The dancer grabbed a brass pole with both hands and lifted herself up. Jolene watched wide-eyed as she climbed the pole and then spun around on it. Men walked over to the stage and sprinkled money on the floor.

The girl opened her shirt, exposing her chest. She slipped her plaid skirt down her long legs. Wearing only a tiny bikini bottom, she hoisted herself up again. Her body was exposed to every eye in the room. Customers left more dollars on the stage. Thighs grasping the pole, the girl pulled strings on each hip. When she flipped back up, the bikini bottom fluttered away. Now completely naked, the dancer spun around with her legs open. With a shock, Jolene realized that was why the men were here:

They come to look at her pussy.

The song ended. The dancer gathered up the money.

Jimmy whispered, "It takes me three hours to make what she did with one dance."

Jolene did not think she could be naked in front of strangers.

The manager appeared. "If you want to stay you have to pay the cover charge."

"We'll go," Jimmy said.

Jolene followed him out, speechless at the thought of what Jimmy wanted her to do.

"You ready to audition?" Amos asked.

"Can I come back later?" she asked the manager.

He handed her the documents. "Let us know when you're ready."

"You got to do this," Jimmy growled.

Jolene leaned in close. "I got hair down there." The dancers had all shaved between their legs. Her crotch was like a lawn that needed mowing.

They went back to the Inca Inn. Jimmy had worked the night before, and he fell asleep without even taking off his clothes.

Jolene went outside, lit a cigarette, and thought about what Jimmy wanted. It would be hard to be naked, and dancing on the pole looked impossible. Yet the men had thrown money, lots of it. That would change her life.

The first step would be to get a sexy outfit, and a pair of shoes like the women in the club. She would have to shave between her legs, and teach herself to dance.

When Jimmy woke up, Jolene explained the situation. Jimmy said they could go shopping for clothes that evening.

"We ain't hardly got any money left," Jolene said. They had to wait until Jimmy got paid.

Over the next few days Jolene practiced dancing. A row of poles outside their room held up a second-floor walkway. She tried swinging around one of them. She couldn't hang upside down like the schoolgirl dancer. The best she could manage was spinning around.

Jimmy would lift the bed on its side before he left for work, making an open space in their room. Jolene pranced in bra and panties, trying some of the moves she had seen the schoolgirl dancer doing. Late in the evening she pulled the mattress down on the floor to sleep. Jimmy would come home and crash beside her.

One morning Jimmy came home bringing breakfast. "I finally got paid," he said.

As they ate she asked, "How much do we have?"

"Two hundred and thirty-three dollars." Jimmy explained that he had repaid Hammerhead's loan, filled the motorcycle's tank and given the Inca Inn a month's rent.

Why did he pay for a whole month? She needed to start dancing right away.

That night they set out to find a dancing costume. Jolene had seen a store that sold sexy clothes, but when they got there they could not believe the prices. The costumes were only a few scraps of cloth and yet terribly expensive. Each pair of shoes was nearly a hundred dollars.

"This place is for tourists," the clerk said. "Go to Goodwill. You can get some real bargains." She gave them the address.

The thrift store had a section with outfits like the ones the girls wore at Sweethearts. Jolene supposed that even dancers got tired of their clothes. She selected a green sequined bikini and a skimpy skirt-and-top in red with black trim. There were also lots of shoes, and Jolene found a pair of platforms. She would learn how to walk in them.

Back at the Inca Inn, she tried on the green bikini. Hair stuck out everywhere. Jimmy borrowed a pair of scissors from the motel office, and she snipped away most of it before lathering on shaving cream. It was hard to reach every spot. By the time she came out of the bathroom, Jimmy had left for work.

Jolene put on the green bikini and strapped on the platform shoes. Teetering, she grabbed the edge of the desk. *How did women dance in shoes like these?* The girls at the club moved like cats. Jolene made circuits of their tiny room. Two hours later she flopped onto the mattress.

When Jimmy came home he fell instantly asleep. Jolene put on her jeans and the platform shoes. Her feet hurt something awful, but she set out to buy coffee. The broken sidewalk made walking difficult. Jolene somehow made it to the 7-Eleven and back home.

Another week passed. Jimmy went to work each night and Jolene practiced. Tying the bikini straps loosely behind her neck, she could release the top with a tug. The cups fell away, revealing her breasts. She also figured out how to remove the bikini bottom over her shoes.

Jimmy woke up one day to find Jolene dressed in her bikini and shoes. She wanted to show him her act. Jolene hummed a tune and wiggled in front of him. His face broke into a grin when she stripped off her bikini. Finished, she struck a little pose naked before him.

Jimmy gathered her into his arms. For the first time Jolene felt like having sex with him. She reached down and squeezed his hard cock. Jimmy groaned with pleasure.

They made love, but it didn't last long. Jimmy came as soon as they began.

To celebrate, he took her to Dinky's Diner. "You want to go back to Sweethearts tomorrow?" he asked.

"They're open right now ain't they?"

Jimmy shook his head. "I gotta work. We'll go in the morning."

~

Jimmy woke her with kisses. Half asleep, she realized he wanted to fuck her again.

"No!" she insisted, pushing him away. "We're going to Sweethearts."

Jolene wore her green bikini under a T-shirt and jeans. Putting the platform shoes into her backpack, she put on sneakers for the ride.

The manager remembered them. Jolene handed over her paper work. Amos asked her to follow him, but stopped Jimmy at the door.

"I can do this on my own," Jolene told him.

Amos led her into the club, where music throbbed. The manager took her to a hidden doorway behind the stage. Knocking, he announced that he was coming in.

The room looked like a Hollywood movie: makeup tables with mirrors and giant light bulbs. On one side stood a row of lockers. Three girls eyed her silently.

"Did you bring a lock?" Amos asked. "The club is not responsible for personal items."

A voice from loudspeaker said, "Epiphany onstage." One of the girls walked through a curtained doorway.

"You can go on after her," the manager said. "I'll be outside watching."

Jolene untied her sneakers, stripped off her jeans, and placed them in a locker. Taking the platform shoes out of her backpack, she strapped them on.

"What do you use on your hair?" someone said. Jolene turned to see two girls looking at her. One wore a white bra and panties. The other was dressed in a leather skirt and matching top. Her right arm was covered with tattoos from shoulder to wrist.

"Shampoo," Jolene answered.

"Shit," said the girl in the leather skirt. Her own hair was stringy.

"What's your name?" asked the girl in white.

"Jolene," she replied, and then remembered that she should have said "Holly."

"I mean what do you use when you dance?"

Jolene didn't know she needed another name, but remembered one she had used before:

"Audrey," she said.

"You'd better tell the DJ," said the girl in white.

Jolene went through the curtain. A man sat there with two record players in front of him.

"What's your name, sweetheart?" he asked.

"Audrey," Jolene told him.

"What music do you want?"

"Whatever."

The song that was playing ended. Epiphany came off stage naked, clutching her clothes and some money. A song started, and Jolene heard the DJ say: "Gentlemen, give a warm welcome to Audrey."

She walked out on shaking legs. The lights were bright in her eyes, and she could see nothing beyond the edge of the stage but blackness. Moving forward, Jolene grabbed the pole and flung herself around. Twirling off, she dropped to her knees and then came up, letting her hair fly out. She reached out for the pole, and spun around it the other way.

Jolene had gone onstage wearing her T-shirt over her bikini. Dropping to her knees, she pulled it off in one quick motion. After twirling the T-shirt around, she threw into the darkness.

The song ended. Jolene saw that men had sprinkled dollars on the stage.

A second song began. Tugging the strings, the bikini top dropped away. Flipping her head down, she tossed her hair. She did a backward somersault, pulling her bikini bottom off as she went. When she came up, she was naked.

I've done it!

Men came from the darkness and threw money. She danced naked, feeling liberated. When the song ended, Jolene collected her clothes and the cash. She had done nothing more than show her naked body, and they had thrown money at her!

In the dressing room the girl in white asked, "How'd it go?"

"Fine," Jolene said. She placed her clothes and money on one of the dressing tables.

"That's Zahara's. Use this one," the girl said, pointing to another space.

After moving her things, Jolene put her bikini on, unstrapped her shoes and stepped into her jeans. Then, she remembered tossing her T-shirt into the audience. Picking up her backpack and coat, she went into the club to find it.

Amos was waiting. "Let's talk in the office," he said.

They went through a door into a hallway lined with metal cans. Amos unlocked another door and they went into a room big enough for a desk, two chairs, and some of filing cabinets.

"You hardly used the pole," he said, pointing to a chair. "But I liked the bit with the T-shirt. It makes you look like a runaway teenager."

"I have to get it back," she said. Sitting in her jeans and bra made her uncomfortable.

"I'll give you some of ours. You can toss one out every dance. It's good advertising."

He opened a cardboard box and handed her one. It had "Sweethearts" written in red surrounded by Valentine hearts. Jolene put it on.

"We don't have many like you, girl-next-door types with natural breasts. Give it to me."

Jolene didn't know what he meant.

"The cash from that dance," he explained. "Audition money goes to the staff."

"I earned that money," she protested.

"It's the same in every club," he insisted. "The other girls will tell you."

Jolene gave him the twelve dollars.

"It's a six-hour shift," he continued. "You dance at least once an hour. You might do three or four. You also have to sell four drinks."

Jolene nodded, trying to take it all in.

"You tip out twenty percent to the house, five to the DJ, and five to the cocktail waitresses. Ten more goes to the bouncers."

"What does 'tip out' mean?" she asked.

"You have to pay the other people who work here."

Jolene didn't like that, but she needed the job.

"I can give you 8:00 a.m. to 2:00 p.m., or 2:00 to 8:00 a.m.," he continued "The day shift gets a lunch crowd. Graveyard is good at first but gets slow later."

"Did you say I could work two to eight?"

Jimmy worked then.

Amos smiled. "The graveyard manager is Louie. I'll tell him you're coming."

Jolene went out into the lobby. Jimmy was asleep. She woke him saying, "I got the job!"

They went back to the Inca Inn, where Jimmy fell asleep. Jazzed up, Jolene walked back to Sweethearts, five miles away. Standing outside, she dreamed about the money she would make. Twelve dollars a dance and at least six dances a night.

Later, she told Jimmy about the dressing room. They bought

a lock in a drug store. He left her in the Sweethearts' parking lot at quarter to twelve.

Inside she met Louie, the night manager: a chubby man in his forties with red hair.

"Audrey, right?" he asked. "Why are you so early?"

Jolene explained her situation with Jimmy's work schedule. She wanted to wait somewhere with her book.

"You can read and you want to work at Sweethearts?" It took Jolene a moment to realize he was making a joke.

Louis took her to the office. "Wait here. The dressing room's a little crowded."

Jolene tried to read but couldn't concentrate. She walked down the hall and peered into the club. Girls sat around the room talking to customers. A dancer twirled on the pole. Men at the edge of the stage threw money.

She noticed one of the women take a customer through a curtained doorway. A man dressed in black—beefy like a football player—jotted something on a clipboard.

Back in the office, Jolene fell asleep. Louie woke her before 2:00 a.m. He handed her a stack of T-shirts. "Amos says you use them. Don't give out more than one a dance."

Jolene went into the dressing room. The night shift girls were going home.

An older woman caught her eye. She wore a black leather outfit and knee-high boots, with a barbed wire tattoo around her upper arm.

"What's your name, honey?" the woman asked.

"Audrey," Jolene replied.

"I'm Janet. My dancing name's Invictus. Hey, Temptation?"

A girl looked up. She had dark hair with red streaks, and patch shaved bald on one side.

"This is Audrey," Invictus explained. "She's new."

"Invictus, onstage," said a voice over the loudspeaker.

"Last dance of the night," the woman said. She rose and walked out.

Jolene stripped down to her green bikini, put on one of the Sweethearts' T-shirts, and strapped on her platform shoes. Stuffing everything into a locker, she snapped the lock closed.

Temptation sat at a mirror putting on eyeliner. Jolene sat next to her. "They told me not to sit in Zahara's spot," she said.

"That bitch thinks she owns the place, but she's not here now."

Invictus came back and plopped into a chair, naked except for her knee-high boots. Opening a little purse, she added money to a roll of bills inside.

"Not a bad night," she said.

Jolene whispered to her, "What do I do now?"

Invictus smiled. "Tell the DJ to put you in the lineup."

Jolene walked through the curtained doorway. A black man with braided hair took her name and asked if she wanted any special music. Jolene said whatever he played would be fine.

"You follow Chanel," he instructed.

Jolene went back into the dressing room. The dancers from the earlier shift had put on their street clothes and were stuffing their costumes into bags. A voice behind her said, "Good luck, honey."

She hardly recognized Invictus. The older woman had scrubbed off her makeup, tied back her hair, and was wearing slacks and an overcoat.

"Get out there," she said with a smile. "Sell some drinks. Get some men to buy dances."

Jolene walked into the crowded club. The men were all watching the stage, where a girl danced naked on the pole. She noticed Temptation and walked over.

"I'm supposed to sell four drinks. How do I do that?"

"Ask a guy to buy them. If he gets one for you and one for himself, that's two." Temptation paused. "Why are you wearing that T-shirt?"

"I use it in my dance," Jolene said.

"Take it off when you're in the club. It's easier to sell if you show them your body."

Jolene stripped off her T-shirt. She could carry it until it was time to go onstage.

"Those are nice," Temptation said. "Who did them?"

"Who did what?" Jolene asked.

"Your boobs. What doctor did your boobs?"

It took Jolene a moment to figure out that the girl thought a doctor had done something with her breasts.

"They're my boobs," she said.

"Jesus. They're that big and natural? You're going to make a fortune."

Jolene smiled, not at the compliment but at the idea she was going to make money.

Temptation walked toward two men just sitting down. She spoke to one of them, pulling up a chair of her own. The man said something and she laughed. It looked easy enough. Screwing up her courage, Jolene walked over to the table.

"Hi, Audrey," Temptation said with a smile. "This is Jack." Speaking to the other man she asked, "I didn't get your name."

"Bill," the man said, his eyes never leaving the dancer onstage.

"This is Audrey. Want to buy her a drink?"

Bill looked at Jolene. "What do you want?"

"Whatever," she answered.

Jolene watched Temptation, lightly running her fingers over Jack's arm while talking to him. When a waitress came by, she ordered four Piña Coladas. The waitress brought frothy glasses loaded with fruit. Jolene sipped one. It was sweet and creamy, like a dessert.

This job is going to be fun.

"Do you want a dance?" Temptation asked Jack.

"How much?" he asked.

"Twenty out here, thirty in the back."

The girls who danced in the back earned more. What was the difference?

"The Champagne Room," Temptation continued, "is a hundred dollars for fifteen minutes."

"Jesus," Bill said. "What happens in there?"

"You can do anything you want," Temptation answered seductively.

Did she have sex with the men?

"I'll buy him a dance," Jack said.

"The Champagne Room?" Temptation asked.

"I'm not that good a friend. I'll buy him one out here."

Jack handed her the twenty, which she put into a little purse. Then she stood up and held out her hand to Bill. "We'll find a more comfortable spot," she said.

Temptation led him to a padded booth. A new song began. She straddled Bill's lap facing him, unclasped her bra and dropped it to the side; her breasts were naked to the stranger. The dancer put her arms on the man's shoulders and began to move her hips back and forth like she was having sex with him. She slid down his body as if getting ready to give him a blowjob, and then stood up and wiggled with her back to him.

Looking around, Jolene saw other girls dancing for men like that.

She felt something on her arm. Jack was caressing her skin, like Temptation had been doing. Jolene almost pulled her arm away, but realized that it was part of the job. The men wanted to touch her. How much depended on how much they paid. Buy a drink, touch an arm. Buy a dance, see the body.

What happened in the back room?

The song ended. Jolene watched as Temptation slid off Bill's lap. The dancer put her bra back on, then they came back to the table where Jolene and Jack waited.

"How was it?" Jack asked his buddy.

"Great," he answered. "You should get one, too."

Jack looked at Jolene. "Maybe I will," he said. "Maybe one in the back."

What if he wanted to go in the Champagne Room?

"Audrey onstage." The DJ's voice rang through the room.

Going backstage, Jolene slipped on the Sweethearts T-shirt. When the song ended, she heard the DJ say, "Gentlemen, give a warm welcome to Audrey."

Jolene walked onstage. The seats at the edge were filled with men watching her. She swung around the pole and then stripped off her T-shirt. Twirling it around her head, she tossed it into the audience. The men scrambled to catch it. Some scattered money at her feet. The first song ended and the second began.

Time to give them what they paid for.

Jolene pulled the string behind her neck and her bra fell. She then did a backward somersault and pulled off her bottoms. Rising, she swung around the pole again, dancing until the song ended.

Money littered the stage. Jolene scooped it up with her hands. Returning to the dressing room, she passed Temptation waiting to go on.

Jolene dumped the pile of crumpled money on a table. She dressed, sat down and pressed each bill smooth. Twenty-seven dollars. It was her salvation.

"I like the T-shirt." Turning, she saw Temptation standing naked, holding her money and clothes. "But you don't use the pole."

"It's my first job," Jolene answered.

"I can show you later, when the crowd thins out."

"What happens in the Champagne Room?" Jolene asked.

"I let the men touch me."

"Do you fuck them?" she whispered, astonished.

Temptation grew serious. "No. It's against the law. Don't start hooking. You can get us all in trouble."

"Try some lap dances first," the dancer continued. "All you take off is your top."

They left the dressing room. Jack and Bill had taken seats at the edge of the stage, watching a dancer shimmy up the pole. Temptation disappeared.

Jolene saw a man sitting by himself. He was really old. The small table in front of him was empty. Jolene walked over.

"Want some company?" she asked.

"I don't think I'm going to buy a dance," he said.

"I'm not sure I want to do one," Jolene replied, sitting down. "Can you buy me a drink?"

The man waved the waitress over.

"I'm Audrey," Jolene said. "What's your name?"

"Robert," he said.

The man told her he sold insurance. He lived in some place called Palmdale. The waitress brought their drinks. After chatting awhile Jolene asked, "Do you want me to dance for you?"

"I've never done that before," he said.

"How about the next song?"

Jolene did what she had seen Temptation do: she led Robert

to one of the padded seats against the wall. When the music began, she straddled Robert's lap. He looked at her with awe. Jolene moved her hips back and forth like she did when she had sex with Jimmy. Reaching down, she grasped the bottom of her T-shirt and pulled it off over her head. It messed up her hair and she shook it out with her hands. She could feel Robert's cock grow hard against her thigh.

Wow. Even a guy this old still can have sex.

Pulling the strings of her bikini top, the cups fell away. Robert made a sound like air leaking from a balloon.

She tried what Temptation had done earlier. Sliding down Robert's legs, she acted like she was going to give him a blowjob. Not touching his penis, she stood up, twirled around and faced away from him. After wiggling a bit, she looked at him. He had not moved, mouth open, eyes wide. Jolene danced in front of him until the song ended. Sitting down, she slipped on her T-shirt without putting her bra back on.

"Twenty dollars," she said.

The man pulled out his wallet and handed her the bill. Not having any place to put it, she stuck it in the waistband of her bikini bottom.

Jolene talked to him for a while, until the DJ called her name. The dance bought in eighteen dollars. It was 4:00 a.m., and most of the customers had gone home. Putting the money in her locker, she went back to Robert who ordered another round of drinks. Jolene danced for him four more times. She did another turn on stage dance at 5:00 a.m. When she returned, Robert was gone. There were hardly any customers at all.

She felt so tired! Going into the dressing room, Jolene put her head down on a makeup table. The DJ's voice woke her up, and she went onstage and danced again. This time, there was no money at all.

In the dressing room, she ran into Temptation, headed for the stage. "I saw you dancing for some guy," she said.

"Made a hundred dollars," Jolene answered.

"You would make more if you took him in the back. In the time you made a hundred, I've made three."

Three hundred dollars in one night!

"Come on," Temptation said. "Let me show you how to work the pole." She led Jolene into the hallway and said to the DJ, "We're going to do a double."

They walked onstage together. No one sat around the edge. Squinting, Jolene could see a few customers at the back.

"One hand high on the pole," the dancer said. "Put the other hand low. It gives you leverage." Temptation grabbed the pole and lifted herself off the ground. "You try it."

Jolene did as she instructed.

"Leaning toward the pole slows you down. Lean away and let gravity carry you." The more experienced dancer grabbed the pole and whipped her body in a circle.

"Giving lessons?" said a voice from the darkness.

"There's nobody here Louie," Temptation said.

"Yeah, all right," said the manager, and he walked away.

"We're not supposed to do this," she explained, "But Louie's cool."

Jolene tried spinning as she had seen the older girl do. She made it halfway around before losing momentum.

"Take three steps before lifting. That gives you the speed to keep going."

This time, Jolene made it around the pole twice. They left the stage after four songs, making no money. In the dressing room Jolene collapsed in a chair. Temptation opened a locker and took out a little bottle. Twisting off the cap, she tapped it against one of her long fingernails. Some white powder spilled out, which she sniffed into her nose.

"Want a bump?" she asked.

Jolene shook her head. Temptation had just snorted cocaine. She had learned about it in Ms. Beckon's health class, and the idea of doing drugs scared her.

Seven o'clock passed. Jolene's body sagged. Her arms ached. She spent the last hour listening to Temptation, who suddenly had a lot to say. As eight o'clock approached the morning shift girls began to trickle in.

"Might as well cash out." Temptation said. "Get your money."

She led Jolene to the bar where Amos had a clipboard. He glanced at it, wrote something down and said, "That's one-nine-ty-five, darling."

Temptation opened her little purse, counted out ten twenties and handed them to Louie. He gave her a five-dollar bill.

The manager looked at his clipboard. "Five on the floor,

none in the back, six onstage. Sixty dollars." Jolene reluctantly handed over nearly half of what she made.

In the dressing room, now crowded with girls, Jolene put on her jeans and sneakers. Coming out of the club with Temptation, the morning sun dazzled her eyes.

"You need a ride?" the older girl asked.

"My boyfriend's coming," Jolene said.

"See you tomorrow." The dancer got into a brand new, nice-looking car.

Jolene sat on a bench. The ground was littered with cigarette butts. She pulled out her pack, realizing she had not smoked all night. Resting her head against the wall, she took a drag.

Someone nudged her shoulder. Jolene sat up, blurry and confused. It was Jimmy.

"How much did you make?" he asked.

"Hello to you, too," Jolene said. She pulled out the wad of bills.

"That's all?"

"It's over a hundred dollars," she said, shocked that he thought it wasn't enough.

Jimmy stuffed the money into his leather jacket. "Let's go home," he said.

Jolene was too tired to argue. They drove to the Inca Inn, where she went into the bathroom. Jimmy was snoring when she came out. Lying beside him, Jolene dropped off in seconds.

CHAPTER TWENTY-NINE

Audrey

WHEN WORKING AT SWEETHEARTS, Jolene thought of herself as Audrey. Not the girl she had known back home but another person, someone not Jolene. Audrey was bold. Audrey was sexy. Audrey loved taking money from men.

All of the other girls each carried a small purse. Before her second night, Jimmy took her to get one and then dropped her off two hours early, as before.

A group of dancers stood outside smoking. There was a moment when no one said anything, and then one of the girls asked:

"You're Audrey, right? I'm Sandy. Alessandria onstage. How do you like it so far?"

"Tipping out sucks."

The girls all laughed. They thought she was making a joke.

"I used to work at Pleasure Chest," said a tall woman, who danced by the name Copenhagen. "House fees were two hundred up front." They started talking about the different clubs and how much the girls had to tip out. Audrey lit a cigarette and listened.

"Why are you here so early?" Copenhagen asked. Audrey explained that her boyfriend dropped her off on his way to work. That started a new conversation about men. The women considered them all worthless.

"Except for sex," said Sandy.

"Yeah, you gotta have that," Audrey quipped, and the girls laughed.

She stood outside, smoking and talking, until 2:00 a.m. The dancers on shift would come and go. At one point a woman wearing a long, tawny coat emerged. She had dark hair, olive skin, and stunning green eyes. Standing apart, she lit a thin cigarette with a golden lighter. When finished, the woman went back inside without saying a word.

The girls exploded in conversation. It was Zahara, who the others feared and hated.

At 2:00 a.m. Audrey went in the dressing room, changed, and walked into the club. The place was packed with men. Her eyes fell on two customers at a table. "Come on," she said to the girl beside her. "Let's go make some money."

Audrey walked straight to the table and sat down. "How about you boys buy us drinks?" One of the men waved a waitress over.

When she had gone, Audrey laid her hand on his arm, as she had seen Temptation do. "Come on," she said. "Let's have a dance."

They went to an empty spot at the back of the room. Audrey removed her T-shirt and bikini top in ways that had already become familiar. His cock grew hard beneath his trousers; she could see the bulge in the dim light. When the song ended, Audrey whispered directly into his ear. She did it so that he could hear her clearly, but saw that the man became more excited. Whispering instantly became another weapon in her arsenal.

"Do you want another dance?" she asked.

"You're so beautiful," the man replied. It was the nicest thing that anyone had said to her in ages.

She danced again, and when the song was over she heard the DJ call, "Audrey onstage."

"I have to go," she said.

"You're coming back?" he asked. Audrey simply replied, "That's two dances. Forty dollars." The man handed her two twenties. She snapped them into her new purse.

Going on stage, Audrey tried the moves Temptation had taught her. Grabbing the pole, she took three steps and hoisted herself into the air. The muscles in her arms screamed in pain. She only made it around once before dropping to the ground. It didn't matter. There was a long night ahead.

After her dances, in the dressing room, she counted out thirty-two dollars. Storing it in her locker, Audrey turned to Temptation:

"What goes on in the back?"

"I'll show you," the dancer said.

Temptation opened the door to the service hallway. The wall had tiny peepholes drilled into it. Looking through one, Audrey saw a small room with a sofa at one end, just big enough for two people. The dancer named Alhambra sat on a client's lap, naked. The man had his hands on her thighs, caressing them gently. Alhambra raised her arms over her head; he slid his hands up her rib cage and took hold of her breasts.

"They can touch you all over in a private room," Temptation whispered. "Not your pussy, but they can play with your tits. If one gets too rough, call for the bouncer."

"What if I don't want them touching my boobs?" Audrey asked.

"That's why they pay thirty dollars a dance."

"What's in the Champagne Room?"

Temptation led her to another peephole. Through it, Audrey could see a larger room with a long, flat couch. "The difference is the dance," she explained. "Run your hands through his hair, brush against his cock. Get him worked up as much as you can."

They went back into the club, where Audrey rejoined her customer. "I'm ready for another drink," she said. The man waved the waitress over.

"How about we go in the back?" Audrey asked when the drinks arrived.

"What happens there?"

"I'll get totally naked for you." Just saying the words got her a little excited. She placed her hand on his thigh and gave it a squeeze. He could hardly say "yes" fast enough.

They went to the curtained doorway. The bouncer stood waiting, clipboard in hand. "It's thirty dollars a dance," he said to the man, who hesitated. Audrey whispered in his ear, "It's going to be worth it."

The man nodded. The bouncer held back the curtain and they went into a room.

A new song started. She stripped off her T-shirt, her top, and then her bikini bottom. Straddling his lap, she started moving against him.

The man's hands lay at his sides. Maybe he didn't know he could touch her. Taking his hands in her own, she placed them directly on her breasts. A sigh of admiration escaped from the man's lips. He caressed her breasts and hefted their heaviness. It felt good. All the time she kept moving with the music.

The song ended. Audrey touched her forehead to his, and locked her fingers behind his neck. Whispering, she asked, "Do you want to keep going?"

"Yes, yes!"

They stayed there through several songs. The man caressed her breasts, waist, and thighs. At one point, he tried to touch between her legs. She stood up and said, "None of that."

The man looked as if he was in some kind of trance. "Maybe we'd better go back to the club," he said.

Audrey put her bikini and T-shirt back on. Turning to him, she said, "That's six dances."

The man roused. "How much is that?"

Audrey added it up quickly. *Thirty and thirty is sixty, plus thirty more was ninety . . .* "A hundred and eighty dollars." The amount surprised her.

"Jesus," he blurted.

"Are you going to pay?" she asked, suddenly concerned. "Do I need to call the bouncer?"

"No, no," the man said. He pulled out his wallet and counted twenties into her hand.

They returned to the club. As she passed the bouncer he asked, "You get a hundred and eighty?" Audrey showed him the wad of cash.

Looking around the room, Audrey saw two men sitting alone. She walked over and sat down. "So where are you boys from?" she asked.

"Minneapolis," one said. He went on to say they worked for a company that sold dishes. When the waitress came by and Audrey coaxed them into buying drinks.

Eventually she turned to one and said, "Hey, let's have a dance."

"Not me," one said. "I lost too much at blackjack."

"You'll win next time," she urged. "Come on."

The men looked at each other. "It's why we came," one of them said.

"Twenty out here, thirty in the back," she offered.

One of the men stood up and said, "Okay, let's go."

Audrey took him to a booth. When the song began, the

T-shirt came off, then the bikini top. The man tried to touch her breasts. She pushed his hands away, saying, "Not in the club."

After the dance, they went in the back, where Audrey allowed him to run his hands over her body as she danced. After awhile the man said he'd had enough. She put on her clothes and informed told him "One out front, three in the back. That's a hundred and ten."

"I don't have it."

Audrey pulled back in shock. She had plainly told him it would be thirty dollars a dance. Striding out of the room, she went straight to the bouncer.

"The guy doesn't have any money," she said.

Without a word the bouncer walked inside. Audrey followed. She let this stranger fondle her naked body, and now he wasn't going to pay?

If the bouncer doesn't kill him, I'll do it myself.

The man explained he had forgotten how much he had lost gambling.

"If you don't pay," the bounder explained, "It's the same as stealing. We call the police."

The man glanced at Audrey. She shot knives at him from her eyes.

"Is there an ATM?" he asked.

So, he had money after all. What a lying son of a bitch.

"Go onstage," the bouncer said to her. "You missed two dances."

"What about my money?"

"I'll take care of it."

Audrey went on stage and looked around. The bouncer was leading the man to the lobby. Grabbing the pole, she hoisted herself with a move that Temptation had taught her.

After the dance, she went to find the bouncer. "Did you get it?" she asked. He handed her five twenties and a ten.

The rest of the evening was slow. Audrey convinced a salesman from Wisconsin to buy three dances. Near the end of the shift a group of college boys who had driven overnight night from Texas came in. They wanted to party the second they hit town. Audrey danced five times. When morning came, she left the club with over three hundred dollars.

When Jimmy arrived, the first thing he said was, "How'd you do?"

"Better," she said.

"Give it to me."

"It's my money, Jimmy," she protested.

"I spent everything I had getting here," he said. "Hand it over."

She didn't feel like fighting. Putting her earnings in Jimmy's hand, she suddenly became Jolene again.

CHAPTER THIRTY

Jimmy

MARCH BECAME APRIL. The nights were so warm Jimmy didn't need his jacket when he went to work. The days got really hot, but they spent most of their time inside.

Jo was bringing in good money now, and about damned time. The trip out had cost him everything. He paid for all the food, gas, and hotel rooms, and bought Jo clothes, makeup, and a helmet. Now she was always griping when he took her pay. Jo simply didn't know how much things cost. His salary at Double Jacks barely covered their rent.

What was worse, she didn't want to fuck him anymore. It took her a long time to get over that shit with Prudome, but eventually she came around. For a while they had sex every night, but they hadn't done anything for the past two weeks. Jo pulled away every time he tried.

Jimmy thought about this, lying in bed. Jo was beside him, and hadn't woken up yet. They slept late into the afternoon every day, and then went out in the evening for dinner. After that, most nights they just came back to their room. Jimmy worked out on the floor while she buried her nose in a library book.

What does she get out of all that reading?

Jimmy went into the bathroom. It must have waked her up, because as soon as he was done she rushed inside. They went to Dinky's for breakfast, at 5:00 in the evening.

Then they returned to the room. As soon as they got inside he put his arms around her, but she pushed him away.

"Come on, Jo," he insisted.

"No," she protested, trying to squirm free.

"What's got into you?"

"I don't want to right now."

"Well, I do."

"Jimmy, get off!"

He grabbed her face with one hand, forcing her lips toward his. She pushed real hard, broke from his grasp, and dashed into the bathroom. Jimmy heard the lock turning.

He rattled the knob, and then pounded on the door. "Come out of there!"

"Leave me alone," she replied, her voice muffled.

Why didn't she want to do it? There could only be one reason.

"Are you fucking the guys at Sweethearts?"

"No! They're disgusting."

Jimmy went outside to smoke, seething with anger.

Why do I put up with her crap? She wouldn't even be here if it wasn't for me.

Ten minutes later Jo came out with her backpack. "Take me to work," she demanded.

"We don't have to go yet."

"Then I'll walk."

"Okay," he said, and went in the room to get his helmet.

At Sweethearts, a group of dancers stood smoking in the parking lot. Jo got off the bike and walked straight toward them. The girls said, "Hello," and "Hi, Audrey," like they were glad to see her. No one looked at him twice.

He had the night off, with nothing to do. Driving to Fremont Street, Jimmy parked his bike and walked into a casino. There was over three hundred dollars in cash in his wallet, Jo's earnings from the night before.

I deserve to have a little fun.

He sat down at the wheel game, which he now knew was called "roulette." Buying a hundred chips, he placed some around the board. Waitresses came by bringing drinks. He kept losing, but didn't care. Jo would bring him more in the morning. Stumbling out of the casino at 4:00 a.m., Jimmy drove home and fell into drunken slumber.

"Hey. Hey!" Jo's voice roused him. Morning sun forced its way into his eyes. "Why didn't you pick me up?" she demanded. "I had to get a ride home with the manager."

"Where's the money?" he asked.

"Jesus. That's all you care about."

Jo opened her purse, pulled out a huge wad of twenties and handed it to him. Jimmy gathered the money to his chest and rolled over.

"I need to buy a hair dryer," she said.

"Later," he mumbled, and fell asleep again.

Waking up late in the afternoon, he looked around trying to make sense of things. His head ached and his mouth felt like sandpaper. The bed was covered with cash.

"You're welcome," someone said.

Through blurred vision he could see Jo in the corner, a book on her lap.

His stomach lurched. He barely made it into the bathroom. When he came out he said, "I need something to eat."

"Right there." She pointed to a brown paper bag on the desk. It contained a bagel and a cup of coffee, gone cold. He drank it anyway.

"I have to get a blow-dryer," Jo said. "Just take me someplace where they sell them."

"You never needed one before," he said.

"I never been a dancer before."

"The money is for other things."

Jo turned her attention back to her book. Jimmy finished his bagel and then went into the shower. When he came out, Jo suggested they get some real food. They drove to Dinky's and enjoyed a hearty meal. By 11:00 p.m., he felt almost human again.

After dropping Jo off, Jimmy clocked in at Double Jacks. Mr. McQueen appeared.

"The toilet overflowed in the men's room," he said.

"What's wrong with Filipe?" Jimmy protested. "It happened on his shift."

"He has the night off."

The washing station was piled high with dirty dishes.

Jimmy wheeled the mop and bucket to the men's room. He could hardly stand the stench, but managed to clean the mess. In the kitchen, he set to work on the mountain of dirty dishes.

Why am I still doing this?

He had almost five hundred dollars in his pocket at that very moment. Jo had earned it in one night by just wiggling her ass. Cleaning up shit didn't make him a fraction of that.

McQueen went home. Ryan, the bartender, was in charge and he liked to boss everyone around. At 3:00 a. m., he told Jimmy to mop the floor.

"I don't do that until four," Jimmy snapped.

"Stop being a dick and do it," the bartender ordered.

"You do it!" Jimmy replied, ripping off his apron. "Then fuck yourself with the mop handle."

"Hey, let's all calm down," Hammerhead said.

"Fuck you, too," Jimmy responded. "I quit!" Grabbing his helmet, he stormed out the back door. Hammerhead followed, trying to get him to change his mind, but Jimmy sparked up his motorcycle and drove away.

On Fremont Street, he found a parking place right in front

of a casino. Going inside, he ordered a beer and put a roll of quarters into a video poker machine.

The sky was growing light as he came out. After stopping by a fast-food place, he drove to Sweethearts. When Jo came out, he collected her earnings and drove them both back to the Inca Inn. They ate, and Jimmy fell asleep.

He woke hours later. Jo wasn't in the room. There was no sandwich this time, because he quit the Double Jacks before getting one. Cupping water in his hands, Jimmy drank from the bathroom tap and began his workout.

Jo came in with a drugstore bag. Jimmy snatched it from her hands.

"What the hell is this?" he demanded, looking inside.

"A blow-dryer," she said. "I told you I needed one."

"Where'd you get the money?"

"It's mine."

"You been holding out on me?"

"I need money too, Jimmy," she protested

"You don't pay the rent, put gas in the motorcycle, or anything else."

Jo rolled her eyes. "How much gas do we need?"

Jimmy picked his jeans off the floor and dug out his wallet. It still had some cash, so he pulled up his pants and slipped on his jacket. "Take it back to wherever you got it," he commanded as he tied his boots. "I'm gonna get us some dinner."

Jimmy picked up a sack of burgers. Returning to their room, he heard the blow-dryer running. The bathroom door was locked. He pounded his fist against it, shouting, "I told you to take that back!"

"I need it!"

"Get out here now!" Jimmy commanded.

The bathroom door opened. Jo came out in just a T-shirt, with her hair blown wild. It made her look amazing. His heart, already pounding, beat even harder. He pulled her to him, kissed her and, for the first time in weeks, she kissed him back.

"Fuck me now," she said, whispering into his ear. "I want it."

Jimmy forgot all about being mad. He ran his hands up under her T-shirt. Jo wasn't wearing a bra and her nipples were already hard. Jimmy thumbed one and she gasped. He tore off his own T-shirt, and his jeans followed. Stripping her naked, he stroked her large, firm breasts. She reminded him to put on a condom. He quickly pulled one out of the desk drawer.

Jo guided him into her. He finished quickly, rolled off and sauntered into the bathroom. Coming back, Jimmy saw her in bed, wrapped in the sheet, hair all messed up and sexy.

"I don't fuck the men at work," she said. "They give me money to dance, and I give it to you. But I need a little something for myself."

Jimmy didn't feel like arguing. They sat on the bed and ate dinner. After, Jo pulled out a bottle of nail polish.

"Where'd you get that?" Jimmy asked.

"The drugstore. The girls at Sweethearts all wear it."

Jimmy decided it wasn't worth fighting about.

Jo struggled to put the polish on. "That's the best I can do," she said, sitting with fingers stiff so the polish could dry.

The time neared midnight. "We'd better go," Jimmy suggested.

Jo still didn't know he had quit Double Jacks. Jimmy figured she didn't need to know. It would only cause a fight. Let her think he was still working.

She made enough money for both of them.

CHAPTER THIRTY-ONE

Audrey

AFTER JIMMY DROPPED HER OFF, Audrey approached the girls in the parking lot. One was Invictus, the woman who had befriended her the first night.

"Jesus," she said as Audrey walked up. "Who did your nails?"

"Me."

Invictus displayed her fingers, beautifully painted. "Why don't you go to a salon?" The woman touched Audrey's hair. "You have all split ends. When did you last get a treatment?"

"Never," Audrey said.

Invictus smiled. "You need a girl's day out."

Audrey realized that Invictus wanted to take her for a hairstyle. She had never been part of anything like that.

"I'll ask Jimmy if I can," she said.

"Why?" Invictus asked, narrowing her eyes as she took a drag from her cigarette.

Audrey sighed. "He's trying to save money."

"What he don't know won't hurt him," Invictus said. Audrey realized that the older woman was right.

If Jimmy finds out and gets mad, all I have to do is fuck him.

"When do you want to go?" she asked.

"I'm off tomorrow," the woman answered. "I'll just have to bring my kid."

They agreed on the time, and Audrey gave her directions to the Inca Inn.

Monday was a slower night and the dressing room was half empty. Taking a seat in the corner, Audrey opened her book.

A few minutes later Zahara came in. The olive-skinned beauty wore a gold bikini. Her hair was big and bushy, like lion's mane.

"What are you doing in here?" she demanded.

Audrey dropped her book. Zahara's green eyes burned holes into her.

"Reading," she said.

"You are a late-shift dancer. You are *not* supposed to be here."

"I ain't in your way."

"Are you questioning *me*?" Zahara asked, incredulous. "Get the fuck out."

"Jesus." Audrey rolled her eyes. "Whatever."

The night air was hot and dry. Girls came and went on

their cigarette breaks. Around 1:30 a.m., Alessandria joined her. Taking a small, crude-looking cigarette from her tiny gold purse, she lit it and inhaled deeply.

"Wanna toke?" Her voice sounded funny, because she was holding in the smoke.

"What is it?" Audrey inquired.

"Just reefer," Alessandria answered, exhaling. "Makes the night go easier."

The cigarette looked like the ones on a slide in Ms. Beckon's health class.

"Go ahead," Alessandria urged.

Audrey drew the smoke into her lungs, and she exploded in a fit of coughing. Alessandria just smiled and took the cigarette. The coughing went on until her throat felt like raw hamburger.

Shit. Why does anyone like this?

Sweethearts was busy for a Tuesday night. Audrey changed, saw a couple of guys sitting alone, joined them, and found herself giggling for no reason.

"Are you okay?" one of them men asked.

"Never better," she said, and meant it. "Come on. Let me give you a dance."

For the next few hours everything happened in a haze. Audrey danced for one guy after another, went up onstage when called, and then floated back into the club.

By 4:00 a.m., her head had cleared. Joining Temptation, Alhambra, and Chanel in the dressing room, she noticed they were all jazzed up. Audrey knew they had been doing coke, but did not ask for a "bump." It was a big deal that she had tried pot.

Remembering Invictus, she thought it would be fun to invite everyone. "Anybody want to have a girl's day out?"

The others looked at her strangely, and then burst into laughter. Once they had calmed down Audrey explained the plan. Chanel wanted to join them. Alhambra said no, because her children would be home from school. Temptation had an audition for a movie.

Jimmy picked her up at the end of the shift. She gave him two hundred of her take, keeping eighty for herself.

The next day Audrey woke up before Jimmy. Excited at the prospect of her afternoon with the girls, she waited anxiously outside.

A sporty blue Camaro pulled up. Audrey got into the passenger side. Invictus nodded toward the back seat. "That's my daughter, Sarah," she said. Audrey turned to see a child about nine years old reading a book.

"This is mom's friend, Audrey," Invictus said. The girl said "hello" without looking up. "That one's a little scholar," Invictus continued. "Don't know where she gets it. Her father was no rocket scientist."

They drove to a beauty parlor called Jacquie's. There were several styling chairs, each with a mirror. At the back, a white-coated woman sat buffing and filing a customer's nails. Invictus told her daughter to sit and read her book, which the little girl did happily.

Chanel and another dancer named Glory had already arrived. Glory was a small, dark-haired woman that Audrey had seen on the evening shift.

The beautician told Audrey to lie back, with her head resting on the padded edge of a sink. The woman washed, conditioned, and styled her hair. When finished, all traces of Jolene had vanished. The girl in the mirror was Audrey through and through.

Next, the girls all had their nails done. Offered a selection of polishes, Audrey picked green. When finished, they compared the results. Janet had gotten another elaborate design. Carol had chosen clear gloss with white tips, and Glory a fiery red.

Taking Janet's daughter, they walked across the parking lot to a Mexican restaurant. Glory ordered a pitcher of sangria. Soon everyone was feeling good. They shared nachos, laughed, and talked about all kinds of things.

Audrey noticed that the other girls all had earrings. Janet wore hoops, Glory had dangling teardrops, and Chanel tiny diamond studs. It was like they belonged to a club.

The sun had gone down when they spilled out into the parking lot. Glory drove off in a green Mustang convertible, headed to Sweethearts for work. Chanel climbed into a Honda, saying that she would see Audrey later that evening.

As they got into Janet's car Audrey asked, "Can I get my ears pierced?"

The older woman looked at her, a smile teasing the corners of her mouth. "Why not?" she said. "We might as well do the whole thing."

They drove to another strip mall. One of the stores had a sign that said "Mandarin Tattoos." Inside, the walls were covered with sketches of snakes and butterflies, angels and devils, flowers and flaming skulls. A beaded curtain parted, opened by an Asian woman with tattoos covering both arms. One ear glittered with tiny diamonds, from the bottom of the lobe to the curve at the top.

"My friend needs her ears pierced," the older woman said.

The Asian woman led them to a counter where Audrey chose a tiny pair of sliver studs. The woman cleaned her ears, and then picked up a device that looked like a gun and fitted it on Audrey's right earlobe. She heard a loud "Bang!" and felt a sharp sting. The woman did the same to the other ear. Looking in the mirror, Audrey saw the tiny silver earrings already in place.

"There you go," she said. "Twenty dollars."

Janet drove Audrey back to the Inca Inn. As they pulled in, the older woman looked concerned. "How long have you lived here?" she asked.

"A couple of months," Audrey replied.

"You can afford a nicer place."

"Jimmy and I got plans to move to Los Angeles."

"Oh, sweetie," Janet said. "There's nothing in LA you can't get here."

Audrey just smiled. "See you at the club," she said, and got out of the car.

Going inside, she found Jimmy eating a burrito. "Where you been?" he asked.

"Met up with some girls from work," she said. Seeing no point in postponing the inevitable, she displayed her newly painted fingernails. "What do you think?"

"How much did that cost?" Jimmy asked.

"Nothing," she lied. "Janet did it as a present. Got my ears pierced, too."

"As long as you didn't spend money."

What he doesn't know won't hurt him.

Sitting on the bed, she put her hands behind Jimmy's neck and looked into his eyes. "I'm glad you like them," she said, and then kissed him. He reacted like she expected, losing all thought of money.

Audrey let him do whatever he wanted. The dances she did at the club were no different. Sex had become a means to an end.

CHAPTER THIRTY-TWO

Jimmy

JIMMY DROPPED JO OFF at Sweethearts, and then headed for a gym he had seen that advertised: "Open 24 hours." He hadn't had a real workout since leaving Florida and ached to lift weights again.

The smell of disinfectant greeted him. The clink of barbells and the soft swoosh of exercise equipment sounded like music. An attendant gave him a tour. There were rows of treadmills and Nautilus machines. Muscular men lifted and curled. Jimmy couldn't wait to start. The attendant had him sign some papers, and Jimmy entered paradise.

A well-built black man asked Jimmy to spot him. The man said his name was Steve and he worked in security at Caesar's

Palace. They lifted together for a while. After, Jimmy took a shower and sat in a TV room to watch a football game. He ate an apple from a bowl of fresh fruit he found there. Before he knew it, it was time to pick up Jo.

This was the beginning of a new routine. Jimmy would drop Jo off and go to the gym. Each morning he would pick her up, collect the money, and they would sleep through the day. When Jo had a night off he would leave before midnight, letting her think he was going to work. When she seemed to be in a good mood, he'd say he had the night off too and they'd spend the evening fucking. It seemed like she never wanted to do it anymore unless she needed something, like more clothes or another pair of shoes.

Jimmy often trained with Steve, or a guy named George who ran a motorcycle shop. Once they took Jimmy's bike in for maintenance.

Some nights he would visit a casino with a sports book. He sat for hours watching games, betting on his favorite teams. He'd also play roulette or video poker, sometimes winning a little but always losing it again.

Damn! When is my luck going to change?

April turned to May, May to June, June to July. The weather went from hot to stifling. Their room had a window air conditioner that had a hard time keeping the temperature down in the daytime, which was when they slept.

In August, Jo said it was her birthday. Jimmy had no idea it was coming up. They told Betty, at Dinky's Diner, who brought out a cupcake with a candle in it, and everyone sang "Happy Birthday." Jo didn't seem to want anything more than that.

One night, Jimmy walked out of the gym just as it was getting light. A limousine was parked beside his bike. A large black man in a dark suit got out from the driver's side and opened the back door. A man who looked like a skeleton got out. It was Prudome.

"You owe me five thousand dollars," he said.

For a minute Jimmy couldn't say anything. "Yeah, I'll get it," he finally answered.

Prudome got back the limo. The driver closed the door and drove away.

Jimmy had forgotten that the man expected money from him. Opening his wallet, he counted a little over three hundred dollars. It was all they had.

Jo would just have to earn it.

She was waiting in the parking lot at Sweethearts, and handed him a hundred and forty.

"This is all you made?"

"Mondays are slow," she answered.

"You got to bring in more than this," Jimmy replied.

They slept through the day, and then went to Dinky's. As they waited, Jimmy thought about how to get five thousand quickly. He asked Jo, "Do you ever work in the Champagne Room?"

"Not yet," she replied, reading the menu.

"You got to start," he urged.

"I don't know what to do in there," she said.

"Whatever it takes," he replied.

Jo peered at him like a cat staring down a snake. "Are you telling me to start hooking?"

"Shit, no," he answered. "But I gotta pay Prudome his money."

Jo's eyes turned away. "I don't want to talk about him."

"He says I still owe him five thousand."

Jo remained silent, lost in thought. Eventually she said, "Why do we got to pay him at all? Let's take the money we already have and go."

The idea brought him up short. Jimmy had never considered simply leaving town. How would Prudome ever find them? Still, they would need money in Los Angeles to tide them over until Jo found another place to dance.

"We got to save a little more first," he insisted.

Jo frowned, but said nothing.

Back in their room, they had sex. Jo didn't seem into it, and went into the shower as soon as they were done. Coming out all she said was, "We'd better get going."

After dropping her off at Sweethearts Jimmy drove to the gym. There was nothing like a good workout.

CHAPTER THIRTY-THREE

Audrey

A FEW DAYS LATER, Audrey had an experience that changed everything.

On a night off from Sweethearts, after Jimmy left for work, she stayed in their room with a library book. She couldn't concentrate on reading. Since Jimmy had said "Prudome" the horrible man kept coming back to mind. It was time to get out of Vegas and leave behind everything she had done there.

She had been giving Jimmy money for months. Each time she asked how much more they needed he always said something like, "A lot more than we got."

How much was enough?

Unable to rest, she decided to walk to the Double Jacks and

ask Jimmy straight out. There would be creepy men everywhere so late at night. Wearing Jimmy's jacket would hide her boobs. Pulling up her hair, she stuffed it under his baseball cap. In summer it stayed hot even at night, but there was no other way. Disguised, Audrey set out into the darkness.

The parking lot at Double Jacks had four cars. She didn't see Jimmy's motorcycle, but he had probably parked in the back. Inside, Audrey asked the bartender if she could talk to Jimmy.

"That son of a bitch quit months ago," he said.

Audrey explained that Jimmy did work there, and that she only wanted to see him for a few minutes on his break.

"I'm telling you he quit," the bartender replied. "If he didn't, he would have been fired."

Audrey walked out. The bartender must be mistaken. Jimmy went to work almost every night. Going around to the back, she noticed his bike was not there. Knocking at the service entrance brought a young Mexican man to the door.

"Is Jimmy here?" she asked.

"No Ingles," the Mexican replied, and waved her inside. In the kitchen was a man she recognized, the cook. She didn't remember his name. The man looked at her surprised, and then realized who she was. "Oh, hey," he said. "What're you doing here?"

"Looking for Jimmy."

"He quit months ago."

"Jimmy quit?"

"Yeah," the man answered. "You and him still seeing each other?"

Audrey was too stunned to reply. She barely noticed anything walking home.

Why did Jimmy quit? Why hadn't he told her? Where had he been going every night?

Back at the Inca Inn, she paced around the tiny room waiting for Jimmy. Eventually a key clicked in the lock. The morning sun spilled in as he entered, carrying his saddlebags and a sack of breakfast.

"Where you been all night?" she asked.

"Working," he replied.

"I went to Double Jacks and you weren't there. They told me you quit months ago."

"You were spying on me?" he said, as if she were the one who had done something wrong.

"Why did you quit?"

"It sucked," he said.

"Why didn't you tell me?"

"Didn't seem important."

"You haven't been making any money at all?"

"I made piddly-shit," Jimmy said. "You make plenty."

"So where you been going every night?"

"To the gym."

Audrey said nothing else. He had lied to her, and wasn't at all bothered about it. She felt confused and betrayed. Jimmy disappeared into the bathroom. Moment later she heard the shower running. Taking a biscuit from the bag she nibbled at it, trying to sort things out.

Jimmy came out of the bathroom, dropped his clothes on the floor and started toweling off. "You need to do laundry again," he said.

Audrey was too stunned to speak. She made all the money and he still expected her to do chores. She watched him take the other biscuit out of the bag, open an orange juice, wolf down his breakfast, and then fall asleep.

Audrey brushed her teeth and climbed into bed. Her mind buzzed for a while keeping her awake, but eventually she drifted into slumber.

They woke and went to Dinky's. She half-listened as he talked about some championship game, her mind still on his betrayal. After dinner, knowing that he would want to fuck, she asked to go shopping. Jimmy drove her to Goodwill. Her mind swirled, but one thought kept returning:

I have to get away from Jimmy.

Where could she go? Maybe one of the girls at Sweethearts would let her stay for a while, or maybe back to Enterprise—

No! I will never go back there, ever!

There was only one answer: Hollywood. It's the place she always wanted to be. Jimmy was supposed to take her, but it was clear that he never intended to live up to his promise. She would need to money for the trip. With less than forty dollars in her pocket—

"This sucks." Jimmy's voice broke into her thoughts. "Come on. I'll take you to work."

They went back to the room for her things. While he was in the bathroom Audrey stuffed her backpack with a second pair of jeans and the two long-sleeved shirts. Her T-shirts were all dirty, but she pulled three out of the laundry and packed them anyway. On top, she placed her green bikini and platform shoes. The ID Prudome had given her went into a side pocket.

When Jimmy came out of the bathroom, Audrey went in to brush her teeth and slipped the toothbrush into her pocket. It made her heart ache to leave the blow-dryer, but she didn't want to draw attention.

At Sweethearts, the last thing Jimmy said was, "You'd better make good money tonight."

A group of girls stood outside. Alessandria was there, holding one of her home-rolled joints. "Wanna get high?" she asked.

Audrey shook her head. She had tried it several times and it made work easier, but tonight she had other things on her mind.

"I want to dance in the Champagne Room," she said, to no one in particular.

"Haven't you ever done that?" asked Exotique.

The girls started sharing Champagne Room experiences. Audrey listened carefully. They didn't seem to do any more than her dances in the regular rooms. Maybe she had been giving the men too much all along. The Champagne Room meant "Touching him a bit," someone said. That was where Audrey had always drawn the line. Her clients could put their hands on her, except for her pussy, but she never, ever fondled them.

The place was packed that night. A back booth had a rowdy group of men. One of them, a fat guy, walked to the stage while Alessandria was dancing. He threw handfuls of money into the air, something the girls called "making it rain."

After changing, Audrey made a beeline for their booth. The night-shift girls had left to tip out, and she slid in beside the heavyset man.

"Hi. I'm Audrey."

The man's eyes lit up. "You the prettiest thing I've ever seen." Audrey could smell liquor on his breath. Sweethearts didn't serve alcohol, so he must have brought his own.

"Want to buy me a drink?" she asked.

The man waved for the waitress.

Chanel and a new girl called Danger joined the party. Audrey chatted with the man who had thrown the storm of money. She learned his name was Albert, and his company had just signed a contract with a large corporation. They had come to celebrate.

The waitress brought Cokes. When she left, Albert pulled out a flask and poured some into each glass. Audrey sipped hers and recognized the taste of rum.

They sat chatting until the DJ called for Audrey. "I have to go," she said. Sliding her hand into Albert's inner thigh, she gave it a squeeze. "Don't forget about me."

Her routine had improved over the months. Climbing to the top of the pole, Audrey spun around high above the stage. She let her upper body fall back until she hung upside down. Taking the bottom of her T-shirt in her hands, she stripped it off showing the men her bikini-clad breasts. She then slid to the floor.

Rising on her knees, Audrey noticed Albert standing at the edge of the stage, a fistful of dollars in each hand. "Let's see 'em!" he shouted. With her eyes locked onto his, Audrey pulled the string at the back of her neck. The bikini top dropped away.

Money fell like New Year's Eve. Audrey climbed the pole again. Looking down, she saw Albert staring up in awe. Flipping over, she dangled with her head down, her breasts exposed. When she reached the floor, she flipped over and came up hair flying.

Crawling to the edge of the stage, she brought her face inches from Albert's. "You want more?" she whispered. Albert pulled out another wad of bills. Money fell around her.

Audrey slipped off her bikini bottoms and spread her legs, moving them slowly as if inviting him in. Taking to the pole again, she danced like the other girls had taught her. When the second song finished, the floor was carpeted with cash.

After stuffing the money in her locker, she went looking for Albert. He was at his booth. Danger sat on one side of him and Chanel on the other. He insisted they make room for her.

"Are you ready for a private dance?" she asked.

"Oh, yeah," Albert said, his eyes twinkling. "How much is it?"

"The Champagne Room is a hundred dollars for fifteen minutes."

"Wow," he replied. "How about an ordinary dance?"

"In the back rooms, thirty dollars a song."

"Let's do that," he said.

She led through the black curtain. A new song started; she stripped off her bikini and climbed on this lap. Gyrating her pelvis back and forth, she felt Albert's cock grow hard.

"God," he said in a breathy voice. He raised his hands to grasp her breasts. Audrey directed his hands to her thighs. "Only in the Champagne Room," she told him.

Albert sat back and watched her dance. Raising her arms above her head, she wiggled on his lap. Albert slid his hands up her rib cage until they were under her breasts, but she pushed them away again. "Let's go in the Champagne Room," she said. "I know you want to." Then she did something that Jimmy had done sometimes when they made love, something that always drove her a little nuts. She gently bit Albert's earlobe.

Albert responded with a sharp intake of breath. "Okay," he said. "Okay, let's go."

Audrey put her bikini back on, saying, "Thirty dollars for the dance in here." Albert paid her. She then led him to the bouncer and requested the Champagne Room.

"Get an hour," Audrey said. "We want to do it right."

"That's four hundred," said the bouncer.

Albert pulled out a wad of money and paid in hundred-dollar bills.

In the Champagne Room, Audrey told him to lie back on the sofa. Kneeling before him, she rubbed her hands on his thick thighs. His boner strained against the fabric of his pants.

"Take it out," he whispered.

"We have an hour," she said. "You won't be disappointed."

Audrey straddled his lap with his erection between her buttocks. She took off her bra, reeing her breasts. Albert reached up to caress them, and this time she allowed it.

One song blended into another. Thrusting her body forward, her chest lay against his, her flat stomach against his fat one. She ran her fingers through her hair, stroked his face and murmured in his ear about how much he turned her on. All the while she rubbed her thigh against his penis, hoping he would come in his pants. If he did, it would be the end of it. It always was with Jimmy.

"I want you to come to my hotel room," Albert said.

"I don't do that," Audrey replied. It was every girl's standard answer. They made their money by teasing, not by turning tricks.

"I'll give you a thousand dollars."

A thousand dollars was a lot of money. She sometimes made that much dancing, but only took home half after tipping out. Going with Albert, she could keep it all.

The bouncer appeared in the door and said, "Time's up."

Audrey watched her client struggle to sit upright, his erection straining against his pants. Gathering her clothes, she hurried out.

"You need to go onstage," the bouncer told her as she passed.

Audrey danced two songs, scooped up the money, shoved it into her locker, and hurried to Albert's table. It was full of men and dancers. The new girl, Danger, sat beside Albert, but eventually the DJ called her to the stage. When Danger rose, Audrey slipped into the spot.

"How about a drink?" she asked. "You can fix it up for me."

"Sorry," Albert said. "I'm empty."

Audrey needed to get him back in the Champagne Room. Leaning into his ear Audrey whispered, "I want to be alone with you again." Moments later she felt something jabbing her hand under the table.

It was a key card to a hotel room. "I'm in 1214," Albert whispered.

Audrey slipped the card into her purse.

"Boys, I've had enough," Albert said. His companions agreed, and they left the club.

By 4:00 a.m. there were more dancers than customers. Going to the dressing room, Audrey opened her locker. Cash spilled all over the floor. She counted three hundred twenty-three one-dollar bills. That alone made it a good night, and there was money coming from the Champagne Room dances.

Would it be enough to get her set up in Los Angeles?

She thought about Albert's offer. With a thousand dollars, she could do anything. Audrey went to find Louie.

"I need to go home," she said.

Louie looked surprised. "You've never asked to leave early before."

"I started," she replied. A girl didn't dance when having her period.

"Yeah, okay," he said, and pointed to the phone. "Need to tell your boyfriend?"

"He's working," she explained. "Can I get a cab?"

"Settle up and I'll call one while you're changing."

Audrey handed him her money. Louie tallied up her dances.

"You finally made it into the Champagne Room I see," he said, counting out her share — a little over six hundred dollars.

In the dressing room, Audrey put on her jeans and the colorful hippie girl shirt.

Outside, the sky had started to lighten. Audrey's cab waited for her. The driver requested her destination. The key card to Albert's room had "The Sands Hotel" printed on the side, so that's where she told him to go.

The *ting-tings* of the machines in the casino greeted her. Audrey looked around. She didn't know where the rooms were, and couldn't remember the number that Albert had whispered to her in the club.

Behind the front desk, a receptionist stared into emptiness. Taking the key card from her purse, Audrey passed it to the young woman saying, "I forgot my room number."

The receptionist put the card in a reader, and then looked back at Audrey. "You're with the Andron Corporation?"

"Sure," Audrey answered, realizing what must be going through the young woman's mind: *Why would a large company have a teenage girl working for them?*

The receptionist apparently decided that she didn't care. "1214," she said.

Audrey paused. The receptionist pointed. "That way."

"Thanks." She walked in the direction indicated.

"Wait," the receptionist ordered.

Had the girl suspected what she was doing? Would she call security?

Audrey turned to see the receptionist holding out the card key.

Dance music with a driving beat played as she went up in the elevator. The doors slid open on an empty hallway. Finding 1214, Audrey knocked. Nothing happened. She knocked louder. The lock went *snick* and the door opened. Albert stood dressed in a white bathrobe. He looked sleepy and confused.

"I didn't think you were coming," he said.

"You still want to see me?"

He opened the door further. The room was clean and looked expensive. A picture of a colorful peacock hung over the king-sized bed.

Audrey dropped her backpack on the floor and turned to him. "You said a thousand."

Albert's eyes roamed down Audrey's body as if eating her alive, "Yeah."

"Money first," she insisted.

Albert opened a closet and leaned inside. She heard a metallic "click." He turned toward her holding a bank envelope, counted out ten one-hundred-dollar bills and put them in her hand. Sticking the money into her backpack, she zipped it shut. Without another word, Audrey sat on the edge of the bed and began to untie her sneakers.

"You got a rubber?" she asked, matter-of-factly.

"Don't you bring them?"

Audrey shook her head. "We can't do it without one."

Albert walked to a small refrigerator at the end of the room. It had a glass door, and inside were bottles of beer, wine, and soda. On top there was a caddy with bags of chips, cookies, and a small box. Albert opened it and pulled out three condoms.

"Got 'em," he said, and turned to her. His face melted in an admiration. Audrey stood naked, letting him look all he wanted.

"Sit on the bed," she instructed.

Kneeling before him, Audrey opened his robe. She never had sex with a fat man but had danced for them often. This didn't seem all that different.

His penis looked like a little turtlehead. She began stroking it, and soon it was hard enough to work with her hand. Rolling a condom over his erection, she took him in her mouth.

Audrey did what she had learned to make Jimmy come faster. Holding Albert's balls in one hand, she worked the shaft with her other while sucking on the head. Before long the man grunted, his cock twitched, and he came. She had been in his room less than fifteen minutes.

Albert lay on the bed, his robe laid open, belly exposed. Audrey slid her arms into her bra and fastened it in the back. Stepping into her jeans she stood, zipped up, and put on the colorful shirt. Sitting on the edge of the bed, she began putting on her sneakers.

The man beside her moved. Audrey did not look at him, but

felt his hand caressing her back. She allowed him to touch her, because asking him to stop would delay her exit. After tying her shoes, she rose and shouldered her backpack.

Albert struggled to rise. "Where are you going?" he mumbled.

"Hollywood," Audrey said, and headed out the door.

The elevator doors opened quickly. Descending into a new life, she went through the lobby as far away from the front desk as possible. There were taxis outside; the big hotels always had some waiting. Audrey got in the back of one and told the driver, "Fremont Street." They reached the destination in minutes.

Even in early dawn there were people roaming about. Stopping to get a bagel and coffee, she also bought a large bottle of water, wedged it into her backpack, and set out for the bus station.

A dozen people were lined up to buy tickets. When Audrey reached the desk the agent asked, "Where to?"

"Los Angeles."

"Next bus leaves in thirteen minutes," he said, pointing to a large window that looked into the bus bays.

"I'll take it."

"Round trip or one-way?"

"Why would I ever come back here?"

She bought a ticket and hurried outside. Showing it to the driver, he tried to take her backpack to load into the luggage compartment. Audrey insisted on keeping it.

Finding a seat by a window, she placed her backpack on

the floor and put her feet on top of it. Her heart thumped in her chest. She was on her way at last.

The bus drove out of the station and on to the highway. Audrey ate her bagel and drank the coffee. An hour later she saw a sign that said, "Welcome to California," and the bus began a slow climb into the mountains.

Jimmy.

They had started their journey together, crossed countless miles, danced in New Orleans, and survived death when his motorcycle nearly went down. He had rescued her from a life of misery and shown her wonders.

I loved him!

A knot formed in her throat. Her eyes filled with tears.

Why did he lie to me? What did he do with all the money I gave him?

Audrey thought of the girls at Sweethearts. For the first time in her life she had friends, and she was leaving them behind forever.

Was getting on the bus a horrible mistake?

She began to sob uncontrollably. Thankfully, no one occupied the seat beside her or across the aisle. No one heard her over the rumble of the road. She took a T-shirt out of her backpack and buried her face in it. After a while she wiped her eyes, blew her nose, and then stared out the window, watching as the bus passed through desert hills in the morning sun.

A great weariness came over her. She had been awake for eighteen hours. Digging out more T-shirts, Audrey balled them into a pillow. She put her backpack on the floor with her feet on top of it, and fell into a deep sleep.

Waking late in the afternoon, there were green hills passing outside the window. Audrey needed to pee and felt terribly thirsty. She took her backpack into the bus bathroom. The toilet was a welcome relief. Opening her water bottle, she drank half of it. After washing her hands and face in the tiny metal basin, she dried off using her T-shirts as towels.

Everything was in her backpack. *What if someone stole it?*

Sorting through her documents, she put the license in her little purse with the six hundred dollars from dancing. Taking off her sneakers, she placed the Social Security card in one shoe and the birth certificate into the other. There was also the thousand from Albert. She tried to stuffing half into each shoe, but then there was no room for her feet. Audrey put the money back into a zippered pocket of her backpack. Her sneakers fit with only the documents inside.

Walking to the front of the bus, she asked the driver, "When do we get to Hollywood?"

"Twenty minutes."

She watched through the window as they passed strip malls and apartment buildings, then drove through a cluster of hills. Coming out the other side, Audrey saw something that made her heart leap. A sign stood on a hill, one she had seen it many times on television. It spelled out the letters of a word that made her heart beat faster: H-O-L-L-Y-W-O-O-D.

She had arrived.

CHAPTER THIRTY-FOUR

Skunk

SKUNK SAT OUTSIDE THE BUS DEPOT, reading an old newspaper taken from a trashcan. He wasn't interested in anything the paper had to say; it helped create the impression that he was waiting for a friend. Skunk came to the Hollywood Greyhound station several times a week to watch the arrivals. He often stayed for hours, waiting for the right person to get off.

Two more busses were expected this evening, one from Phoenix and one from Las Vegas. The first arrived with only a few riders, all too old. Twenty minutes later the Vegas bus came in. Among the passengers was a blonde girl dressed in a hippie shirt carrying an overstuffed backpack. A word came to Skunk's mind as he watched the motion of her hips: "Silky."

He approached her as she stood on the sidewalk looking lost.

"Hey," he said. "You need help?"

The girl turned to him, on guard and a little scared. Skunk knew he had hit the jackpot. He smiled and asked, "Where you headed?"

"Hollywood," the girl said.

She hadn't said a street name or something like "my aunt's house." She was on her own.

"You made it," he said. "Come on, I'll show you around."

The girl hesitated, clutching the straps of her backpack.

"No? Okay, see ya." Skunk turned and walked away. He had hooked her; now he needed to reel her in. Leaving the bus station, he went to the curb and lingered as if waiting for the light to change. A few moments later the girl came up beside him.

"Is this Hollywood?" she asked.

"Just up the street," he said, with a friendly grin. "Movie stars on every corner." What he said was a lie, but it's what kids like her wanted to hear. When the light changed, he crossed the street, and the girl followed.

Perfect.

CHAPTER THIRTY-FIVE

Audrey

WATCHING THROUGH THE BUS WINDOW, Audrey waited for some indication that she was actually in Hollywood. The view was nothing like the movie magazines. The street was dark and dirty, the sidewalks littered with trash. People hurried along wearing ordinary clothes, not one of them in a nice suit or beautiful gown.

Where are the limousines and swirling spotlights?

She would just have to walk around until she found them.

After leaving the bus Audrey stood on the sidewalk, backpack on her shoulders. There was a line of stores across the street, neon glowing sickly from the windows. A giant Kentucky Fried Chicken bucket rotated slowly in the night above her head.

Which way do I go?

Her stomach growled in hunger. She hadn't eaten anything since the bagel that morning, and nothing for hours before that. Although she had slept on the bus she still felt tired.

"Hey, you need help?"

She turned to see a boy smiling at her. He had a yellow stripe in his hair.

"Where you headed?" he asked.

"Hollywood," she replied.

"You made it. Come on, I'll show you around."

Audrey grasped her backpack tightly. She didn't want to go off with a stranger. There had to be a motel someplace, where she could check in and get her bearings.

"No? Okay, see ya," the boy said, and left without a second glance.

The street to the right was dark and empty. The way to the left was brighter, but still didn't look like anything she had seen about Hollywood. The giant bucket groaned as it made another revolution above her head. She needed to ask someone where to rent a room.

Where did that boy go?

He was standing on the curb half a block away. Audrey caught up with him. "Is this Hollywood?" she asked.

"Just up the street," he said. "Movie stars on every corner." He smiled again, warm and friendly. Traffic rushed by them, three lanes each way. The light changed, and the boy went off toward what he said was Hollywood. Audrey followed, because he seemed to know where he was going.

"This is Sunset Boulevard," he said, while they were in the crosswalk. "Did you ever see the movie, *Sunset Boulevard*?"

Audrey had never seen any movie. "No," she answered.

"That's Vine Street," he said, and then pointed to the sidewalk. "Those stars mean we're on the Walk of Fame."

Audrey looked down. Dingy pink markers were set in the cracked and broken concrete. Each had a name on it; the one at her feet said "Anne Jeffries."

The boy walked fast. Audrey found herself hurrying to keep up with him.

"Do you know where I can find a motel?" she asked.

"Sure," he said. "This way."

He kept chatting as she walked along beside him, telling her he played in a band. "That's why I have this hair," he explained. "My name's Skunk."

"The corner of Hollywood and Vine," he announced. On one side was wig shop, on the other an office building. There wasn't anything special about it as far as she could tell.

"Hey, I'll bet you're hungry," the boy said.

"Starving," she answered.

He took her to a pizza joint that was brightly lit and filled with people. Audrey relaxed a bit. *What could happen in a place like this?*

The menu included sandwiches. She ordered a turkey club, and Skunk got a sub. When the food came, he paid for both of them.

"My treat," he said. "You're new in town."

Audrey ate her sandwich ravenously, listening to Skunk talk about Hollywood, rattling off the names of movies stars like he knew them personally. When she had finished every bite, she said, "I need a cigarette."

"Me too," the boy replied. "Come on, let's go outside." He had hardly touched his sandwich, and wrapped it up in the paper.

Outside, Skunk pulled out a pack of cigarettes, shook one up for her, and then struck a flame on his lighter. Audrey drew in the smoke gratefully.

"Where is the motel?" she asked.

"You can get a room where I live, if you want. Nothing fancy, but it's cheap."

Do I want to live in the same place as this guy?

"It's a hotel, really," he continued. "You can rent by the night, the week, or the month."

That's how it was at the Inca Inn.

She decided to go with him, at least to check it out. They walked several blocks to a building with the word "Hotel" on the side in faded paint. It was five stories tall, with bars on the lower windows like the place where she and Jimmy stayed in New Orleans.

Skunk took out a key and unlocked the front door. The first door to their right had a sign that said "manager" on it. Skunk knocked, but no one answered.

"Guess he's not in the office," Skunk said. "Don't worry, I know which apartment he lives in." The boy waved toward the stairs. "After you."

Audrey climbed, the backpack feeling heavy on her shoulders. It would be a relief to get a room, put down her things, and rest for a bit.

They got to the top of the last flight of stairs. At the end of the hall was Apartment 5C, with two locks on the door. His keys still in his hand, Skunk opened one of them.

Why would he have a key to the manager's apartment?

This was wrong, really wrong.

Audrey tried to run.

Like lightning, Skunk grabbed her backpack and jerked hard. It was heavy, and threw her off balance. She screamed. The boy slapped his hand over her mouth and hissed, "Shut up, you stupid bitch!"

He shoved her into the apartment. Audrey hit the floor hard, a sharp pain stinging through her left wrist. Skunk slammed the door behind her. She heard the sound of a lock snapping into place. Before she could get up, Skunk was on top of her.

He grasped her neck and forced her face against the floor. "Listen, bitch!" he rasped. "You're mine now. You do everything I say."

He tried to rip the backpack off her shoulders. Audrey shouted, "No!" Skunk whirled her around, and she saw his fist heading toward her eye.

There was a bright flash of light. The side of her face exploded in pain, and she screamed in agony. Skunk's strong fingers closed around her throat.

"What did I say, bitch?" he snarled, his angry face inches

from hers. "Are you stupid? Are you deaf?"

Skunk slammed his fist into her eye, the same one as before. He obviously intended to hurt her badly. He hit the same eye again, and then again.

"No! No! Please," she begged. "Don't hit me! Please don't!"

"Do what I say and I won't hit you," he said.

"Please!"

"Stop talking," he growled, and punched her eye again. He then flipped her over, face to the floor, and pulled on the straps of her backpack. Her wrist, the one that had jammed against the floor when she fell, jolted in pain. Unable to resist, Audrey gave up the backpack.

"What's your name?" he asked.

A sob came from her throat.

"I said tell me your name, you stupid cunt!"

"Jo . . . Jolene." In terror and confusion, she used the name Momma had given her.

"Jo . . . Jolene," he mocked. "That's no name I've ever heard. Jo . . . Jolene." She felt his fingers dig into her neck. She shrieked in terror.

"I said no talking! Don't make a sound! Do you hear me?"

The eye he hit had swollen shut, and burned with pain. The other one was pouring tears.

"I said, 'Do you hear me?'" he pressed.

She nodded her head "Yes," not daring to speak.

"I am going to tell you your name. It is the name you will use from now on. Do you understand? *Do you understand?*"

"Yes," she managed to say.

"Your name is Silky. Say it! Your name is Silky."

What!?

"I said 'Your name is Silky.' Say it!"

"S . . . Silky," she managed to utter.

"See? When you do what I say, you won't get hit." He still held his deathly grip on her neck. "Do something else—" He slammed her face into the floor, on the side with her damaged eye. Pain shot through her skull.

He released her neck, grabbed her by the shoulders and hoisted her up. His face was a sneer of pure evil, his eyes stabbing into hers like knives.

"Take off your clothes," he demanded.

She wasn't sure if she had heard him right.

"Stupid bitch," he said. "I said strip!" His hand slapped her wounded eye.

"Please don't hit me!"

Skunk let go and stood looking at her silently. Involuntarily she began to sob.

"Shut up!" he said. "Take that shirt off! Now!"

She reached down and grabbed the bottom of her colorful, long-sleeved shirt and struggled to pull it up.

"Come on!" he said, and yanked the shirt over her head. Her arms tangled in the sleeves. Her tormentor yanked harder, ripping it away.

"Keep going!" he demanded.

Sitting on the bed, she untied her sneakers with fumbling

fingers. Skunk waited until she had loosed the laces of one, then yanked it from her foot and threw it across the room.

"Did I tell you to stop?" he commanded.

She unlaced the other shoe. Skunk tossed it away.

"Stand up!"

In nothing but jeans and a bra, she did as he asked.

A new shock of terror shot through her as the boy took a switchblade from his back pocket. It opened with a *snick*, and he placed the knife against her throat. She sobbed aloud in fear, instinctively raising her hands to protect herself.

"Hands down!" he demanded.

Skunk ran the tip of the knife down her skin. Putting it between the cups of her bra, he jerked upward. The band snapped and the cups fell off her breasts.

"Lose it," he said, and she slipped the bra straps from her shoulders. He lowered the knife and put the tip under her right nipple.

He was going to cut it off!

"Please," she moaned, through tears. "I'll do anything you say."

He dropped his hand. Snapping the blade closed, he put the knife away.

"Take off your pants!"

Hands trembling, she opened the snap of her jeans. Skunk pushed her back on the bed and stripped them away, her panties with them. She lay naked before him, and knew with absolute certainty what was coming next.

Thankfully, he pulled a condom out of his pocket. "Gotta

wear one of the these," he snarled. "I don't know what kind of junkies have been fucking you."

After tearing the packet with his teeth, he opened his zipper and shoved his jeans down his thighs. His cock was hard and ready. After rolling the condom over it, he thrust into her, with no time to prepare. It felt like sandpaper.

Skunk pounded brutally into her, driving home the message that he was now in charge of everything in her life. She turned her face away, closing the eye he hadn't hit so that she wouldn't have to look at him.

Skunk finished, pulled out, stripped off the condom, and threw it on her stomach. It hit her skin with a wet plop.

"Don't move!" he ordered, and then walked into the bathroom. She didn't dare twitch a muscle. He came out, put his clothes back on, and then picked up his jacket. Taking his uneaten sandwich from the pocket, he put it into a small refrigerator against the far wall.

Suddenly needing to throw up, she dashed into the bathroom, knelt over the toilet and vomited. When finished, she wiped her mouth with the back of her hand.

Skunk stood in the bathroom doorway watching her. "That was disgusting," he said. "I paid for that dinner. Why'd you waste it like that?"

She didn't know what to say.

"I don't buy you food so you can throw it up. God, that was repulsive. Clean yourself!"

Rising, she washed her face in the sink and rinsed her

mouth. Then she turned around, looking for something to dry off with.

Skunk held out her colorful, hippie-girl shirt. "Use this," he said. "You'll never wear it again." He snatched the shirt back when she was done.

"Get out here," he said, and she walked naked into the middle of the room.

Skunk held her clothes in a clump in one hand. Reaching down, he snatched her backpack up in the other and hoisted it over his shoulder.

"I'm going out," he said. "You will do nothing. You will not speak. If you try to call for help, I'll hear you. Do you understand me?"

"Yes," she whispered.

She dared not raise her head. The door opened, and then closed again, followed by the sound of a lock snapping into place.

CHAPTER THIRTY-SIX

Skunk

SKUNK SAT ON THE LANDING AND LISTENED. He waited an hour to see if the girl would try to escape, or call for help. She did nothing. Convinced that he had sufficiently terrified her into submission, he lifted the backpack and descended the stairs.

The street outside hummed with life. Going into an alley, Skunk knelt behind a dumpster and went through her clothes, finding a lipstick and the key to a hotel room in the pockets of her jeans. He tossed them into the dumpster. Opening the backpack, he found clothes, a little red purse, cigarettes, and a lighter. The cigarettes and lighter went into his jacket. There was a green sequined bikini and a pair of platform shoes like a dancer in a titty bar would wear. He threw them away. Whatever she had done in her old life didn't matter. She was Silky now, one of his kids. She would do only what he wanted, and wear only what he allowed her to put on.

At the bottom of the backpack he found a book: *M'Lady's Passion* by Emily O'Hara. The cover had a woman in an old-timey dress and a guy with no shirt. Inside, it said "Las Vegas Public Library." None of the other kids ever had a book. He made a mental note to watch for other surprises, and threw it into the trash. Then, he opened the little red purse.

Jesus! The girl had real money on her!

He counted four hundred and eighty-seven dollars, and shoved the bills into his pocket. He also found a driver's license for Holly Susan McMillan, eighteen years old. Using the lighter, Skunk held the flame under a corner of the card. It smoldered and stank as it burned. When it was no longer recognizable, he threw what was left away.

Skunk looked up. Two of his kids had entered the alley, which was their usual meeting spot. The first was Oxie, a skinny boy about sixteen with red hair, freckles, and a chipped front tooth. The other was Candy, a heavy black girl with a frizzy Afro.

"Hand it over," he said. Digging into their pockets, they pulled out a few bills and lots of change, a little over thirteen dollars. It was money they had collected panhandling.

LightLight showed up last, a girl with pale blue eyes and hair so blonde it was almost white. There was something wrong with LightLight's brain, because she never said anything. When panhandling, she simply stood in front of her mark with her hand out and waited for the person to respond. She gave Skunk seven dollars and change.

Sooner or later a car would stop at the curb. In the meantime, Skunk went through the rest of the backpack. The front had two zippered pockets. The top one had only a toothbrush. The one on the bottom held a wad of one-hundred-dollar bills.

"Wow!" Oxie said. Skunk looked up to see the kids gaping. He shoved the money deep into the pocket of his jacket.

"You didn't see anything," he said, flashing his terrible glare. "Not a fucking thing." They all looked frightened. Skunk left abruptly, walking several blocks away to throw the backpack into a different dumpster.

Returning to the alley he acted as if nothing had happened. None of the kids would dare mention the money again.

The first car pulled up around midnight. Skunk sent LightLight to service the client. Twenty minutes later, another car stopped and he sent Candy. LightLight came back, and handed him fifty dollars. The next client wanted Oxie. Around 1:00 a. m. LightLight went out again.

Things picked up after 2:00. All three of the kids were with clients, and Skunk used the time to sell reefer to the people coming out of the clubs. He never sold harder drugs; it was too dangerous.

By 3:00 a. m. the street was empty. All of the kids had come back. Skunk counted the night's take, over three hundred dollars.

"Go on, get out of here," he said. The kids went off to a room Skunk leased for them by the week for them.

He headed home, stopping at an all-night taco stand. The girl locked in his room would be hungry, and had probably eaten the sandwich in the fridge. He could use that as an excuse to discipline her. She needed to learn that good things came only through obeying him.

CHAPTER THIRTY-SEVEN

Silky

SHE STOOD IN THE MIDDLE OF THE FLOOR, arms clutched around her chest, the condom still stuck to her skin. Sniffling, she tried to not cry out, afraid that the boy might return. Thirty minutes passed. Her body trembled and her knees grew weak. She sat on the bed, ready to jump up at the sound of the door opening. The boy did not come back. Unable to keep control, she broke into sobs.

What the hell had happened?

He had been so nice at first, explaining things to her, buying a sandwich. He had also told her they were in Hollywood, but that must have been a lie. The place was nothing like she thought it would be. The bus driver had made a mistake. But how could that be? She had seen the big sign with white letters on the hill.

The side of her face throbbed. She longed to go into the bathroom, run some cold water over it, inspect the damage. Still, she dared not move.

An hour passed. Her mind cleared a bit. Pulling the sheet from the bed, she wrapped it around her naked body and went into the bathroom to look in the mirror.

Skunk had beaten half her face into a distorted mask. Her good eye looked back with sorrow. She wasn't Audrey anymore, and certainly wasn't Jolene. Her identity was the name Skunk had called her:

Silky.

She plucked the condom from her body and threw it in the toilet. Wetting a corner of the sheet, she wiped Skunk's stickiness away, and cleaned between her legs. Silky then wrapped the sheet more tightly around her body.

Her stomach growled. The only thing she had eaten had been the sandwich, and she had thrown it up. There was no kitchen, only the small refrigerator and a locked cabinet beside it. Skunk's sandwich was in the fridge. Silky grabbed it, but stopped before taking a bite. Maybe it was a trap. She put it back.

The apartment didn't have much in it. The bed stood against one side, the refrigerator against another, and a third was a hallway leading to the door. The remaining wall had a single window, covered by a sheet of plywood screwed to the frame. A slanted gap between one edge and the frame allowed a bit of light through. Silky pressed her good eye to it. She could see the brick wall of the building next door.

A small table and two chairs stood under the covered window. A single, exposed bulb in an overhead socket lighted the room. A worn carpet covered the floor.

The bathroom had a toilet, a tub with a shower, and a sink with a medicine cabinet. There was one small window with frosted glass. Silky pried it up a few inches, could see a parking lot behind the building and a street beyond. People walked along the sidewalk on the other side of the lot. She called "Help!" but no one heard her.

Returning to the main room, Silky sat on the bed. Skunk had taken everything she owned: her backpack, her clothes, and her money. After a few minutes, she noticed her shoes.

Why hadn't he taken them?

Picking up one, Silky found her birth certificate inside. The other shoe lay under the small table. It still held her Social Security card.

Where could she put them?

Nothing in the main room seemed secure. The bathroom had a medicine chest with a mirrored door. It contained a bottle of aspirin, a nearly empty bottle of antacid, a few baggies with dust inside them, a tube of toothpaste, and a frayed toothbrush.

Lifting the top of the toilet, the inside of the tank was stained with rust and filled with water. Taking one of the baggies from the medicine chest, she opened it. It smelled like one of Alessandra's hand-rolled cigarettes. Putting the documents inside, Silky sealed it and folded it in two. Leaning over the tank, she looked for some place to wedge it in. All she could do was drop it into the water. That wouldn't be safe.

The tiny bathroom window was her last chance. Maybe she could throw the packet to the ground and pick it up later. But what if her captor kept her there for weeks, or even months? She had seen a program on television about some girls who had been kept inside a house for years. What if that happened to her? Her ID needed to be hidden where it would be safe.

There was a drainpipe outside the window. Taking the baggie with her documents in one hand, she reached out as far as possible. Steadying herself against the sill brought a sharp pain to her left wrist. Nevertheless, she managed to wedge the packet between the pipe and the wall.

Returning to the main room, Silky sat on the bed. She would bide her time, do whatever he asked, and look for an opportunity to escape.

CHAPTER THIRTY-EIGHT

Skunk

SKUNK CLIMBED THE STAIRS and stood outside the door to his apartment. The girl was probably asleep. Or, she might be waiting for him, ready to strike. Oxie had done that. He worked a leg from the table loose and attempted to clobber Skunk when he entered. After a solid beating, Oxie never tried again.

Skunk entered to find the girl asleep.

Good, I can wake her for more instruction.

He did not want to hit her with his fist again. The eye needed to heal. Clients wouldn't take a kid with obvious bruising.

Skunk unlocked the cabinet. Inside were cans of food, an opener, and a cigar box with loose change and a few bills. He put Silky's cash in and locked the cabinet.

His leftover sandwich was still in the refrigerator. The next stage of his plan depended on it being gone. It didn't matter that she hadn't eaten anything. A false accusation would be just as good, maybe better. Skunk dumped the food into the trash chute in the hallway, then returned and locked the door. Grabbing the girl by the shoulders, he roused her violently.

"Where is my goddamned sandwich?" he said. The girl looked at him, one eye still swollen shut, the other now open and registering terror. "Did you eat it?"

"I didn't. I swear. Please don't hit me."

"Tell me the truth or I'll slap you across the room."

"I, I . . ."

"Tell me!"

"Yes. Yes. I ate it. I'm sorry. I was hungry."

She lied to give him what he wanted, which meant the girl was under his control.

"What is this?" he said, lifting a corner of the sheet wrapped around her body.

"I was cold."

"When I leave you naked, you to stay naked," he said, jerking the sheet away. The girl tried to cover up with her hands. The eye that Skunk had not damaged began to tear up.

"Stop that," he commanded. He grabbed her jaw and forced her face up. "Do you know how to suck cock?"

The girl nodded "Yes," not daring to speak.

"Get on your knees," he commanded.

Silky knelt on the floor, opened his pants, took his hard cock in her hand, and worked it up and down. She then opened her lips and moved her head forward. Skunk grabbed her jaw in his hand, forcing her to look in his eyes.

"Never suck cock without a rubber. Do you hear me? Never."

The girl looked back, her eye pleading for him not to hit her. Skunk reached into the pocket of his jacket. He took out three condoms and placed them in her hand.

"Always keep some with you," he instructed. "Put one of them on me."

The girl rolled the rubber over his hard cock.

"Good," he said. "Start sucking."

She took his penis into her mouth. Sucking hard on the head, she moved her hand up and down on the shaft while holding his balls with the other.

She has experience.

It didn't take him long. Silky remained on her knees, her head down, as he pulled the condom off and then zipped up his pants.

"Give me your hands," he said.

She raised them in the air in front of him, palms down.

"Turn them over, you stupid cow."

The girl obeyed. Skunk plopped the used condom into her palm.

"Don't move until I come back." He walked into the bathroom and used the toilet. Coming out he saw that she had stayed on her knees, holding the rubber.

"Take that into the bathroom and flush it. Wash your hands."

The girl did as he ordered. While she was in the bathroom he sat at his table, unwrapped a burrito, and popped open a can of soda.

"Come here," he said when she returned. "Sit."

The girl obeyed. He knew that she was starving, but still waited quietly for instruction.

"Go on," he said. "You've earned it."

Silky looked at him as if needing reassurance.

"Eat," he said, and pushed the burrito closer. The girl flinched, but was apparently convinced that he meant no harm. She bit into the meal eagerly.

Skunk unwrapped another burrito. "If you do what I tell you, you will always be rewarded," he said. "Do anything to cross me and a bruised eye will be nothing."

When she had finished, Silky sat waiting for his next instruction.

Normally he wouldn't ask anything about a kid's past life. He instruction depended on them forgetting all about what they had been before. But the backpack had held a lot of money.

"Where did you get a thousand dollars?" he asked.

"Sucking cock," she answered.

So that's why she's good. She was a whore for somebody else.

"Go to bed," he ordered.

The girl did as she was told. Skunk lifted the sheet and a blanket over her, tucking her in. He then flopped down beside her and slept soundly.

CHAPTER THIRTY-NINE

Silky

SILKY STAYED SKUNK'S PRISONER for weeks. He came and went, once leaving for an entire day, not returning until she was crazy with boredom. Her eye gradually healed, turning from purple to red and then to normal.

Skunk fucked her before going out and when he came back. Sometimes he took her in the pussy, sometimes in the mouth and, often, in the ass. It hurt every time, but she did not dare complain. She was just grateful he always used a condom.

She had nothing to wear. When he was out she wrapped the sheet around herself, putting it back when she heard his keys in the door.

The fourth week Skunk came in carrying several bags.

Opening one, he handed her a package of underwear. They were a size too small, but she didn't complain. Wearing panties again felt wonderful. Next, he tossed a packet of socks her way. With his permission, she slipped on a pair. Then he took out jeans and a blue T-shirt. Silky almost squealed in glee when he handed them to her. The jeans were baggy and the T-shirt way too large. She didn't care. She was happy just to be dressed.

"You still have your shoes, right?" he asked.

Did he know about her birth certificate and Social Security card?

Silky said cautiously, "You left them on the floor."

"Put 'em on."

She took them out from under the bed, slid her feet into them, and tied up the laces.

Skunk looked her up and down. "Okay," he said. "Take 'em off again."

"But why?" Silky blurted out, instantly regretting it.

"Never question me," he said. She whimpered, raising her hands to protect her face.

"Take the clothes off," he repeated. "Do it!"

Through tears, she stripped off the T-shirt. Untying her shoes, she set them on the floor. Sliding the jeans down, she handed them to the man who stood before her.

"The socks and underwear, too," he said. "You will get the clothes back when you learn to behave."

"Yes, sir." She had started calling him "sir" because Prudome made her say it. Skunk apparently liked it, as he never told her to stop.

He locked the clothes in his cabinet and left the apartment. Silky gazed out the tiny bathroom window, her only connection to the outside world. She could see cars driving by, and buses stopping at a corner several blocks away.

Skunk returned bringing Chinese take-out. They ate, and when finished, he announced that she would dress and go with him that night.

Silky could hardly believe her ears. "Really?" she asked.

Skunk nodded, wearing a mischievous grin. Silky could hardly contain her excitement.

"You're allowed to thank me," he said.

"Thank you, sir," she responded, breaking into a smile.

Skunk handed her the clothes. When she was dressed, he gave her a fringed bag with a long shoulder strap.

"You need something for your stuff," he explained.

Silky slipped it over her head so that the strap ran across her chest, the bag on her left hip. Skunk told her to put her spare underwear and socks in it. He then handed her a dozen condoms.

"Remember to use one every time," he instructed.

They went outside. The city swirled around her. Her head went dizzy with the sights and sounds and smells.

Skunk led her to a driveway with a locked gate at the far end. "You start work tonight. I'll point out the cars for you. Tell the driver to come here. Left at the first light, right at the next corner. Take his money, suck him off, and get out as quick as you can."

Silky nodded solemnly, taking it all in.

"You've done this before," he concluded. "You're just doing it for me now."

Skunk then led her to a street with a blue sign that said "Hollywood."

"Hey, Shirley!" Skunk called. A tall black woman in a pink dress waved to him. As they drew closer, Silky noticed the woman was a man wearing a wig.

"This is Silky. She's working for me," Skunk said, and then turned to Silky. "You get in trouble and can't find me, go to Shirley."

"I'll take care of you, honey," the man/woman said. "We girls got to stick together." As they left, she saw Skunk give Shirley a twenty-dollar bill.

They came to an alley. Three kids her age stood a little way inside.

"This is Silky," Skunk announced.

The others looked at her without speaking. One was a teenager with hair so blonde it was almost white. Skunk called her LightLight. A black girl with frizzy hair regarded her coldly; Skunk introduced her as Candy. The oldest was a skinny boy with freckles named Oxie.

"Give her a cigarette," Skunk said. Oxie pulled out a pack. Candy struck a lighter, and Silky pulled the fumes gratefully into her lungs—her first since becoming Skunk's prisoner.

They stood smoking, saying nothing. The others watched her and she did the same.

A beat-up Monte Carlo stopped at the curb. Skunk walked

over, talked to the driver, and then approached Silky.

"Be sure to get at least fifty," he said. "If you have trouble, get out and run away."

Silky walked to the car, opened the passenger door, and slid in. The upholstery was worn and stained. The driver was an older man with silver hair. She did not ask him his name.

"Turn left at the first light," she said, as Skunk had instructed her. The man did that. She told him to turn right at the next corner. Seeing the driveway Skunk had shown her, Silky told the driver to pull in. He did, and shut off the engine.

"Money first," she said. "A hundred bucks."

"It was fifty the last time."

"A hundred or I walk."

"How about eighty?" the man asked.

Silky opened the door. The light went on, flooding the car with brilliance.

"Okay, a hundred," the man said. She closed the door.

The man handed her five twenties. Silky stuffed them into her pocket. She reached into her fringed bag and took out a condom. The man unbuttoned his pants. Silky pulled his penis out and began working it up and down. Slipping the condom over it, she sucked hard to make him finish quickly.

The man fondled her breasts. "Let them fiddle," Skunk had said. "It makes them come faster." Her nipples were soft, her pussy dry. She might have been a machine for all that she put into it. The man groaned, and the twitching began. The job done, Silky got out and walked away.

The thought crossed her mind to run. The hundred dollars in her pocket wouldn't be much, but it would be a start.

"Did you get fifty?" a voice said. Silky turned, shocked to see Skunk walking beside her. If she had tried to escape he would have caught her.

"Give it to me," he said.

Silky pulled out the wad of twenties and handed them to him.

"A hundred?" he said, and then smiled at her. "You done good."

As the hours crawled by, one kid after another went out, returning to hand over the money he or she had earned. Silky turned one more trick. A man in a blue Mercedes stopped at the curb. The car was new, the interior spotless. She asked for two hundred, and got it. The blowjob she delivered was no different from any other.

Eventually Skunk said they were done. He told Silky to go with the others and walked away. Watching him leave, she felt a tinge of sadness. Although he had beaten and abused her, Skunk had filled her nights and days for weeks. There was comfort in the familiar.

The kids took her down a side street to an old hotel with fading paint. Oxie pressed a doorbell. Silky heard a harsh *click* and a prolonged buzzing. The kids entered a dimly lit foyer. On one side was a Plexiglas window with a hole in it that reminded Silky of the office at the Inca Inn. A man sat behind it, taking no notice as they passed.

The worn-down room had two beds with threadbare blankets. Candy and Oxie took the far one. LightLight dropped onto the other. Oxie pulled a bottle of wine from his backpack. Taking a drink, he handed the bottle to Candy. She swallowed some and gave it to LightLight. The girl took a swig and offered it to Silky. After a moment's hesitation, Silky drank. She didn't want wine but felt a need to join the ritual.

"Where is you from?" Candy asked.

"Las Vegas. My boyfriend and me wound up there. Worked as a dancer for a while."

"What kinda dancing?"

Silky told her, but it seemed like some other girl had lived that life, or maybe she had dreamed it. When finished, Silky saw that Oxie had dropped off in his clothes. Candy lay down beside him saying, "I is g'wan get some sleep."

Silky went into the bathroom. After using the toilet, she looked in the mirror and thought: *This is my life now.*

She could simply leave, but to where? Skunk had taken all her money. At least she had a place to sleep. Even if she did go, what would she do? She needed the birth certificate and Social Security card hidden behind the drainpipe outside Skunk's bathroom window. If she had them, maybe there would be a chance. She would have to bide her time and hope that Skunk would give her an opportunity.

CHAPTER FORTY

Silky

THE MORNING AFTER Silky's first night with the others, Oxie took her to a store several blocks away from Hollywood Boulevard.

"I'm gonna get us some breakfast," Oxie said. "Go in and fuck with the clerk."

Silky went inside. The place was old and worn down. Spanish music played over a radio. Silky approached a dark-skinned man behind the counter. "How much is this?" she asked, pointing to a beaded necklace on a rack.

"Nine ninety-five," the man said.

Silky looked at him in the way she used to do with the men at Sweethearts. "I only have eight. Can I have it for eight?"

The man hesitated. He was almost under her spell, but snapped out of it.

"Nine ninety-five," he demanded.

Silky pouted. "Can't you help me out?"

"Nine ninety-five," the man intoned.

Silky sighed. "All right," she said, and left the store.

She met Oxie down the block. He had slipped in while she was talking to the man and stolen a box of donuts.

Over the next few months Silky learned how to shoplift, acquiring a hairbrush and makeup one item at a time. She also stole a kitchen knife and, with Skunk's permission, kept it in the bottom of her fringed bag. It made her feel safer.

Summer turned to winter, and the kids went out in jackets that Skunk provided. When the weather grew warmer, they went back to wearing T-shirts. Silky kept hoping that Skunk would take her home one night, so she could steal a moment alone in the bathroom to grab her ID from outside the window. But he never let any of the kids stay with him.

She even asked. Skunk glared and said, "You got your own place." Silky did not ask again. Over time, the idea of getting her identification crossed her mind less often.

Every night she serviced men in their cars. Some became regular customers, like the man in the Monte Carlo. Once in a while a client would want more than a blowjob. He would pay for a room at the cheap hotel, which rented by the hour and never asked questions.

One evening a client picked Silky up. She instructed him to

park in the usual spot. Just as they were getting started a police car pulled in behind them. Bright red and blue lights swirled and the siren burped, scaring her half to death.

The cops approached the driver's side window and the client rolled it down.

"License, registration, and proof of insurance," the officer said. The client handed them over. The cop gave them to his partner, then asked the driver what he was doing there.

"We just stopped to talk," the client said.

The officer shined his flashlight into Silky's eyes. "You okay, miss?" he asked.

"That's my daughter," the man said quickly.

"That true?" the cop asked. "You his daughter?"

Silky nodded "Yes," too terrified to speak.

The cop's partner came back and reported the man was "clean." The officer looked at them a few moments, shining his flashlight from one face to the other. He then handed the man his paperwork, saying that the driveway was a no-parking zone and he needed to move.

The man waited for the cops to leave. He backed into the street, drove a few blocks, and pulled up to a curb. Shaking, he told Silky to get out.

She went to where Skunk waited and told him the story. He believed it and did not hassle her for returning without cash. Silky didn't go out again that night, and the next day Skunk showed her a different place to service clients.

When it rained, Skunk would give them money for a movie.

The first time, Silky was expecting it to be like the films her teachers showed in school. She had never been in a theatre, and was astonished by how big it was inside. The movie was about a policeman who was made into a robot. She'd never seen anything so *real*. Silky thought the bullets might fly right out of the screen and hit her. Thrilled, she couldn't wait until Skunk would let them go to one again.

Sometimes an entire block of Hollywood Boulevard would be fenced off for a premiere. The sidewalks filled with people watching the limousines driving slowly down the street. Standing on tiptoe to peer above the crowd, Silky saw handsome men and beautiful women, walking down a red carpet to disappear inside one of the big theatres. She even recognized some of them from the magazines she used to read, or the movies she now occasionally saw. Her heart always ached, watching them. She still dreamed of being one of those people.

Her sixteenth birthday came and went, and then her seventeenth. She barely noticed, remembering only when she saw the date on a newspaper.

Candy, the black girl, disappeared. Skunk said nothing, and the kids were too scared to ask. Later that night, they talked about it but had no answers. A few weeks later Skunk showed up with someone new, a whiny little boy named Drivel.

One night a silver Porsche pulled up to the curb and sat idling, like a sleeper caught between dreaming and waking. The driver in silhouette waited for one of the kids to make the move. Skunk spoke to him, then turned and fixed her with his steely gaze.

"Shit. I knew it," she said, and took a final drag off her cigarette.

"Come on," Skunk said, as he approached. "You got a chance to do good."

Dropping her smoke, she ground it into the pavement with the toe of her sneaker. There were pink stars in the sidewalk with the names of actors set in them, stained with spit and old gum. "David Niven" read the one below her foot. She had no idea who that was.

Silky walked toward the car, opened the door, and got inside.

CHAPTER FORTY-ONE

Susie

SUSIE'S SKIN HAD TURNED BROWN from the summer sun. She sat on Charlie's deck, his latest recommendation on her lap, a collection of stories called *The Dubliners*.

After finishing *To Kill a Mockingbird,* she asked him again to give her a romance novel.

"You need to be reading better writers," he scolded. For a few days she refused to read anything, but in the end, boredom wore her down and she picked up the book he had given her.

The door behind her slid open. Charlie came out and placed a wrapped package on the table. "Happy birthday," he said.

Susie looked up in astonishment. She had told him the date months ago.

"What's this?" she asked.

He replied, "Open it."

Susie tore the brightly colored paper. It was a brand-new, hardcover book called *Hollywood Wives*, by Jackie Collins.

"I guess it doesn't hurt to occasionally indulge in mind candy," Charlie explained. Susie turned the book over to read about the author, and was unprepared for what Charlie said next:

"You're eighteen today, if I've figured correctly."

Charlie sat back in his chair, legs crossed, as always wearing slacks and a dress shirt. He had a mischievous look in his eyes, and Susie thought she knew what it meant.

He's been waiting for me to turn legal age.

She didn't know how to feel about that. Months earlier, Susie wanted him to make love to her but Charlie never tried. In the time that passed they had developed a student-and-teacher relationship that was familiar and comfortable. If Charlie wanted to fuck her she wouldn't say no, but the idea would take some getting used to.

He surprised her again by bringing up a totally different subject: "I'm throwing a party Saturday. I could get a cake and have everybody sing for you."

Susie frowned. The only birthday celebration she had ever had was in Enterprise. Momma and Daddy gave her presents, but it felt like they were doing it out of obligation. And on the street, her birthday was just like any other day.

"I don't like making a big deal out of it," she said.

"Fair enough," Charlie agreed.

"Why are you having a party?" she asked. Susie had lived with Charlie almost a year and he never had a visitor.

"The studio is starting production on my script, and everybody wants to talk to me. It will be tedious, but I understand the necessity."

Charlie stood up. "I'll schedule an appointment at Eternity that morning. You'll have to stay there awhile, because I'll be busy." He slid the door open and walked back into the house.

Susie smiled. She liked nothing so much as going to the mall.

On Saturday, Susie rose early for a swim. Sunbathers lay scattered across the beach. Children ran about, chasing each other. A group of surfers bobbed in the water, nearer than before. After laying out a towel, she plunged into the ocean. Coming up, she noticed that one of the surfers had drifted close, on a bright orange board. He had a shaggy haircut, and wore baggie trunks.

A swell caught up to him. The boy took several strokes with his strong arms and stood up. Susie could see the muscles in his legs straining to keep balance. When the wave died out, the surfer noticed her watching and paddled over.

"Hi," he said, sitting up on his board. "I've seen you out here a lot."

"Really?" she replied.

"You live on the beach?"

"Yeah," she replied. "You're good at surfing."

"Thanks. I'm Carson."

"Susie."

He slid off his board into the waist-deep water. "I can show you how, if you want."

"I'm going somewhere. Just came down for a dip."

"Okay. Next time," Carson smiled, his white teeth standing out in contrast to his tanned skin. He lay on his surfboard and paddled away, back toward his friends.

Returning to the beach, Susie picked up her towel. Carson seemed like a nice boy, close to her age. The only friend she had was Sandrine. Maybe it was time to start building a life of her own. She couldn't live with Charlie forever. Getting a job and moving into her own place made sense, and she would like to have a boyfriend again—if she could find a better one than Jimmy.

Susie headed for the house. After taking a shower on the deck, she joined Charlie who had brought breakfast on a tray.

"The people coming to the party all work in the movie business," he said, buttering an English muffin. "I'm concerned you won't have much in common with them."

"I'll just talk about what I've been reading," she countered.

"They're not big on literature."

"Then why are you friends with them?"

"They aren't friends," he answered, frowning. "They're business associates." Gazing out at the ocean he said, "I have never been as comfortable with anyone as I am with you."

Susie didn't know what to make of that, so she didn't answer.

"We need to leave soon," he said abruptly. "Your appointment is eleven."

Susie went upstairs, brushed her teeth, and put on a summery dress.

The women at Eternity greeted her warmly. Although Susie had told them she was Charlie's research assistant, they didn't seem to really believe it. As a joke, Sandrine sometimes called Charlie her "sugar daddy."

After an hour of pampering, Susie took Sandrine to lunch. They ate in one of the nicer restaurants, and Susie picked up the check. After, the two young women wandered the mall to look in store windows.

Sandrine knew everything about fashion. Susie had seen names like Donna Karan, Giorgio Armani, and Ralph Lauren in her magazines. Sandrine could identify each designer by his or her work. Neither of them had been to college, and they sometimes talked about going together.

They walked back to Eternity. Charlie had still not returned. Sandrine had another client, so Susie went into the boutique next door. Finding a dress with a halter and a plunging neckline, she held it up to admire.

A familiar voice behind her said: "Why don't you try it on?"

Turning, she saw Charlie. Going into the changing room, she put on the dress and came out to show off for him.

"You must have that," he said, and glanced at the saleslady. "Can it be altered and delivered by five?"

"I don't think so," the woman replied. "It takes a few days."

"How much?"

"Sixteen hundred."

Sixteen hundred dollars!

Susie was so astounded that she couldn't speak. That was so much money! Charlie shouldn't spend it all on one dress.

Had he been paying that much for her clothes all along?

Before she could say anything, he had taken out a credit card. As the saleslady reached for it, Charlie pulled it back.

"Only if you deliver before five," he said.

Susie's street sense kicked in. Skunk had always said, "Never get involved in anybody's business." It was Charlie's money, and she shouldn't interfere.

The woman didn't want to lose the sale. A seamstress was called, who tugged and pinned. When she was done, Susie changed back into her summery dress and handed over the evening gown.

On the ride home, Susie thought about all she had been through since leaving Enterprise. Charlie listened to everything and never judged her. At times she had given him shit, but he never raised his voice. He was patient, kind — and living with him had made her a better person.

Charlie had changed as well. The night they met, he was so nervous his hands were shaking. When she touched him on the shoulder once he nearly jumped through the roof. Now he had relaxed confidence. They went places together, and she had met some of Charlie's friends. Whatever he had offered her, in a way she had given him just as much.

Arriving home, they drove past a valet parking station that had been set up near the road. A truck with the words "Sunshine Catering" on the side sat in the driveway. Inside the house, white-coated servers bustled about setting up steam trays and silver urns.

Susie went to her bedroom and tried to read, but could not concentrate. Going out on the upper deck, she lit a cigarette. Having managed to cut back to only a few each day, she decided it would be the last one until the party was over.

Voices drifted up from downstairs as the guests arrived. The deliveryman finally came bringing her new dress. Susie put it on, with black heels and a pair of onyx earrings. Looking in the mirror, she saw an elegant young woman in a lovely evening gown. There was no trace of Silky the street whore, Audrey the dancer, Jo the girl on the back of a motorcycle, or even of Jolene, the child she had once been. She was Susie, and belonged in this house.

Stepping out on the upper landing she surveyed the room below, now filled with people. At the bottom of the stairs stood a handsome man that Susie remembered from the pages of her magazines. A young woman in a lavender dress beamed at his every word. Glancing around, Susie noticed others who looked familiar. With a shock, she realized that the party was exactly like the ones she had read about so many times, what her magazines called "a star-studded event." Without knowing it, Charlie had given her the best birthday present ever.

Or had he planned it all along?

As she descended, the handsome man noticed her. He smiled with the radiance of a thousand suns.

"Hi, I'm Tom," he said, extending his hand.

"Susie," she replied, feeling electricity in his grasp.

"How do you know Charlie?" Tom inquired.

"I'm his research assistant."

"I would have guessed that you were an actress."

"Why would you think that?" Susie asked, genuinely puzzled.

"Because you're so beautiful," Tom said. He seemed to be waiting for her to react.

"Well, I'm not an actress." It was the only thing she could think of to say.

"This is Lenora." Tom indicated the girl in the lavender dress. Susie smiled and said, "Hello." Lenora returned her greeting, trying to be pleasant but coming across as cold.

Charlie's familiar voice spoke behind her: "I see you two have met."

"Where did you find such a creature?" Tom asked.

"She came recommended," Charlie replied. Susie had no idea what that meant.

"You should bring her to my premiere," Tom offered.

"Thanks, but I'll pass."

"Then maybe she'd come as my guest. I could find a few moments to escort her in."

"Maybe next time." Charlie steered Susie away.

"What did he want us to do?" Susie whispered.

"He has a movie opening next weekend." Charlie hesitated, and then added, "A red-carpet event."

Susie's heart almost leapt out of her chest.

"I know that's something you would like to do," he continued cautiously.

"Oh, Charlie, could we?" She had waited her whole life to see one.

"I hate those things," he said. "I hoped the party would be enough."

"Please?"

His expression softened. With a sigh, he said, "I'll call Tom's publicist and set it up."

Susie felt like hugging him, but knew that it would make him uncomfortable.

Charlie led to her to a group standing near the sliding glass door and introduced each one by name. Susie tried to remember them, but couldn't.

"What have you worked on lately?" The sentence cut through the fog of distraction. A beautiful woman had asked her a question.

"I'm Charlie's research assistant," she explained.

"Really?" the beautiful woman replied. "I assumed you were an actress."

Why do people keep saying that?

Charlie continued the conversation, his hand resting on the small of her back. Susie listened without hearing. Her head swam with excitement.

A waitress came by with tall, skinny glasses of wine. She took one and sipped it. Bubbles tickled her nose, and Susie realized she was drinking champagne. Mentioned often in her books, this was the first time she had tasted it.

Charlie led her outside. A buffet had been set up, with shrimp, oysters, clams, and crab legs on cracked ice. Charlie recommended she take some of each. After helping her to a table, he excused himself.

Susie had never eaten an oyster. It slid in gooey and salty, and reminded her of when Jimmy would shoot off in her mouth. She liked the clams better, especially with cocktail sauce. Taking up one of the crab legs, she had no idea how to open it.

"Susie, right?" said a voice behind her.

A black man smiled down at her. His beard could not hide the dimples beneath it.

"Stanley," she said. His name had come to her surprisingly easy. She had only met him once, on the day Charlie took her to Beverly Hills.

"Good memory," he said. "Of course, a research assistant would have one." He sat in the chair across from her. "The trick to these," Stanley continued, picking up one of the crab legs, "Is to work a tine into one end. Then bring it up sharp." He stabbed a fork into the bottom of a leg and ripped it open. "Dig the meat out with your fingers. You can't be dainty eating crab."

Susie did as he instructed. The crab had a heavenly flavor.

"Do you like working with Charlie?" Stanley asked.

"Yup," she said, popping another piece into her mouth.

"Let me guess. You're doing it to pay the bills but you're really an actress."

"Why does everyone keep saying that?"

"Most pretty girls in Hollywood aspire to the trade."

"I'm a research assistant."

"And you have never wanted to be in front of the camera?"

"Nope."

"If you ever want to try it, let me know," he said, "I could probably find you something." He took a business card from his pocket and held it out to her. Susie set it on the table.

Charlie arrived. "Keeping Susie company?" he asked.

"Join us, please," Stanley said. Charlie pulled up a chair.

"When will you be casting?" Stanley continued.

"Not until fall," Charlie said.

"Is anyone attached?"

"The studio wants an unknown for the lead."

"How about Susie?"

"You're kidding, right?" Charlie said.

She felt a sudden tension between them. Charlie didn't like Stanley's suggestion. Susie placed her napkin over Stanley's card. She didn't want him to get in trouble.

Stanley beamed his dimpled smile. "I haven't seen the script, Charlie. Melinda's told me about it, that's all."

"I'll ask her. If the studio agrees, she can send it over."

"That would be great." Stanley rose. "I'd better keep working the room."

After he had gone Susie said, "I need to wash my hands."

Rising, she picked up her napkin and the card along with it.

Making her way through the party, Susie noticed a heavyset woman across the room wearing a flowing black dress. It was Melinda, Charlie's agent. She thought it would be a good idea to say hello, but went upstairs first. She put Stanley's card into her fringed bag, now filled with cash Charlie had been paying her every week. It hung on a hook at the back of her closet, hidden behind the clothes.

Susie went back downstairs. Melinda was chatting with a man about twenty years old. As she approached, the agent greeted her warmly.

"This is Jason," Melinda said, indicating the young man beside her. "Susie is Charlie's research assistant. You still are, right?"

"Yes."

"And you live here, at his house?"

Susie could tell that Melinda wanted to know if she and Charlie were lovers. Well, it was none of her business.

"I just wanted to welcome you to the party." Turning to the young man she asked, "Are you having a good time?"

Jason's words came out in a rush: "Charlie is the most wonderful writer in the business. I loved *The Consignation*, loved it, loved it, loved it. And he has a new script. I would give anything to work with him. He's awesome."

"The crab legs are delicious," was all Susie could think to say.

A snicker came from Melinda's lips, which she quickly stifled. Then she said, "For Charlie's script, where did you find all that information about strip clubs?"

Susie knew Charlie was writing about the things she told him, but he had never allowed her to read anything. Every time she asked he would say something like, "Maybe when it's further along." And yet Melinda had read it, and he was having her send it to Stanley.

Was he hiding something from her?

Forcing a smile, Susie replied, "I'd better find Charlie. Good to see you again."

He was on the deck, chatting to an older man. Susie sat off to the side and watched as people came up to talk to him. She knew Charlie didn't like having people in his house, and admired his ability to keep everything under control. She decided to wait until later to ask him about the script.

The sun became an orange ball and dropped into the water. White-coated waiters lit Tiki torches placed in the sand. The party went on for several hours, but eventually people began saying "good night." Tom and Lenora disappeared. Melinda made a big show of leaving, saying "good-bye" to everyone. Stanley walked out with the young man named Jason. The caterers began hauling platters in from the deck. Tables and chairs were folded and stacked in the truck.

Charlie came up beside her. "Why don't you go to bed?" he suggested. "I'll see you in the morning."

"It was a fun party," she replied, and squeezed his hand. Charlie smiled.

In her bedroom, Susie lowered the blinds. The sound of a vacuum lulled her to sleep as the cleaning crew worked long into the night.

CHAPTER FORTY-TWO

Susie

THE EXCITEMENT OF ATTENDING her first premiere made Susie anxious. She couldn't read, and turned to the television for distraction. She had stopped watching *All My Children*, because Charlie's books were more interesting. It seemed stupid now to her, so she switched to talk shows. In her growing anticipation, she completely forgot to ask Charlie about his script.

On Tuesday they went to Papillion, her favorite clothing store, and selected a stunning red gown. It gathered on one shoulder, the fabric falling across her torso like a sash. The hem was cut to flash her thigh every time she took a step. They left the dress for alterations.

Every day she went swimming in the ocean. She looked for

the surfers, hoping to talk to Carson again. They never came. The water was unusually calm, and maybe the waves weren't big enough to make it worth their time.

On Friday, Susie bounded out of bed early. After lunch, Charlie took her to Eternity. Sandrine did her hair and makeup, and a manicurist applied polish that matched a fabric swatch from her new dress. Charlie was waiting when she finished. He had stopped by Papillion to pick up her gown, and carried it in a garment bag.

On the drive back, Susie asked a thousand questions about who would attend the premiere and what might happen. Charlie told her that the people in the movie would be there, and others in "the industry," as he called it. They would stay after for a party.

At Charlie's house, Susie went upstairs and put on the dress. They wouldn't be leaving for an hour, and she fretted about smoking a cigarette. Finally giving in, she lit up on the upper deck. Thankfully, the ocean breeze didn't do too much damage to her hair, carefully styled to fall gently around her shoulders.

Charlie appeared at her door dressed in a tuxedo and looking handsome. He offered his arm. They walked together down the long, curving stairway to the living room.

A white limousine stood in the driveway. "If we're going to do it, we might as well do it right," Charlie said. The uniformed driver opened the door and they got in.

Susie had never been in a limo. Charlie sat beside her, and she laced her fingers in his. They rode that way, hand in hand, saying nothing.

Forty minutes later they pulled onto a familiar street. Susie gazed out the window nervously. For two years she had lived there, asking strangers for money, shoplifting necessities, and selling her body. It frightened her to be back in Skunk's world, and she squeezed Charlie's hand more tightly.

The limo stopped at the entrance to the Chinese Theatre. Cameras flashed as they got out. She could not stop smiling as they made their way down the red carpet. People lined the walkway on both sides. Susie could hear many asking, "Who is she?"

The theatre lobby was filled with elegantly dressed people. At one end stood a little stage with a backdrop showing the name of the movie: *Stardust*. An actress in a yellow gown posed in front of it as cameras flashed and whirred. Tom stood nearby greeting admirers. He had a beautiful woman on his arm. She was not the girl from the party.

"Charlie. So glad you changed your mind," Tom said as they approached. He then turned his million-kilowatt smile on Susie. "You look smashing."

"Thank you," she uttered, feeling her face grow warm.

Susie and Charlie entered the theatre and took their seats. The lights dimmed, and a spotlight illuminated the area in front of the screen. A man walked in and everyone applauded.

"He's the director," Charlie whispered.

The man talked about why he made the movie, and then introduced Tom. The actor told a story about falling off a piece of scenery and everyone laughed. Tom then introduced the actress in the yellow gown. Susie began to wonder if they were ever going to show the movie at all.

It turned out to be thrilling. Tom played an astronaut, and the actress in the yellow dress was his spaceship captain. They flew around the galaxy with other astronauts, looking for a planet to live on. They found one inhabited with dangerous alien creatures. The astronauts died one by one, killed by the monsters. Only Tom and the captain survived. Although they had spent the movie arguing, they fell in love in the end.

Everyone clapped when it was over. Susie joined in enthusiastically.

They walked back into the lobby, which had been set up for a party. Susie marveled at all of the handsome men and lovely women in their beautiful gowns. Waiters walked around with trays offering snacks: melon wrapped in thinly cut ham, chicken on pointy sticks, and little crackers with some kind of tasty meat on them.

One person after another said hello to Charlie. Susie watched as he chatted politely, knowing that he wasn't having much fun. Eventually he asked, "Are you ready to leave?"

She didn't ever want to leave. The evening had been magical. She nodded, thinking it might be possible to talk him into taking her to other premieres. After all, he had said it was important for his business.

For now, they headed out. Charlie spoke to a man, and a few minutes later their limo pulled up. They rode back together in comfortable silence. Susie leaned against Charlie and he put his arm around her. She lay with her head on his chest, and he didn't pull away.

At home, Charlie thanked the driver and gave him some money. The limo left, and they entered the house.

Susie walked through the living room, slid open the glass door, and went onto the deck. A full moon shone on the calm ocean, casting a long ribbon of light against the water. The waves rolled in with a gentle rumble. Moments later Charlie came up beside her.

"Did you enjoy the evening?" he asked.

"Yes, very much," she said, turning to look at him.

Susie waited for Charlie to say something. She waited for him to *do* something. The feelings she had months ago of wanting Charlie to make love to her were now back, in full force.

She gazed into his eyes, sending a silent invitation: *I'm ready.*

"It's been a long night," he said. "We'd better get some sleep."

He turned and went into the house. Susie watched through the glass wall as Charlie walked across the living room. In his tuxedo, he looked like a black ghost against the whiteness of the furniture. There was a glow when he turned on the light in his bedroom. The light snuffed out when the door closed.

Going upstairs, she hung the beautiful dress in the closet, removed her makeup, and crawled into bed.

Sleep didn't come right away. So much had happened that day: the limo ride, the walk down the red carpet, the flash of the cameras, the people, and the delicious food. This had been the night she had always wanted.

Finally drifting off, she dreamed about Charlie. They were at the party with the beautiful people. Charlie turned to her and said, "You are safe. I am here. I'm never going away."

Susie sat upright in bed, fully awake. The room was dark, the sound of the ocean coming faintly through the windows.

Why am I alone?

Rising, she put on a bathrobe, tied loosely around her waist. Walking barefoot down the inside stairs, she went to the door of the guest room and tried the knob. It opened.

Charlie lay on his back, sleeping. She sat beside him on the bed.

"Charlie. Wake up. Okay?"

Susie caressed his face with her hand. Her touch roused him. His eyes looked back with surprise, and then concern.

"What is it?"

"Shh," she answered, and lowered her lips toward his.

He pulled away, saying, "I don't think we should."

"Of course we should." She kissed him, and he responded.

Susie drew back the sheet, and unbuttoned the top of Charlie's pajamas. His body wasn't like Jimmy's—her boyfriend had been rock-hard with muscle. Charlie was soft, and looked more like the men she used to dance for at Sweethearts. The thought sent a chill down her spine:

Maybe this is a bad idea after all.

No. Charlie was nothing like the men at Sweethearts, who came to leer and drool. Charlie was kind. Charlie cared for her.

She straddled his body, placed her hands on his shoulders,

and trailed kisses along his jaw, down his neck, up to his ear.

"I want you to make love to me," she whispered.

She had said such things before as Audrey, enticing the men so that they would pay her more money. This was not the same. Her words were sincere.

Charlie pulled away, asking: "Who are you?"

Why would he say a thing like that?

Did he still think of her as Silky, the street whore? Charlie would never make love to a woman like that. But she wasn't Silky. She was the woman Charlie had allowed her to become.

"I'm Susie," she whispered in his ear, "and I'll be your girl-friend if you want me."

She opened his pajama bottoms and grasped his cock. The many erections she had stroked since Jimmy meant nothing to her, but Charlie's felt precious in her hand.

The slickness between her legs flowed freely. She guided his penis into her body and pushed down until Charlie filled her completely, gasping aloud with the sensation of it.

She did not ask him put on a condom. With Jimmy it had been a necessity, and certainly with her clients. This was differ-ent. Susie didn't care if she got pregnant. She knew with absolute certainty that if she did, Charlie would always take care of her.

The golden wave she felt with Jimmy began to build inside. Moving her hips faster, she rubbed her pelvis against his. A warm, wonderful cloud filled her mind. Jimmy would have finished by now. Charlie showed no signs of stopping.

What if he kept going all night? Was that even possible?

She felt his hands caress her thighs, her breasts, and her back. He ran his fingers down her stomach, and stopped with his thumb at the top of her pussy, on the little nub there, which was as hard as it had ever been. He began rubbing it, fast. Her juices made it slick, his thumb slid easily, and she felt herself growing more excited—

Something happened inside her, a new sensation. There was a clutching in her vagina, a squeezing feeling, thrilling unlike anything she had ever experienced. Her mind went blank and she left the world behind, soaring into heaven. She heard her own voice as if coming from another woman, screaming "Jesus, *Jesus, JESUS!*" She could not stop.

Am I dying?

She felt Charlie throb inside her and he cried out, too.

Then, he grew soft. The spasms subsided. Still, she did not pull away. They stayed in each other's arms, her legs around him, cheek against cheek. Taking his face in his hands, she kissed him murmuring, "Thank you, Charlie. You are so good to me. Thank you."

Nestling in his arms, she laid her head on his chest. They stayed together, not speaking because they had no need for words.

CHAPTER FORTY-THREE

Charlie

CHARLIE RAN THOUGH A DARK FOREST, stumbling. Skeleton fingers scratched his skin. There was no way out. He couldn't *breathe*.

Then he was lying on a bed of grass. Ancient trees covered with moss twisted upward, golden shafts of light coming down as if through the windows of a cathedral. Hummingbirds flitted about—but were they birds? They had human faces, and yet were not human.

He felt something tugging on his penis. Between his legs, a fairy with stained glass wings stroked his cock. It looked up at him with Susie's smile.

Charlie awoke to see sunlight filtering through the blinds.

Susie knelt on the bed, his erection in her mouth. She pulled her lips away and said, "Good morning."

He couldn't find his voice to answer.

She gazed back at him confident and happy, her hand never leaving his cock, moving slowly up and down. She took him in her mouth once more.

This wasn't right. They had not even discussed sex. She had taken the initiative, and he had not refused, but, but—

Charlie surrendered. Pulling Susie up, he kissed her. She responded eagerly. Then he guided her down until she was lying on her back, and trailed kisses along her neck, her shoulders and her breasts. Susie gasped as he took her nipple into his lips. At the same time, he slid a finger into her vagina to stroke a place inside her. She said "Oh," when he did, more in surprise than passion. The sounds that came after were deep and sincere.

Charlie continued down until his head was between her legs. Susie tensed for a moment when he kissed her there, then relaxed. Pressing his mouth against her vulva, he flicked his tongue quickly inside and out, teasing the folds of flesh with little nips of his lips.

Susie responded with gasp that turned to moans, which became cries of "Oh, Jesus, oh, OH, *OH!*" as her orgasm began. Charlie pumped his fingers inside her, running his tongue over her clit as she shuddered and screamed. Then he slowed, letting her waves of passion subside, and moved up on his knees, between her legs—

She grasped his erection and guided it in. He heard her gasp, and cry out, "Oh, my God," felt her vagina clutching again, and the sensation triggered his climax.

When finished they lay together, exhausted and exhilarated.

He went into the bathroom to freshen up, returning with his pajamas buttoned. Susie bounded in next, and moments later he heard the shower running.

The enormity of what they had done came crashing down on him. Driven by some primal urge, he had fucked Susie—*twice!*—and without a condom. What if he had caught some terrible disease?

He shook the idea away. He knew both of them were healthy. But then, he might have gotten her pregnant. She was not on any kind of birth control—

It didn't matter. If Susie had his baby, he would dedicate his life to seeing that she and their child had everything they needed.

My God, I'm in love with her!

The realization rolled over him like thunder. The idea thrilled him, and then filled him with dread. He had been in love before, and it had not ended well.

In high school, he had fallen hard for a spunky, brown-eyed classmate named Dale. It took him months to work up the courage to ask her out. They only went on one date, during which Dale made it clear she wasn't interested in being his steady girl. Charlie was devastated and threw himself into his schoolwork, graduating cum laude.

In his freshman year at college, he met an adorable young lady named Betsy. She enthusiastically introduced him to the pleasures of sex. They spent long hours in bed exploring each other's bodies, and Charlie learned how to make a woman happy. Betsy, however, had aspirations that could not be met in North Carolina. She dropped out of school and moved to New York, leaving Charlie behind.

On the rebound, he started dating Clarissa, who had a beautiful signing voice. Eventually she moved into Charlie's apartment. Shortly after they had settled in, Clarissa began acting differently. She took offense at unexpected things. There were several heated arguments. Charlie told himself that any couple has fights, and that it was part of building a relationship. It didn't seem all that serious until the quarrel about the musical.

Clarissa tried out for a leading role, but was cast in the chorus. She came home seething with anger and unloaded on Charlie. He tried to reason with her, but she could not contain her rage and flung a cereal bowl across the room. Charlie was too astonished to duck, and the bowl struck his head. Later Clarissa apologized, and Charlie forgave her.

Although she had promised to never do such a thing again, her unexpected and violent reactions continued. On his birthday she gave him a sweater, which he didn't like very much. When he asked if she kept the receipt, Clarissa slapped him across the face. That should have been the end, but Charlie foolishly felt that they loved each enough to work things through. Then one day, during an argument over something he couldn't even remember, she scratched his neck. He wore a dress shirt and tie in an attempt to hide it, but people noticed.

Later that day he asked her to move out. Clarissa refused, saying, "This is my place, too." Over the next week Charlie found another apartment, and took his things there one evening while Clarissa was at rehearsal. She was furious, and—

That had happened a lifetime ago. He was in Malibu now, with another woman who knew nothing about his past.

Susie came into the room, towel-drying her hair with a satisfied smile.

God. She's beautiful.

He wanted to tell her that he loved her, but something held him back. He needed time to think. "I . . . I'll make breakfast," he stammered, and started to rise.

Susie put her hand on his shoulder. "Let me fix something today." Helpless to refuse her, Charlie sat back down on the bed.

With Susie in the kitchen, his mind raced. How would she react if he told her he was in love? At times Charlie had said or done things that upset her. Once, when Susie touched him on the shoulder, he jumped a mile. She did not speak again for hours. After he refused to provide her with a romance novel, they spent three days in icy silence.

Then again, she had said, "I'll be your girlfriend." Maybe she loved him, too. And yet, he had heard such things before, from Betsy and Clarissa.

Charlie decided to keep his feelings to himself, and least for now. Some day she might give him a sign as to the depth of her feelings for him.

Susie returned with coffee, artisan toast, butter, and jam.

They ate, and talked about senseless things. When finished, she caressed his thigh. Their eyes met, and Susie leaned in to be kissed.

Reaching into the pocket of her robe, Susie produced several packs of condoms. "Maybe we'd better use these," she suggested.

"Where did you get them?"

"I still had them, you know, from the night you picked me up."

It made Charlie uneasy, to be reminded of Susie's former profession. Her proposal, however, was a wise one. He wore a condom when they made love again. Then they rested, and ate, and had sex *again*, as the sun crossed the sky and fell into the ocean.

CHAPTER FORTY-FOUR

Susie

SUSIE AND CHARLIE MADE LOVE every day. Although she had sex often before, Susie had never learned much about it. Charlie gave her words for everything: the little nub was called a clitoris, the place inside her vagina that felt so good was her G-spot, and the glorious explosion an orgasm.

Her romance novels had described orgasms as crashing waves or fireworks. Susie always thought the authors were making a big deal out of nothing. With Jimmy it had been nice, but she had never experienced what the writers depicted. It seemed now that every book had fallen short.

One day, Charlie announced that he was going into town. The movie was in "pre-production," he explained, which meant he had to attend meetings at the studio.

It changed everything. Charlie left after breakfast and stayed gone until late in the day. Susie would go to the beach, watch TV, or read. When Charlie came home he would fix dinner, but his mind was always somewhere else. He still kept his things in the downstairs bedroom, and the upstairs remained hers. They started sleeping apart, because Charlie needed his rest.

She spent her days alone, with no one to talk to. *Hollywood Wives* turned out to be a disappointment. It took place in modern times, not in the olden days, and had a thrown-together feeling, like the author wrote it in a hurry. Still, some of it was sexy. Susie found herself getting excited, and tried rubbing her clitoris like she had that one night in New Orleans. It didn't take her long to figure out how to bring herself to climax.

One night at dinner, Charlie started complaining that one of the studio executives wanted to add more strip club scenes. "It's an insightful look at a woman's experience," he groused. "Not a peep show." It was the first time he had ever mentioned his work.

Susie asked, "How much of it is about me, anyway?"

Charlie looked like he had forgotten who she was. "I told you," he replied. "It's about another girl named Zoe."

"Why haven't you let me read it?"

Charlie paused, and then said, "My contract with the studio has an exclusivity clause. I can't give it to anyone without their approval."

Susie felt her anger rise. "You sound like Jimmy, whenever I asked him if we had enough money to leave Vegas."

They didn't talk for the rest of the meal. When finished, Susie left Charlie to clear the table. Turning on the living room TV, she flicked mindlessly through the channels.

Charlie came in with tea. Susie rose, and took a book off the shelf at random.

"I'm going upstairs to read," she said. "I want to be alone tonight."

The next morning she stayed in bed. Charlie knocked on her door. "Do you want breakfast?"

"No."

Susie heard the SUV leave. Downstairs, she made coffee and toast and took them outside on the deck, along with the book she had picked off the shelf. It was called *A Tale of Two Cities*, and she immediately became engrossed in the story.

After a few chapters, Susie gazed out at the water. The surfers had been back for a couple of weeks. Every day she looked for Carson's bright orange surfboard, but he was never there. She thought about going over and introducing herself anyway, but decided against it. Walking up to a bunch of strange men didn't seem like a good idea.

Today, Carson was among them. Susie hurried inside and put on her bathing suit.

Diving into the water, she swam to where the surfers had gathered. Carson was sitting on his board, bobbing up and down in the swells.

"Hey, there Blondie," Carson called.

"The name's Susie," she answered. "You still want to show me how to surf?"

"Sure. Nothing but beach break anyway."

Carson taught her how to float on the board, read the waves, and paddle. When he surfed it looked easy, but for Susie it was hard just to stay on the board lying flat. She couldn't hit the sweet spot in a wave, and when she finally caught one, still couldn't stand.

"Pretty good," Carson reassured her. "It takes a while to get the hang of it."

"I haven't seen you for a long time."

"Were you looking?" he asked with a grin.

"Well, yeah."

"Went to Hawaii to surf the Pipeline," he answered, eyes shining. "Totally cranking, every day. Didn't want to come back, but school started."

"Where do you go?"

"SMC," he said. "Workin' on my GE's."

Susie didn't know what that meant, so she changed the subject.

"I'm gonna try another wave."

Turning the board toward the beach, Susie waited for the right-sized swell. She caught it perfectly this time. The wave took her all the way to the shore.

Carson came up beside her. "I gotta go. I have class."

"Will you come back tomorrow?" Susie asked.

"If you're gonna be here, sure." Carson grinned. "In the afternoon, though."

"Okay, I'll see you then."

"It's a date." Carson hefted his board under his arm and took off for the dunes.

Susie watched him leave. It felt good to have met a boy her own age. She walked back up to Charlie's house, showered, and put on shorts and a Hawaiian shirt.

The afternoon passed quickly. *A Tale of Two Cities* turned out to be fascinating. It was more like the novels she used to read, set long ago, with a love story and lots of danger.

Charlie came home at sunset. "You're in a good mood," he said.

"I had a good day," she answered. "What's the Old Bailey?"

"What are you reading?"

She told him, and Charlie began to explain the British court system. They continued to talk as Charlie made dinner, salmon with dill sauce and peppered Brussels sprouts.

When they finished eating, he produced some legal documents.

"I had my lawyer prepare a contract," he said. "If you sign it, you will officially be my research assistant. Then I can let you read my screenplay."

Susie looked at the pages, filled with tiny printing. The signature page said "Jolene Turley"—her real name, which she had mentioned to Charlie.

"It also contains an exclusivity clause," he explained.

"That means you can't tell anyone what's in the script without permission."

Susie tried to read the contract. It was difficult to understand.

"You can have a lawyer look it over, if you want," Charlie continued.

"That's okay, Charlie," Susie said, picking up a pen. "I trust you." She signed "Jolene Turley" on both copies.

"Keep this," Charlie said, handing her one of them. "And don't ever sign a contract again without having a lawyer read it first."

He gave her the screenplay the next morning. Susie put on her swimsuit and took the script to the beach. It was called *Sunrise*, and was clearly about her life. Zoe, the girl in the story, ran away with a boy on a motorcycle, became a dancer in Las Vegas, had sex for money, and then left her boyfriend for Hollywood. That's where Charlie ended the movie, with Zoe leaving to live a life of independence.

The screenplay left her feeling a little betrayed. She had known that Charlie had been writing about the things she told him, but the story hit deeper than expected.

Susie made a sandwich and ate on the deck, keeping an eye out for Carson. He finally came up the beach, surfboard under his arm.

"Ready for another lesson?" he called.

Susie slipped off the shirt she was wearing and ran down to the beach.

Carson did not let her go in the water at first. Laying his

board flat on the sand, he showed her how to lift herself to a standing position. After an hour of practice, he finally let her take the board out in the water. It was still difficult to catch a wave, and when she did, impossible to stand.

"Don't lean back when you get up," he said, when she came back to the beach. "It's throwing you off balance."

"I didn't know this was such hard work," she replied.

"You'll figure it out," Carson answered. "Ready for a beer?"

"Where?" Susie asked.

"We brought a cooler." Carson pointed toward the beach. "Sun's going down, anyway."

Susie saw that he was right. Charlie would be home soon. Then again, he might not. These days he sometimes didn't return until after dark.

"A beer sounds good," she said.

They went into shore. Susie met his friends: Ritchie, Bruce, and a guy they called Hot Dog. Carson gave her a towel, and a cold Corona.

A few minutes later a girl in a black bathing suit walked up carrying a surfboard. She had a dozen rubber bracelets on one wrist. Carson introduced her as Cathy. The others treated her like one of the guys.

"Where are you from?" Cathy asked, accepting a beer from Carson.

"Florida," Susie said, "But I've lived here for a while."

"What do you do?" Cathy continued. Susie sensed that she was glad to have another girl join the group.

"I'm a research assistant," she answered.

"What's that?"

"I work for a writer, giving him ideas. His name is Charlie Warren."

"The guy who wrote *The Consignation*?" Hot Dog gushed. "Wow!"

Everyone was impressed. They seemed to be waiting for further information. "I met him after," Susie explained. "I haven't seen it."

"I thought everyone in the world had seen it," Hot Dog said.

Cathy asked her why she came to LA, and Susie told them she wanted to get out of the small town where she grew up. Uncomfortable talking about herself, she changed the subject.

"Did you go to Hawaii, too?" Susie asked Cathy.

"I wish."

"Bruce went with me," Carson said.

He started talking about their trip. Relieved that they weren't asking any more questions, Susie relaxed and finished her beer. Carson handed her another, and she listened to stories of their adventures until the cooler was empty.

"We'd better split," Ritchie said. "It's getting dark."

Carson shoved the towels into a duffel bag, and Ritchie dumped the ice from the cooler. Picking up their boards, the gang headed for a path between the dunes. Carson lingered behind the others, duffel bag on his shoulder.

"Are you coming back tomorrow?" Susie asked.

"Sure," he said, grinning. "Same time?"

Susie didn't want him to go, and Carson acted like he didn't want to leave, either.

"See ya then," he finally said, and hurried after his friends.

Susie walked back up the beach in the growing gloom. Every light was on in the house. She used the shower on the deck to wash off the sand, and when she emerged, Charlie was standing at the open sliding door.

"Where have you been?" he demanded.

"On the beach." Grabbing a towel from the cabinet, the entire stack fell out. "Oops," Susie said, giggling.

"Have you been drinking?" Charlie accused.

"I had a couple of beers," Susie answered.

"Where did you get them?"

"Met some people. They showed me how to surf."

"You aren't old enough to be drinking."

"For God's sake, Charlie. You've been giving me wine for months."

"In my house, where I can keep an eye on you."

"Go fuck yourself." Suddenly, she was Silky again.

Who did Charlie think he was, anyway?

"I'm making dinner," he said impatiently. "Get dressed."

Susie didn't like being told what to do, but needed to get away from him. Leaving the towels in a pile, she hurried up the outside stairs to her room.

As she dressed, Susie thought again that she had no purpose at Charlie's house. He picked her up because he wanted her story. Now that he had it, Charlie didn't need her anymore.

People had always used her. Her parents did it to fulfill their twisted desires. Jimmy treated her like an ATM machine. Skunk was the worst of all, forcing her to have sex for money. Charlie was nicer, and it had taken her longer to notice, but he exploited her like all the others. He hadn't taken her body; she had given that freely. Charlie had taken her *story*, stolen her *life*.

Downstairs, Charlie had made Chicken Parmesan, one of her favorites. She sat down without a word, and so did he. After eating in silence for a while, Susie decided she had to confront him:

"I don't want you to make this movie."

Charlie looked at her strangely. Finally, he said, "It's not up to you."

"It's my story, Charlie. Mine."

"You didn't write the script."

"Still, it's about me," she pressed.

"People say to me all the time, 'I've got a great idea for a movie.' It's not the story. It's the way the story's told."

"I told you everything, and you used it. *Everything*."

"And I paid you for it," he said, a hard edge to his voice. "What do you think a research assistant does, anyway?"

Susie stopped talking. Charlie was so defensive. She had never seen him like this. They finished the meal in silence.

"I'm going upstairs to read," she said after.

In her room, Susie lay on the bed thinking. She would always be grateful to Charlie for rescuing her from the street, but it wasn't like she owed him anything. She had taken care of herself for a long time before she met him. In a way, it would be easier than when she ran away from home, or when she left Jimmy. She had money, and a friend in Sandrine.

"I could probably find you something."

Stanley's words at the party came to mind. Maybe he would know where she could get another job as a research assistant.

Discussing it with Charlie would be pointless. He would only try to talk her out of it. Having done it three times before, she knew the best way to go: simply walk away.

His knock woke her the next morning. "Do you want breakfast?" he asked through the door.

"No, thanks."

After hearing Charlie's SUV leave, Susie took a shower. She put on jeans and a designer T-shirt, both of which Charlie had bought for her. They would be appropriate in any situation. There was a set of luggage on an upper shelf, and Susie pulled down a small, wheeled suitcase. It had a handle that could be pulled out for rolling.

Sandrine had told her that every woman needed a little black dress. Susie packed the one Charlie had given her, with a pair of matching heels. She considered taking the black onyx earrings, but decided against it. Maybe Charlie could sell them and get some of his money back. She also left the expensive dress he had bought her for the party; maybe he could return it. The red dress for the premier went into the suitcase—Susie couldn't bear to part with it. She also packed casual clothes, a bathing suit, and underwear. Her toothbrush, toothpaste and other grooming items fit into the bigger outside pocket, and her makeup kit into the smaller.

Susie took her fringed bag off the hook at the back of the closet. It was surprisingly light in weight, considering that it was filled with money. Charlie had been paying her $400 a week for months, and she hadn't spent much of it. There must be at least ten thousand in one-hundred-dollar bills. She considered putting the money into a second suitcase, but decided not to. Her fringed bag was the only thing she had from her days with Skunk, and needed it to remind herself how far she'd come.

Going downstairs, Susie looked up the number of a cab company and asked for a driver to come at 11:00. She ate breakfast, and finished the coffee Charlie had made. After brushing her teeth, Susie took a pen and paper, sat at the dining table, and wrote a letter:

Dear Charlie—

I borrowed one of your suitcases, and packed some of the clothes you gave me. Just to be sure you don't think I stole them, here is a thousand dollars to cover the cost. The rest of my things, you can return them or sell them. They're really yours, anyway.

I appreciate everything you've done. The night you picked me up changed everything, but it's time for me to go. I hope you understand.

I'll be in touch once I'm settled somewhere.
All my best, Susie.

It took her three tries to get it right. The first one didn't make much sense, and she crumbled the page in frustration. The second was better, but she wrote it again just to be sure. She placed the letter in the center of the dining room table, so that Charlie would see it when he came home. Above it she laid the white envelope he had given her the night they met, with the same ten one-hundred-dollar bills inside.

A car horn tooted outside. Susie hoisted the strap of the fringed bag over her head, and pulled the suitcase behind her.

The cab driver loaded her luggage into the trunk. She took the fringed bag with her into the backseat.

"Where to, Miss?" he asked, as they pulled out of Charlie's driveway.

"Hollywood," she replied.

"All the pretty girls want to go to Hollywood."

"You can drop me at the corner of Vine and Selma."

The ocean passed outside the window. Carson would be expecting her that afternoon. She wished it were possible, but there were too many other things to do. Maybe she could come back some day and explain why it was so important that she leave right then. Susie wondered where SMC was, and if she could find an apartment near it.

A place to live was top priority. Sandrine might have some ideas; she could go to the mall and ask her.

It wasn't smart to carry around thousands of dollars in cash; she needed to open a bank account. What would a banker think if she tried to deposit it all at once? Maybe putting a little in different banks would be good idea.

The cab turned into the hills. As they climbed, Susie remembered the bus ride three years earlier, when she left everything she knew behind. Her throat grew a tight, and tears came when she thought about leaving Charlie. He had been so good to her.

It doesn't have to be forever.

Susie pulled herself together. There was immediate business at hand. Everything she wanted to do—finding an apartment, opening a bank account, and getting a job—depended on having identification. As far as she knew, the Social Security card and birth certificate for Holly Susan McMillan was still in the plastic baggie under the drainpipe outside Skunk's bathroom window. She would have to find some way inside the building. It was absolutely necessary that she not cross paths with Skunk, but she thought it would be possible to avoid him.

The taxi drove down familiar streets. The driver pulled up and asked, "This good?"

"Fine," she said. "How much?"

"Sixty-two fifty."

Susie handed him a hundred-dollar bill. "Sorry," she said. "It's the smallest I have."

"Money is money," he answered, taking it. He gave her change, and she handed him a ten-dollar bill as a tip. The driver pulled her suitcase from the trunk and set it on the sidewalk.

Susie rolled it along behind her, walking several blocks until Skunk's building loomed in front of her. It was a little after noon, and Skunk would be emerging soon to begin his day. She would go in after he left.

She went into the alley across the street and stashed the suitcase behind a dumpster. No one would see it there. There was nothing more to do but wait.

THE END